PRAISE FOR *THE EPIC STORY OF 1780-1783*

"I stand in awe! These bright and ambitious young historians have crafted a delightful anthology of masterful portrayals that bring key Revolutionary figures to life. Huzzah for the talented writers of the next generation! Savor this bold and insightful work declaring their own "INDEPENDENCE!""

— **Libby McNamee**, Richmond, VA
Author of *The Union Spymistress, Susanna's Midnight Ride,* and *Dolley Madison and the War of 1812.*

"The dedication in this book is incredible; each and every story was written with care evident in each page. The amount of time, research, and revising shows so well, the stories are fascinating. Each character grips you—and you're getting views you'd never thought you'd get. Traitors and well known heroes, as well as the quiet heroes you may never have heard of before! All to say, this story is indeed EPIC."

— **Kayleigh H**, 16, IL
Homeschooled

"I really enjoyed the stories, continuing on through the early American battles for freedom, learning more about our historical figures, both good and not-so-good. The sidekick animals added some fun humor. You can tell these writers did a lot of research on their characters."

— **Mary H**, Elgin, IL
Homeschooled

"*The Epic Story of America: 1780-1783* breathes life to historical figures that would otherwise just be names in a textbook. Readers will be immersed into the world of the American Revolution as they follow each central character and learn how each person played a part in the struggle for American Independence."

— Nadianne P.
History University Student

"A great historical fiction compilation that's inspiring, moving, and engaging. Would recommend for any history lover and those generally interested in quality reading material. Loved reading this!"

— Sophia W, 18, Inman, SC
Bob Jones University

"This book is such a great, glorious pile of wonderful information! After reading through it, I would say that this is a must-have for anyone who is a fan of American History. I tip my old-fashioned American top hat to this year's participants in the Epic Patriotic Camp!"

— Marcus C, 13, Brighton, TN
Homeschooled

"Containing interesting information from each character's personal perspective, this book is a treasure trove! *The Epic Story of America 1780-1783* incorporates beautiful writing styles which showcase an epic literary journey teaching us what our forefathers sacrificed to liberate this country and truly make it the home of the free and the brave."

— Xavian Cox, 15, Brighton, TN
Homeschooled

"I was very impressed by the authors' close adherence to historical accuracy. This book read very professionally; I could tell the authors had put in much time and research. I hadn't known of many of the historical figures listed and enjoyed getting to learn more about them through this book."

— **Olivia Tonn**, 16
Advance Reader

"The first two books in the trilogy were amazing, but this one takes the cake! This book is FANTASTIC!! The incredible penmanship of the authors is amazing. I felt as if I were taken back in time. Once again, this book is fantastic!! I would highly recommend this book to any history lovers."

— **Tess Dobler**, 18, Peoria, IL
Homeschool Graduate

Commit thy works unto the LORD,
And thy thoughts shall be established.
Proverbs 16:3

THE EPIC STORY OF AMERICA
INDEPENDENCE

1780–1783

CHRISTOPHER J. WATT   ELLA QUILL

ALEXANDRA ROBERSON   CAMERON GRAHAM

CHASE ADAM   EDAN MACNAUGHTON

EMMANUEL MORISSET   HANNAH SCHNEIDER

MADELEINE ROSE WENZEL

MIKAYLA BADENHORST   PAYTON GRACE

ROXANNE MESSIER

EPIC PATRIOT PRESS

A catalogue record for this book is available from the National Library of Australia

CONTENTS

FOREWORD

CENTURIES BEFORE ANCIENT ROME made the eagle famous for imperial power, ancient civilizations used the majestic raptor as a symbol of divine power and royal authority. The feathered emblem was such a clever idea that succeeding empires adopted it as well: the Byzantine Empire, the Holy Roman Empire, and the Russian Empire, along with a smattering of other European states. The eagle has soared through the pages of history as a national icon depicting strength, courage, power, and *independence.* So, when the newly *independent* United States of America needed a symbol for its Great Seal in 1782, it also chose the eagle. But the *American* eagle was different—this was a bird of a different feather found only on American soil: the oh-so-cool-looking bald eagle.

Many people are surprised to learn that bald eagles aren't born looking that cool with their handsome white heads and tail feathers, piercing pale eyes and intimidating yellow talons. Baby bald eaglets begin life and remain brown through their juvenile stage when they fledge the nest at around fourteen weeks. They slowly mature with mottled white feathers as they strike out on their own, but it takes up to five years before they have full, majestic, white plumage. Do you know why young bald eagles fledge the nest? The mother eagle "stirs the nest," making it uncomfortable.

When a pair of bald eagles prepare a nest for their offspring, they carefully place the large branches pointing outward. They ensure that their babies are safe and comfortable while they attend to their every need with food and warmth. As the eaglets start to grow, the nest gets crowded. When it's time for the fledglings to start learning how to be eagles, the mother eagle first must make them *want* to leave the nest. She points the large branches inward to poke the young eagles, prodding them to hop out onto the surrounding branches. And guess what that enables the pushed-out-of-the-nest fledgling eagles to do? From where they sit outside on the branches, they can then observe and learn how their parents hunt. They see how it's done and slowly decide that they want to try it themselves. The day finally comes when the young bald eagles take flight for the first time while under the watchful eye of their parents. Those first few moments must feel unnerving to the young eagles, but as they begin to feel the wind under their wings, they soon understand that they were built for flight. They weren't meant to sit in a comfortable nest, fed by their parents forever. They were created for *independence*.

The book you hold in your hands is the result of young writing eagles fledging the writing nest, prodded to pursue publishing *independence.* For two summers, author Libby McNamee and I led twenty-five aspiring young authors in an online summer writing experience called Epic Patriot Camp. The purpose was to teach the next generation of historians and authors how it's done, and to inspire them to want to try it themselves. In year one (2022), we taught our quill-wielding eaglets how to research, write, and edit their work. We published their book *The Epic Story of 1776: 25 People, 13 Colonies and 1 War (The Epic Story of America),* on Amazon. We also laid the groundwork to get their book into several historical site bookstores including The American Revolution Museum in Yorktown, Mount Vernon, and the Boston Tea Party Museum. The Epic Patriot Camp eaglets even had their first book signing in the prestigious Yorktown museum. In year two (2023), the eaglets grew into fledglings, increasing their knowledge and experience of editing, proofing, and marketing their second book, *The Epic Story of 1777–1779: Trials, Turning Points, and Triumphs (The Epic Story of America).* When summer 2024 came along, Libby and I needed to focus on our own writing projects. Although we labored with love "for the children," we were unable to lead camp that year, even though we knew that completing the trilogy of *The Epic Story of America* books required a third and final Epic Patriot Camp. It was then we realized that the remaining education our young eagles needed was to take what they had learned and take flight themselves. It was time for our fledglings to leave the nest and gain their *independence.*

We proposed the idea of Epic Patriot Camp 2025: INDEPEN-DENCE to the older leaders of the previous camps. Christopher Watt and Ella Quill rose to the occasion, making the bold decision to lead camp themselves with a small team of colleagues. They knew it would require a tremendous amount of time, work, and uncomfortable uncertainty with untried wings; but as they lifted off from the branches, their excitement immediately sent them soaring. They have surpassed our expectations with their group of ten campers to prepare, lead, write, edit, proof, publish and market this final book in the trilogy of America's story as told by the next generation.

Libby and I are so immensely proud of our eaglets all grown up! They've come so far, and it is our hope and prayer that this next generation of writing eagles will grow into their white feathers as they soar across new pages of history, authoring countless books in the years to come. Thank you for encouraging these young writers by reading, reviewing, and sharing their books with others. History's future is always dependent on the next generation, and from where I sit in this empty nest watching them fly, the future looks very bright indeed.

Soar, children, soar!

Jenny L. Cote is the Award-Winning Author of the
Epic Order of the Seven® historical fiction series.

*This book is FOR THE CHILDREN
of history's next generation. HUZZAH!*

BENEDICT ARNOLD & PEGGY SHIPPEN

WHO CAN WE TRUST NOW?

by Ella Quill

I dedicate this chapter to the one person who put in the most work for Epic Patriot Camp. Christopher, I know how many hours you've spent overthinking every little aspect of Epic Patriot Camp, and I'm so excited to see our hard work come to fruition! Thank you for being an epic co-host and friend. HUZZAH!

LETTERS TO JOHN ANDERSON

PHILADELPHIA
JUNE, 1780

PEGGY SHIPPEN ARNOLD PUT a hand on her growing stomach. "Put the tea there…yes, and the apple fritters there." She pointed, directing the maid servant, who nodded and arranged the dishes how Peggy had indicated.

Rubbing her hand once more over her stomach, Peggy exhaled and gripped the back of the chair at the table.

The maid servant noticed, straightening and crossing over to her. "Are you alright, Mrs. Arnold?"

Peggy waved her off dismissively. "Oh, it's all right. I'm quite well, thank you."

The maid nodded respectfully and hastily left for the kitchen quarters.

Peggy fanned herself as she murmured, "Goodness, now where is that husband of mine?" She wandered into the parlor, where Benedict, her husband, sat at the writing desk. He was deep in thought, with his back turned to her. His quill scratched across the paper and every few moments he dunked it into the inkwell. He muttered, tweaking his wig, which was askew.

Peggy smiled. He had not noticed her yet. Quietly, she came up behind him, then curled her fingers onto his shoulder.

He reacted immediately, jerking and whirling around. "Blast it! I said to leave me–" He halted when he noticed it was Peggy and relaxed. "Oh, hello dear."

She leaned over his shoulder to peer at his writings. "What are you writing, Mr. Arnold?"

He quickly swept his arm over the desk and gathered the scattered papers, shoving them into the drawer of the writing desk. "Nothing, my dear. Just informing a few colleagues of the baby's progress."

"Hmm, a few colleagues? Like who?" Peggy toyed with the ribbon in his hair. "A certain…John Anderson?"

"Hush now, Peggy." Benedict whispered, using a rag to mop up the ink that had spilled.

Peggy leaned in closer to say in a soft tone, "And it's not really our baby that you're writing about, is it?"

He looked up and his eyes met hers. He didn't say a word, but she understood him.

He laid his hand over hers. "You know I care about our child too."

"Of course, dear." She fingered his hair ribbon again, then asked softly, "Have you heard anything from General Washington?"

He stood, stuffing the letters into his coat pocket. "Nay, not of late. But I shall ride later this month to West Point."

"Again?" Peggy sighed, walking with him to the doorway. "He trusts you too much."

A pained look crossed Benedict's face and he nodded. "I know." Then, he jerked his wig back into place, roughly put his hat on, then tramped out the door.

***

WEST POINT
JULY 1780

"It is good to see you again, Arnold." The stoic General Washington towered over Arnold as he courteously extended a hand.

Arnold nodded, shaking the general's hand. "As to you, General." His palm was clammy with sweat, and the moment the handshake was released, he ran his hand down the thick woolen pant leg of his uniform.

General Washington didn't seem to notice Arnold's nervous state, which was good. *Any moment now and he shall offer me command of West Point.* Arnold thought of the letter he had recently sent to British General John André. He was confident that Washington would offer him the position.

General Washington began to leisurely walk the grounds of the fort, Arnold by his side. "Is Mrs. Arnold doing well?" He inquired politely.

"Yes, she is quite well." Arnold replied, trying not to fidget with the collar of his coat. Sweat trickled down his back. It wasn't just this warm weather that was causing his unease. Plans for what was plainly treason was about to fall into place, and Arnold could not let down his guard.

"Good." General Washington smiled briefly, then glanced down at Arnold. "How is your leg?"

He was referring to the time Arnold seriously injured his left leg in the battle of Saratoga. At the mention of it, Arnold's leg began to throb, but he shrugged. "Quite well, General."

"I see." General Washington's lips formed a tight line, then he stopped walking and turned to face Arnold. "Major Arnold, I have a proposition to make."

This is the moment. Arnold looked up at the General's grave face. "Sir." He could feel beads of sweat forming on his forehead. *He has to give me West Point.*

General Washington took a deep breath, then said, "It is my pleasure that you are to command the left wing, the position of honor."

No. Arnold's heart dropped, and his face grew warm. His eyes widened as he quickly turned away from the General, clenching his fists. *No! He was supposed to offer me West Point. This could ruin everything.*

"Major?" General Washington inquired, and Arnold shook his

head, at a loss for words, his nostrils flaring as he turned on his heel and walked quietly off, leaving the bemused General behind.

General Washington called on him later that evening, asking again if Arnold would take the position.

Arnold stood by the window, arms crossed as he gazed outside. There was nothing outside to be seen except for the dark, moonless sky.

"My apologies, General," He replied, moving to cross the room and stand by the table, at which a lit lantern rested. "My leg is still too weak for such a position."

General Washington eyed him as Arnold once again crossed to the window. "I see. Major Arnold, if you would just–"

Arnold interrupted him by firmly putting up a hand. "I'm afraid I would be of no use on the battlefield, given that my injury bothers me frequently."

General Washington was silent for a moment, staring into the flickering flames of the lantern. Then, with a sigh, he stood. "Very well. I will call again tomorrow, Major." With a polite nod of his head, he ducked through Arnold's door and out.

Arnold sat at the table, muttered a curse before arranging a blank sheet of paper on the table and reaching for his quill.

With a tap of the quill to rid it of excess ink, he began to pen a letter home to his wife, Peggy.

SHOCKING NEWS

MRS. ARNOLD, DID YOU not see the new fabrics in the tailor's windows?" Mrs. Morris asked, taking another dainty sip of her tea.

Peggy adjusted her bonnet, nodding. "Yes, Mrs. Morris, I did indeed. The blue muslin looks quite nice."

"Indeed!" Mrs. Morris replied, "Quite a high price as well. You have expensive taste, Mrs. Arnold." She sipped once more from her cup, then turned to her husband, Robert Morris, who sat reclining at the head of the table, smoking his pipe. "Mr. Morris, did you see that new lace trim at the tailor? Oh, it would look lovely on my bonnet. I'm afraid my old bonnet is fading."

"Yes, my dear." Robert said absentmindedly.

"And oh! Did you hear that poor Mrs. Smith's daughter has taken ill with croup? We better make sure our girls don't go near them. It would be a pity if our girls caught the nasty cough."

"Yes, my dear." Replied her husband amicably, watching the smoke drifting from his pipe.

"Good heavens! Polly, what is it?" Mrs. Morris addressed the maid who had just entered the room.

"A letter for Mrs. Arnold, ma'am." The maid nodded and held out a sealed letter to Peggy, who rose to take the paper.

Her hands trembled as she opened it and she tried to ignore Mrs. Morris' curious questions as Peggy scanned the letter. *Benedict has been offered to command the left wing?* Her heart began to race and she pressed a shaking hand to her forehead. "Oh gracious, *no*." Her legs gave way and she collapsed back into her chair, the tea in her stomach cold.

"What is it, Mrs. Arnold?" cried Mrs. Morris, alarmed. "Are you quite ill?"

Peggy quickly folded the letter and tucked it into her dress.

"I'm afraid so. Polly, can you please fetch my carriage?" She tried to keep her voice even, but she still had a tone of urgency, which caused Mrs. Morris to stand.

"Mrs. Arnold! What is it? Who is it from?" She hurried to Peggy's side and gripped the back of Peggy's chair.

"From my husband." Peggy replied, as Polly rushed off.

Robert Morris seemed to finally pay attention and he sat up, leaning forward. "Oh? What did he write?"

Tears pricked at Peggy's eyes and she swallowed, saying, "He has a new assignment: command of the whole left wing."

Robert Morris' eyes widened. "The whole left wing? By jove, that's wonderful!"

"No, it's not!" Peggy suddenly burst out, sobbing. "Good heavens, no it's not!" She covered her face with her gloved hands as she wept bitterly.

"Now, Robert!" Mrs. Morris admonished her husband. "While it's an honor, it is also a *dangerous* duty." She took Peggy's hand and patted it comfortingly as Polly re-entered.

"Your carriage is ready, ma'am."

"Oh, thank you." Peggy dabbed at her wet eyes as Mrs. Morris escorted her out.

THE RIVER AMBUSH

ENEDICT ARNOLD STARED LISTLESSLY out the window, his quill pen hovering right above the blank parchment page. Outside, a storm raged. The wind howled and shook the branches of the trees as if they were made of straw. Rain pattered against the window, hitting hard like bullets. The candle that rested upon his writing desk flickered, casting dancing shadows across the walls.

Arnold's gaze seemed to go beyond the wall, seeing right through the storm and the darkness, through the rain and the wind. In his mind's eye, he could picture his wife Peggy, presumably sitting by her own window. Perhaps she was thinking of him at this moment.

What would she think? What would the children think?

"She will be coming soon to West Point." Benedict reasoned, " Only a few days away." Arnold set the quill pen back into the ink-well. This letter could wait for Peggy.

* * *

THE HOME OF JOSHUA HETT SMITH
11 SEPTEMBER, 1780

Arnold raised the iron knocker on the door and knocked heavily on Smith's door. While he waited for a reply, he subtly risked a glance over his right shoulder. His conversation with General Washington replayed in his mind.

"Ah, Major Arnold, how are you this morning?"

Arnold adjusted a button on his coat, clearing his throat. "Fine, General. Do you have plans for this afternoon?"

Washington, always walking with his hands crossed behind his back, looked up at the sky, which was a stark blue. "I do have to meet with a few of my lieutenants. What about you, sir?"

Arnold also looked up at the sky, noting the wisps of cloud on the horizon. "Ah, I have decided that some signals need to be set up at Dobbs Ferry, in case the British decide to come up the river."

Washington glanced down at him. "Very wise, I see. Very well! I hope it goes successfully."

Arnold attempted a polite bow. "Thank you, General. I hope so as well."

Arnold wasn't at Dobbs Ferry. Instead, here he was, standing at the doorstep of Joshua Hett Smith's home, waiting for information on his barge. Arnold shifted, tugging on the collar of his coat as he glanced around. With the barge, he would have a chance to meet up with John André, whom he had been corresponding with under the name "John Anderson". If all went according to plan…this would be their first time meeting.

Smith opened the door, raising an eyebrow. "Ah, Major Arnold, you're right on time."

Arnold nodded as he stepped inside, removing his hat. "Yes, is the barge ready?"

"It shall be but a moment, Major." Smith replied, looking Arnold up and down. "Headed up to Haverstraw, are you?"

"Ah, yes." Arnold fidgeted with his cravat, the Smith home being very warm inside.

"Well, then, right this way." Smith led him outside, down toward the riverside. "And that lovely wife of yours is expected soon, I wager?"

"Yes, yes she is." Arnold replied. His wife, Peggy, and their infant son were to stop at the Smith house before going to West Point.

* * *

Soon, Arnold was being rowed by several men to his meeting spot with André. All seemed to be according to plan.

"Sir!" One of the men exclaimed, pointing. "It's the British!"

Arnold quickly stood, causing the barge to wobble. The men

around him struggled to keep the boat balanced.

"Sir!" The man shouted. "They're—" He was cut off as several shots rang out, and the man tumbled back as a bullet whizzed past his cheek, barely missing him. The men panicked as more bullets zipped past, splashing into the water around them. Arnold rushed to sit back down, as the British continued to fire.

"Go back!" Arnold shouted. "Fall back!"

The water churned as the British fired. One of the men cried out in pain, dropping his oar, which clattered to the deck. A dark red spot was already growing from where the man had been hit.

"Fall back!" Arnold ordered, standing up and grabbing the oar, and shoving it into the water to row.

The men needed no further encouragement as they rowed for their lives, pumping their arms, sweat glistening on their brows, the veins on their arms clearly outlined.

Arnold glanced back at the firing ship, silently cursing that they had ruined his opportunity to meet with André. He shook a passionate fist, then watched as they grew closer to shore. *We will have to wait before returning.*

BENEDICT ARNOLD

SECRETS IN THE INK

THE HOME OF JOSHUA HETT SMITH
12 SEPTEMBER, 1780

BENEDICT!" PEGGY GREETED HER husband with a kiss to both cheeks, cradling their son Edward in her arms. "Oh, I am so thrilled to see you again."

Benedict put his arm around his wife and returned the kiss. "And I, you, my dear. How was the trip for you?"

Peggy brushed back a stray lock of hair as Arnold led her toward their room. They would be staying the night at Smith's and go on to West Point in the morning, when Peggy felt well enough.

"It was quite rough, I'm afraid. Edward was fussy most of the time." She glanced down at the babe and sighed. She did look a bit worn, and thinner than she used to be.

He reached for her thin hand and wrapped his strong fingers around hers. "I am sorry that the travel made you unwell. Do you want to rest for a moment?"

"Perhaps." She nodded faintly. "We do have some letters to write, don't we?"

Arnold unlocked their room and led her inside, motioning to the bed. "There, you lie there while I prepare the writing supplies."

He helped his wife into the bed with the baby and checked to make sure she was comfortable. Then he crossed to the desk and pulled out a fresh sheet of parchment, laying it on the desk.

He uncorked the inkwell, fetched a feather quill pen, and on a scratch piece of paper, did a few practice strokes with the pen, leaving a few inkblots. The colored ink that splattered on the paper looked eerily like blood, and Arnold's insides turned.

He didn't realize he was gripping the quill so tightly his knuckles were white until Peggy spoke from the bed behind him,

"Benedict, are you quite well?"

"I…" Arnold let go of the pen and it clattered to the desk, sending ink splatters across the practice page. A few blots stained the back of his hand and he quickly dabbed at his skin with a rag, turning to face Peggy. "Yes, my dear. I am. Just a bit of a…sore wrist, I'm afraid." He rubbed his wrist for good measure.

Peggy arched an eyebrow. "You're not having second thoughts about this letter, are you?" The baby lay beside her in the bed and whimpered as she shifted, sitting up. "Benedict," her voice lowered, "*this* is what you've worked for. What *we've* worked for." Edward gave a cry, shaking his balled fists up toward the ceiling.

"I know. Trust me, I know!" Arnold said, a little louder than he meant to. He pushed away from the desk and stood. The baby continued to cry as Arnold came closer to the bed, meeting Peggy's fiery gaze. His dark eyebrows knit together as he slightly leaned forward and said in a lower tone, "I'm not going back on this." Her bright eyes searched his, and she didn't break the gaze. "Not after–" Arnold broke off, then stiffened and straightened. "Peggy, the baby, dear."

Peggy was silent, eyeing him as she eased back against the pillows and soothed baby Edward.

Arnold heaved a sigh as he turned back to the desk, picking up the pen once more and rested it on the page. "How shall we begin this time?"

From the bed, Peggy rubbed her forehead and pointed to a chest in the corner. "I brought the dictionary with me. We shall use it again."

Arnold set the quill into the inkwell and knelt by the chest, unlocking and opening it. Inside were a variety of things that Peggy had packed. Extra clothes for the baby, several hats and bonnets, a couple cosmetic supplies, and there, at the bottom, was a thick book.

He pulled it out, dusted off the cover, and cracked it open. "Well, what shall we say?"

Peggy sat up slightly, beckoning to him. "Come."

He arched an eyebrow and leaned in closer. She tenderly clutched his face, sliding her finger down his jawline, her lips coming close to his own.

Then she slightly tilted her head so that her ruby-red lips brushed his ear, and she whispered the message to him, just barely audible.

"Ah." Arnold nodded. "I see." As she drew back, his eyes fell on her vibrant blue eyes. *Such a clever woman.* He reached to take her hand and kissed it. "It shall be as you say."

The two worked for nearly an hour, as the wax candle dripped, growing smaller by the minute. It flickered, casting dancing shadows across the room.

The pocketwatch inside Arnold's coat ticked slowly, and baby Edward's eyes drooped until he fell asleep, unaware of his parents' labor on the letter.

Finally, Peggy shut the dictionary and quietly rearranged her trunk, hiding it again at the bottom, under several pairs of the baby's clothes. Then she slipped under the covers of the bed, alongside Edward.

Arnold set the quill back in the inkwell, ignoring the ink smudges that stained the side of his hand. It was done.

As he bent to blow out the candle, his eyes fell on the fresh message drying on the parchment sheet:

176.30.3 9.5.12 64.3.4 119.2.3 225.21.4 158.23.2
138.20.9 52.12.13 97.2.12

* * *

ARNOLD'S HOME AT WEST POINT
20 SEPTEMBER, 1780

"Are you sure it's quite safe?" Peggy asked softly, clutching crying baby Edward to her chest as Arnold paced the room, searching for his hat.

Arnold spun to face her. "Quite safe? No, it is far from safe." He snapped, lifting up one of his breeches and looking under it. "Blast it! Where is my hat?"

Peggy furrowed her brow. "Well, I–"

Arnold found the hat thrust underneath the writing desk from where they had only been sitting several weeks ago, writing that notorious letter. "Peggy, darling, *this* is what we have worked for. Do not tell me that you are having second thoughts!" He clenched his fist, for once grateful for the racket Edward was making. The baby's cries helped cover up their treasonous conversation.

Peggy bounced Edward a bit, tears springing to her eyes. "Oh, I know! I perfectly understand! But Benedict! Think of what could happen if you're discovered! What could happen to *us*! To your child!" Beseechingly, she held the bawling baby out towards him.

Arnold gently pushed her aside, going for the door.

Peggy rushed to stand in front of him, blocking the way. "Oh please, just be careful! Promise me you'll come back." Her blue eyes sparkled with tears, which rolled down her pale face. She clutched Edward to her, no longer attempting to soothe his cries.

Arnold sighed, rubbing his forehead. "Crying women are always a pain…and something no man can ignore." He muttered, then he stepped closer to Peggy, leaning in. He wasn't much taller than she was, but it was still a great enough difference that Peggy had to look up at him.

She was still blinking back her tears, almost on the verge of crying like Edward. "Benedict," She whispered, desperate. "Please, come back to us." Her lip trembled, and her chest shook with silent sobs.

Arnold looked gravely at her, attempting to keep a stoic expression as he tenderly kissed her. "I will do my best, my dear."

She stepped aside as he put on his hat, opened the door, and went out, his wife's cries echoing behind him.

Arnold walked outside, down the path to the stables, trying to avoid meeting with anyone else. *Just walk with a purpose.* He squared his shoulders and strode confidently toward the barn, where his horse, Justice, was waiting.

"Hey, boy." Arnold said softly, holding out his hand to reveal an apple for Justice. The horse nickered and eagerly nudged his hand, his warm lips brushing Arnold's open palm. The apple was gone quickly, and after running his hand down the horse's nose, he swung himself into the saddle and patted Justice's side.

"Alright, boy, let's go." he prodded the horse forward, and as he was preparing to exit the stable, he heard a familiar shout.

"Major Arnold?" came General Washington's voice.

Arnold's stomach sank. "Go, Justice! Go!" He nudged the horse's side and Justice rushed out of the stable, running past where Washington was striding up.

Washington watched them go past, his brow knit as Arnold gave a friendly tip of his hat. "Good afternoon, General!"

The General raised his hand in greeting as they rode past, and when they were further from him, Arnold let out a sigh of relief. Now was *not* the time to speak with General Washington.

Soon enough, Arnold rode up to Smith's home. Justice was breathing heavily, his mane lathered with foaming sweat. Arnold slowed his cantering horse to a stop, then slid off leading Justice over to the water trough and tying his reins to a post.

Arnold, himself drenched in sweat, adjusted his coat before grabbing the iron knocker and clanging on the door.

Smith greeted him at the door, opening it. "Major Arnold, welcome."

Arnold nodded, stepping inside and following Smith. "Hello, sir." He shook Smith's hand firmly, and walked into the parlor, where a maid was bringing in the afternoon tea.

Tea. As Arnold sat in one of the chairs by the table, he glanced down at the steaming cup by his place. It had been a while since he had drunk tea. The Patriots had boycotted it, especially after the infamous Boston Tea Party.

"Cream, or sugar?" Smith asked, pouring some cream into his own cup.

Arnold blinked, snapping out of his reverie. "Ah, both. Thank you." He nodded as Smith passed the sugar jar. Arnold took it, spooned a generous amount into his tea, and lifted the cup to his lips, not hesitating even a moment before drinking it.

"Now..." Smith began, setting down his cup. "Everything is settled. Mr. Anderson is arranged to meet you at the decided place."

"Wonderful." Arnold took another sip of his tea, relishing the freedom to drink whatever he liked. It seemed that all was going to fall into place.

✱✱✱

ARNOLD'S HOME AT WEST POINT
21 SEPTEMBER, 1780

Unfortunately, everything did not go as planned, nor as Arnold had hoped. Smith had been recruited to convey André to Arnold, but could not find a boat.

"So he sent me here." The farmer Samuel Cahoon explained apologetically, shrugging.

Arnold gripped the letter tightly, his knuckles white. "What do you mean?" He asked, anger burning at the edge of his voice like fire that quickly devours paper.

"Just that, sir." Cahoon replied, hitching up his pants and motioning to the letter in Arnold's hands. "He wanted me to deliver this letter to you, and so I did."

"A moment, then." Arnold said, then turned and left the poor farmer standing in the parlor.

Arnold slammed open the door to his study, startling Peggy, who sat nearby, rocking baby Edward's cradle. "Gracious, Benedict! What is the matter?"

Arnold vigorously shook the letter from Smith. "This! Blasted man couldn't find a boat!" He cursed, crumpling the letter and tossing it into the fireplace. The flames eagerly licked up the letter, which was soon ashes.

Arnold crossed to his writing desk and shoved the books off, which clattered to the floor.

Peggy stood, reaching to grab baby Edward from his cradle. "Perhaps, I should go to the other room and leave you to destroy things in peace."

"Perhaps you should." Arnold snapped in reply, and his wife hastily left the room while Arnold gathered his writing supplies and quickly scratched out a letter to Smith.

> *My dear man,*
> *I urge you to try again tonight. I assure you that you have permission to pass at any time, be it day or night. It is vital that this mission be carried out.*
> *-B. Arnold*

Arnold folded the letter, sealed it, and stormed back to the parlor where Cahoon had been waiting uncomfortably.

Arnold thrust the letter into Cahoon's hands. "Take this to Smith, at once."

Cahoon glanced down at the sealed letter, turning it slightly in his hands. "If this is about escorting that Mr. Anderson I'm not sure if I can do it tonight. You see, sir, my wife doesn't want me to be involved with these sort of things. Makes it dangerous for a man."

Arnold's eyebrows shot up, and he jabbed a finger at Cahoon's chest. "You *will* go tonight, and I'll see to it if you don't." He muttered a threat under his breath, and the farmer quickly backed up, nodding.

"Alright, alright, I'll go this night. Soon as it's dark." Cahoon tipped his hat to Arnold, then went off.

Arnold firmly nodded and watched Cahoon mount his horse and ride off. Then he shut the door behind him and ran a hand through his long dark hair. He clenched his fist and stomped up the stairs.

At each creaking step, he recounted the plans for tonight. *André will be waiting on the Vulture, a British ship.*

Another creaking step, which bent slightly under his weight. *Cahoon will take Smith to meet with André.*

This step wasn't as squeaky, it was quite firm. *Smith will convey André to me.*

It should all go according to plan. How could anything go wrong?

Arnold crossed the last step, one that was slightly unbalanced and shifted slightly under him. He walked into his study room, and glanced around. Now it was just time to wait for the sun to set.

* * *

There was movement on the pathway ahead. Arnold stood, slowly swinging his lantern. He saw Smith point, and the two men started making their way toward Arnold.

As the two came into the puddle of the lamplight glow, Arnold saw André for the first time. He was slim, fairskinned, and carried himself with an elegant demeanor. Arnold motioned for Smith to wait a few yards away, and Smith nodded, retreating down the pathway a bit. Arnold looked André up and down, then scoffed. "So you're the man my wife so admired."

André gave a stiff bow. "Indeed, Major, I hope Mrs. Arnold is well. And I believe *you* are our contact we have kept in touch with these past months." He arched an eyebrow. "Clinton would like to offer you £16,000."

Arnold stepped back slightly, his face growing red. "That's £4,000 less than your original offer! No, I will only do this if you give me my promised £20,000!"

André shrugged, slightly dusting off the collar of his coat jacket. "I will ask Clinton to consider providing the promised sum. Now, the documents?"

Arnold looked him firmly in the eye. "You *will* talk to Clinton about my twenty-thousand pounds."

André nodded primly. "*Oui.* I promise."

"Good." Arnold hung the lantern on a low hanging branch of a tree, then shifted and pulled out several parchments from inside his coat. "Here." he unfolded the parchment and handed it over to André, who took it, intrigued. "This page is all about West Point's weaknesses and strengths. And this one," Arnold unfolded another, "is about its garrison and defenses. This is what I'm thinking…"

Over the next few hours, the two started a deep conversation about Arnold's strategic plans over how the British should attack and take over West Point.

"And so, if we march in from the east side…" André murmured, looking at the rough diagram of the fort that Arnold had drawn in the dirt.

Smith came running up, and Arnold looked up, startled. "What is it?" He asked, quickly dusting away the diagram.

André glanced up too, getting up off his knees and standing quickly.

"It's getting light! Smith pointed to the sky."We need to hurry!" He hissed.

Arnold was already scuffing with his boots the map he had drawn on the ground. Then he blew out the lantern light while André hastily folded the documents and stuffed them into his pockets.

"Quick! I must get back to the *Vulture*!"

Smith led the way back to where Samuel Cahoon and his brother Joseph were waiting for them. Both were fast asleep, slumped against trees while their raft bobbed softly in the shallow water.

"Samuel!" Arnold hissed, and the farmer sat upright, his head banging against a low branch.

"Good heavens! What is it?" Cahoon asked, cursing as he rubbed the spot where his head had hit the tree. He stood and yawned, stretching.

"We need to leave, now!" Arnold ordered, but the man shook his head.

"Sorry, we can't take you now. The tide has changed and it will be too hard for us to take you back." Cahoon shrugged and Arnold balled his fists and kicked angrily at the ground.

"André! You'll have to come with us back to Smith's home." He said to the British officer, who nodded.

"I agree. It will be the safer route." André replied, adjusting his wig.

"Let's go, then." Arnold gestured to Smith. "Smith, I want you to help the Cahoon brothers return the boat. André and I will start back to your home."

Smith nodded, "Will do, Major."

"Come, this way." Arnold said, beckoning to André, and the two began the six mile hike back to Smith's.

André fretted the whole way, glancing back at the river every now and then to catch a glimpse of the *Vulture*. "If I get caught this will not go well." He muttered, and Arnold furrowed his brow.

"Let's hurry, then. I think I can see the house!" He pointed up ahead, where indeed, the Smith home rested, the morning light reflecting in the glass windows.

Suddenly, shots rang out, echoing across the river. "The *Vulture*!" André cried, dashing ahead and to the house.

Arnold followed, and they burst through the front door and up the stairs to an empty room. André shoved aside the curtains and pointed out the window to where they could see the river.

"The Americans are firing at them!" André exclaimed, desperate. "What are we going to do now? I cannot approach the ship while they're firing!"

"We must wait and see if the fire ceases." Arnold replied, trying to ignore the growing amount of panic welling inside. His palms were sweaty, and he anxiously rubbed them down his pant legs. *This was not part of the plan.*

The American fleet and the British continued to fight, the gunshots pounding, making the glass windows vibrate.

When Smith arrived, he was also anxious about the gunshots. "This cannot be good." He muttered, and Arnold cursed.

While Arnold paced the room, André stayed like glue to the window, watching the fight. Suddenly, he clamped his hand to his mouth and exclaimed, "The *Vulture*! They're leaving!"

Arnold rushed to the window, shoving André out of the way to see. Indeed, the British ship was sailing away. Away from them. Away from *André*. Arnold glanced at the British officer, who had turned a very sickening pale shade.

Arnold's mouth was dry as he searched for words. "You and Smith can cross the river by ferry. Once you're in no-man's-land, you should be able to cross safely into the British lines."

Smith furrowed his brow, scratching his head. "You cannot go dressed like *that*, though." He motioned to André's British uniform. "You can borrow a coat of mine to wear over it."

Arnold stroked his chin. "And you cannot have those documents in your pockets, in case they'll search you."

André took out the papers, then glanced down at himself. "What if I hide them in my stockings and boots?"

"Do it." Arnold nodded, and André proceeded to tuck the folded papers into his stockings, concealing them with his boots.

"You'll have to take my horse." Arnold said, as he and Smith escorted him out to the stables. It was getting lighter by the moment, and they had no time to lose before the river was bound to be patrolled by American forces.

André gawked at the beautiful stallion. Justice was black with a white star on his forehead. Justice neighed and tossed his head as André ran his hand down the horse's mane. "He's a fine stallion. What's his name?"

"Justice." Arnold said firmly, and André glanced at him.

"Is this what you seek? Justice for how the Americans have treated you?" He held out his palm and the horse sniffed it.

Arnold shrugged. "Well, justice, and my own independence, I suppose. I seek both, because even though these colonies are seeking freedom, they don't give others the independence they need."

André nodded slowly. "I see…I doubt you will find much freedom in the British army, but you will find justice." He swung himself into the saddle and patted Justice's neck. "Let's go." He dug in his heel and the horse took off. Smith went after him on his own horse.

PEGGY THROWS A FIT

ARNOLD'S HOME AT WEST POINT
25 SEPTEMBER, 1780

ARNOLD FOLDED THE LETTER from Smith with satisfaction. According to Smith, all was well with André. Things were going smoothly, and Arnold couldn't help but pride himself. With a satisfied smile, he glanced in the looking glass and adjusted the ribbon holding his hair back.

"Are you aware, my dear," he said, addressing Peggy who was dressing little Edward for the day. "That Washington and his aides are coming to dine with us for breakfast?"

"Yes, my love." his little wife replied, and Arnold glanced at her through the looking glass. She was much thinner than she had been, and instead of rosy cheeks, she was quite pale. She had not adjusted well to living at West Point.

A knock resounded on their bedroom door and Arnold crossed to answer it. A servant stood there, and she nodded toward the downstairs. "Hamilton, Knox, and Lafayette are here, sir. They said that General Washington shall arrive shortly."

"Ah, splendid. Peggy, would you come down and say hello?" Arnold turned to her.

Peggy cradled Edward and nodded. "Of course."

The couple met the group downstairs, and Arnold engaged in conversation with Hamilton and Lafayette, while Knox greeted Peggy and baby Edward.

"Why hello, Mrs. Arnold!" The cheerful man said, and he leaned forward to playfully shake Edward's hand. "And Mister Edward as well! How are you?"

"Quite well, Mr. Knox, thank you." Peggy replied, attempting a sweet smile. Edward began to cry softly and she bounced him. "Hush now, child."

From across the room, Arnold raised an eyebrow at Peggy. Edward was causing too much of a ruckus.

Peggy turned to Henry Knox and started to back up slowly. "I'm so sorry, Mr. Knox, but I think I need to go tend to the baby." She glanced over at Arnold. "You all can start eating. I will be down shortly." She smiled at them all and headed back up the stairs to take care of Edward.

When she was settled in a cozy chair in their bedroom, she began to feed Edward, who immediately quieted. She sat a few moments in silence, listening to the clatter of utensils and dishes as the men downstairs began their meal. She brushed back a strand of hair that clung to her sweaty forehead. She had not yet eaten, and her hands shook slightly.

The wind blew outside, as the morning sun shone through the window. Peggy rocked back and forth, and Edward was soon asleep.

She stood to lay him in his cradle when heavy footsteps came up the stairs. Arnold burst through the door, closing it firmly behind him. Peggy blinked. "Benedict, what is the matter?"

Arnold crossed to her, gripping her shoulders tightly. His face was ashen grey, and his eyes wide. "Peggy, I must go, *now*."

Peggy shook her head, her mouth suddenly very dry. "Must go *where*? I don't understand!"

Arnold lowered his tone and said barely above a whisper. "André was found and captured. Peggy, I must *go*. I have to leave to join the British immediately."

Peggy's head swam, and the room seemed to spin. She tried to form words but found that she couldn't. Her legs gave way and she collapsed into Arnold's arms, as her world faded to black.

* * *

Peggy snapped awake, her heart racing and chest heaving. She pressed a palm to her forehead. Her skin was hot to the touch and her hair clung to her sweaty brow.

Edward's cry came from his cradle, and Peggy swung her legs

over the side of the bed looking around. *What happened? And* where *was Benedict?* She tried to stand, weakly, her mind racing.

Then Peggy remembered, and her legs collapsed beneath her. "No!" She cried out, falling to the bed, trembling. "No." She sobbed, tears stinging her dry face. "No, Benedict!"

Edward cried louder from his cradle, and a soft knock resounded at the door.

"Mrs. Arnold?" Alexander Hamilton cracked open the door, and her heart breaking cries caused the good man to step inside. "Mrs. Arnold, are you quite ill?"

Peggy buried her face in the pillows of their bed, the pillow itself reminding her of her beloved Benedict.

"I'm not well, at all! I'm all alone, and the child—ooh, the child!" She broke into fresh sobs, banging her fist against the mattress of the bed.

Hamilton glanced over at the cradle, where Edward hollered, his red face all scrunched up. "Er, Mrs. Arnold, may I comfort the child?"

Peggy's answer was inaudible from the bed, so Hamilton gently took up Edward and walked him out of the room, bouncing the baby and attempting to calm him.

General Washington greeted him out in the hall. "How is she?" He asked quietly.

Hamilton shrugged, awkwardly rocking the baby. "She is in great distress. Perhaps you can calm her, or get something out of her cries."

Washington nodded, and softly cracked open the door to the

bedroom. "Mrs. Arnold?" He walked over to her bedside and knelt by where Peggy was still trembling and sobbing.

"I–I–I'm all alone!" She cried out, curled up and rocking back and forth. "There's no one! The child–he's all alone."

"What are you talking about?" Washington asked gently. "We are here, we are your friends. And there is your husband, Major Arnold–"

Peggy suddenly scooted back and through breaking hiccups, she shook her head, eyes wild. "N-n-no, he is gone! Gone forever!" She broke into fresh cries and thrust herself upon the bed.

"What do you mean, he's gone?" Washington stood, his firm blue-gray eyes on Peggy as she cried, and then a shout from downstairs caught Washington's attention. He walked out and met a messenger who was waving around several papers.

"General, Sir!" The messenger handed Washington the papers and reported his message breathlessly. "These papers were found on a British spy, Major John André. He says that he was in contact with Major Arnold, who gave him these." The messenger tapped the papers.

"What?" Washington quickly flipped through the papers, his eyes widening.

Lafayette, Knox, and Hamilton were standing nearby. Lafayette gasped, and exclaimed in French, "That must be why Mrs. Arnold is in such distress! Her husband has fled to the other side!"

Hamilton cursed, stamping his foot. "That blasted traitor! Let me go after Arnold!" He passed baby Edward to Knox and rushed out the door, putting on his hat before Washington could give further orders.

Baby Edward was quite calm now, and Knox laid him in another cradle as Washington turned to them gravely.

"Arnold has betrayed us. Who can we trust now?"

ABOUT

BENEDICT ARNOLD

Benedict Arnold was an infamous hero of the Revolution until he turned traitor against the Patriots. He was a man who was always seeking independence and glory, and when he did not receive those from the Continental Army, he began a secret correspondence with the British, and attempted to betray the Patriots in September 1783. After this attempt, he fled to London, where he lived for the rest of his life and died in 1801.

ABOUT THE AUTHOR

ELLA QUILL

Ella Quill is a young writer who is passionate about using her God-given gift to serve her readers. She's always grown up telling stories to herself and others but started pursuing writing more seriously in 2020. A published author outside of Epic Patriot Camp, she is currently working towards publishing the second book in her fantasy series, *The Lavender Dawn Saga.* When she isn't writing, she loves to sing, knit, eat chocolate, and read good books. You can learn more about Ella and her writing at LavenderDawn.NobleKnoll.com

BENEDICT ARNOLD & PEGGY SHIPPEN

NOTES FROM THE AUTHOR

Benedict Arnold…the Notorious Traitor of the American Revolution. This chapter took a lot of work and a lot of research, but not all of my chapter may be entirely true.

There are a lot of debates of whether Arnold's wife, Peggy, was included in his treacherous plan or not. Some historians think that she was completely innocent of the whole scheme, while others think that she helped Arnold with his correspondence to Andre. In my chapter, I went with the route that she did know and supported him, especially since she is from a Loyalist family.

In my chapter, there is a coded message that Arnold and Peggy collaborated and wrote. Although they did use this method to write letters to John Andre, this letter itself is a piece of fiction. You, my dear reader, can actually decode this message if you own a copy of *1777-1779; Trials, Turning Points, and Triumphs* by the Epic Patriot Campers. Simply use the method below to decode and enjoy!

Page Number. Line Number. Word Number.

Arnold *did* have a horse, but his horse's name was not Justice. That was my own name given to his horse. He did lend his horse to John Andre.

The scene when Peggy is hysterical and Washington, Hamilton, Lafayette, and Knox attempt to console her is a true event, though I as the author have taken creative liberty with how this scene is depicted.

I once heard an account that Benedict Arnold, as he was dying, said that he preferred to be buried in his Continental Army uniform, for it was in that Army that he did greater things. I did not include this snippet in my chapter, because it is not a confirmed story, but it is still a story that echoes in my mind, and I hope in the threads of my story.

JOHN ANDRÉ

BETRAYAL — A SPY'S RECKONING

by Cameron Graham

Thank you to my parents for all of the support you give me.

JOHN ANDRÉ

PROLOGUE

2 OCTOBER, 1780

THE SOUND OF MARCHING filled the air. Major John André was making his way down a dirt path, with a guard on either side. When they turned the corner, he started back for a second.

"Why this emotion, sir?" asked the officer standing by his side.

"I am reconciled to my death, but I detest the mode," André said, looking straight ahead.

In front of them was a large crowd of soldiers and civilians, and in the middle was the gallows. To the right were high-ranking rebel officers on horseback; all of them were familiar faces. One of them was Nathanael Greene, the president of the jury. As he approached

Greene, he gave a puzzled look as he caught sight of a small turtle in Greene's saddlebag.

How did I come to this end? André thought to himself as they passed the downcast crowd. As André approached the wagon, which was serving as a make-shift platform, he managed to hop up with as much dignity as he could muster and place the noose around his neck. A Colonel, whom André knew as Scammel, came up.

"You may speak if you wish," he said.

André's mind swelled with the statement, and his head raced back through the days prior.

HUNDLEY'S MISSION

21 SEPTEMBER, 1780

WATER LAPPED AT THE sides of the *HMS Vulture* as the sun began to set.

"Now, Captain," the 31-year-old André said, "Here is the plan once more before I go ashore. The meeting will last until tomorrow morning. I will come down here at some time in the night and conceal myself over in those reeds. Then, you will pick me up, and we can be off."

"Very well, Sir." The captain replied, "Safe travels and Godspeed on your return. We will see you tomorrow."

With that, André climbed into a small fishing boat that had pulled alongside the ship. He nodded at the Cahoon brothers, who had been hired to transport him, to push off. When they reached the shore, André got out quickly, before anyone could spot him, and began his journey inland. As he walked through the woods, a squirrel ran past him chattering loudly, bringing a smile to his face. *There are still things to smile about in this war,* he thought to himself, *I could use more of those moments.* And he was right; his job had been taking a toll on him for a long time now. *I have to finish this mission and I can relax,* he told himself. The mission he was a part of was the biggest break the British had ever gotten, and it rested squarely on his shoulders to complete it. *West Point will be ours by the month's end. The war could even be over by New Year's.* But he knew that this was hopeful thinking, the same thing had been said about the 1777 campaign. As he thought, he made his way silently through the shadows on the side of the path. Even though he had an overcoat, he felt more comfortable staying out of sight due to the bright red uniform he wore underneath. He was on the very edge of British territory, and didn't want to be caught by a rebel raiding party.

Little did André know that a rebel at that very moment was tailing him. That chattery, red squirrel was on a mission of his own, and hot on his trail. Hundley had joined the rebel forces back at the beginning of the war. His friend, George, a small box turtle, was adopted by none other than General Nathanael Greene. Greene confided in George his worries and concerns about the progress of the war, and then George would pass them along to Hundley. He had been dreaming of this opportunity for years; his only desire was to obtain information to aid the Patriots in their fight for independence. Now was his chance, he couldn't afford to lose the trail now.

Soon, the forest path led to a rutted dirt road, and André spotted a house across the way. *This is it, it has to be.* He went to the front door and knocked. A second later a maid opened the door.

"Come in, quickly." she whispered, showing him in, "Mr. Smith is upstairs, in the guest room. I will announce your arrival."

As André stepped aside so she could close the door, a blur of red shot past. Blinking, he stared.

"Are you well, Mr. André?" the maid questioned.

"Yes, I just thought…" André paused. "It's nothing. Now, please show me where they are meeting."

They went up the stairs, into the guest bedroom. Joshua Smith, stood in the middle of the room. The curtains were drawn, and a table was set up in the middle of the room. Another man was seated in one of the two chairs, with his face towards the fire.

"Here you are," Smith said, "We were getting worried about you. If there is anything I can get you gentlemen, then ring this bell and I will see what I can do. Now, I will let you two be." Smith left the room and André sat down. The man seated next to him turned to face the small table and frowned.

"Well, General Arnold," André said, "Let us get to business." Lowering their voices, the two began their negotiations.

And just as quietly, a spy listened to their conversation. Under the washstand, Hundley was making careful notes of their plans. And as the night dragged on, his squirrel energy started to get to him. *I have to get out of here to tell George!* He thought, trying not to say it out loud. His moment came when the two men rang the little bell. When Smith entered the room to see what they wanted, Hundley scurried out as fast as he could and made his way out of the back door, past the well, and into the woods. Then he came to his friend, George, who was waiting by some rocks on the river.

"George," Hundley said, nearly colliding with his friend's shell, "Arnold wants £20,000 for West Point. Can you believe that?!"

"That is a lot of money, Hundley," George said slowly, "but we need to know when they are planning to hand over the fort."

"I think it will be the 22nd of September."

"That's tomorrow Hundley!" George said "We must move quickly, you must go back and find out where André is headed…. Wait," he paused, listening, "Hundley, what is that noise?" Men's voices could be heard just beyond a small meadow to their left. "Fire!" one of the men shouted. Then the world exploded.

Cannons opened fire on the dark outline of the *HMS Vulture*, sitting on the Hudson River. The pressure wave shook the ground as shots soared overhead. They were right in front of a Patriot cannon battery!

"Hundley, go find out what they are planning." George yelled. Hundley could only manage to read his lips "I will be fine."

"George, I-" but Hundley stopped, and realized George's point: they had come too far to stop now.

Turning, he ran back to the house, leaving George in the middle of a cannon duel on the false assurance of shell-safety standards. When he got back to the house, he could see that the candles in the guest room were still burning. *Good, I haven't missed him.* He thought.

Getting back in the house was easy. It was harder waiting for morning, and wondering about George. Upstairs in the guest room, Hundley found that André had decided to stay the night, and was now sleeping in the four-poster bed with the curtains drawn. As for Arnold, he was nowhere to be found. *He must have gone back to West Point.*

In the morning, as the sun began to rise, the people in the house started to stir.

"Good Morrow. The battle seemed very near in the night," Mr. Smith replied, coming into the dining room. "It kept the whole house up."

"Yes..." André said, sipping his tea at the table. "But I think it has caused a lot more trouble than keeping the house up. That was cannon fire and the only thing out here worth firing upon at 3:00 clock in the morning is most certainly the *Vulture.*"

"You are right. I will send someone down to make sure that it is still here and in one piece, but you might want to make other plans."

"I have." André answered. "My pass is on the dresser. As soon as your person gets back with the news, then I will be setting off."

"You can't go in those clothes, you can use some of mine." Smith offered "And I will accompany you until you reach the British line. That is about 15 miles."

The two men kept talking, but Hundley had moved on, *I must see his pass.* He came to the dresser and found multiple papers just where André had said they'd be. Opening the first, he began to read.

To Colonel Elisha Sheldon Sept. 9th 1780
Sir

"I am told my name is made known to you, and that I may hope your indulgence in permitting me to meet a friend near your posts. I will endeavor to obtain permission to go out with a flag which will be sent to Dobb's ferry on Monday next, the 11th, at 12 o'clock, then I shall be happy to meet Mr. G—t. should I not be allowed to go, the officer who is to command the escort, between whom and myself no distnotion need be made, can speak on the affair

Let me entreat you, Sir, to favor a matter so interesting to the parties concerned, and which is of so private a nature that the public on neither side can be injured by it

'I shall be happy on my part in doing any act of kindness to you in a family or property concern of a similar nature. I trust I shall not be detained, but should any old grudge be a cause for it, I shall rather risk that, than neglect the business in question, or assume a mysterious character to carry on an innocent affair, and, as friends have advised, get to your lines by stealth.

I am, sir, with all regard, your most obedient humble servant,

John Anderson

Who is Anderson? wondered Hundley. He then looked through the rest of the papers on the dresser and found that they were maps of West Point, as well as a letter dated several days earlier:

176.30.3 9.5.12 64.3.4 119.2.3 225.21.4 158.23.2
138.20.9 52.12.13 97.2.12

"A secret message!" Hundley exclaimed. But his excitement was cut short with the sound of talking coming from the stair hall. "I have to get to George!" Hundley cried as he climbed out the window, then ran down the wood siding and began searching for George.

"George, George! Where are you, George?!" Hundley searched frantically through the carnage of the battle for his friend.

"Here I am, Hundley, don't worry." George said, coming out from a splintered and battered fallen tree, "I took shelter here early in the battle. But enough about that, what is André doing?"

"He has a pass and papers regarding West Point." Hundley reported, "If the ship is gone, then he will go down to New York by land."

"Well, the ship left after the cannonade," interrupted Geroge, "so we will have to move quickly if we want to catch him."

"How, George?" Hundley asked, "Mrs. Greene isn't here to help us get this news to them on time." Hundley recalled when Catharine, wife of Nathanael Greene, had been in New Jersey to settle a debt owed by the army to the family and so got the security (George) back, and brought him safely back to her husband.

"You will have to go without me Hundley," George said, "I'm too slow, besides you did a great job last night. You can do it."

"Oh thank you George for having so much faith in me, but I can't."

"You must Hundley, this is your chance to make Greene proud and be the spy you always wanted to be."

"Ok George, I will do it for Greene." Then Hundley bounded away in search of André. He didn't have to look far, his target was just saddling a horse when Hundley got there.

Once saddled, André and Smith moved out. Hundley followed them down the road; roughly four hours later, Smith turned around and André moved on alone. He seemed to relax in the saddle. *I'm home free, I'm in British lines, I'm there!* Then suddenly, his horse reared and snapped him out of his thoughts.

"Whoa, boy," he said, "what is that squirrel doing?"

Hundley had run in front of his horse and was acting like his true self, a crazy squirrel. *Come on, you three,* Hundley thought to himself as he ran. Then just as he planned, three men dressed in red coats came out from their hiding places to see what the commotion was about. Hundley had acquired intel, after a conversation with George, that not all men in red coats are fighting for the British. Greene even had a red coat as part of his militia group uniform. And with years of looking at it, Hundley could tell the difference between British and militia uniforms. And these men were definitely militia. However, André was distracted and didn't notice the difference in time.

"Move aside soldiers" André ordered "I have important business."

The three men remained in his path undaunted.

"What are you doing?!" André asks, frustrated and anxious to move forward.

"The real question is what are you doing?" one of the men replied.

At this André's heart skipped a beat. *What have I done?*

Hundley watching the unsuspecting André being captured was enjoying a mini celebration. "They got him, they got him! I have to tell George, I did it!"

***

SALEM, NEW YORK
24 SEPTEMBER, 1780

André sat down exhausted from the day's ride. He could hear men downstairs moving their baggage and securing their horses. He heard the voice of Major Benjamin Tallmadge, the commander of his guard, posting sentries outside his door. Deeply troubled knowing his fate, the death sentence was clear; but he hoped to persuade his captor to let him die an honorable death. So he took up his quill and began his plea to Washington,

> *Dear Sir,*
>
> *Buoy'd above the Terror of Death by the Consciousness of a Life devoted to honorable pursuits and Stained with no Action that can give me Remorse, I trust the request I make to your Excellency at this Serious period and which is to Soften my last moments will not be rejected.*
>
> *Sympathy towards a Soldier will Surely induce Your Excellency and a military Tribunal to adapt the Mode of my death to the feelings of a Man of honour.*
>
> *Let me hope Sir, that if ought in my Character impresses you with Esteem towards me, if ought in my*

Misfortunes marks me as the Victim of policy and not of resentment, I shall experience the Operation of these Feelings in your Breast by being informed that I am not to die on a Gibbet.I have the honour to be Your Excellency Most obedient and most humble Servant
    John André Adj. Gen. to the Brit: Army

* * *

REFORMED CHURCH, TAPPAN, NEW YORK
29 SEPTEMBER, 1780

"Hundley you did a great job" George said as they sat outside the courtroom. "You did just the right things."

"Oh, thank you!" Hundley said, "Quiet George, they are starting the trial."

"Gentlemen," the officer of the court stood and began to read Washington's letter addressing the board members:

Major André, adjutant general to the British army will be brought before you for your examination. He came within our lines in the night, on an interview with major General Arnold, and in an assumed character; and was taken within our lines, in a disguised habit, with a pass under a feigned name, and with the inclosed papers concealed upon him. After a careful examination, you will be pleased as speedily as possible, to report a precise state of his case, together with your opinion of the light In which he ought to be considered, and the punishment that ought to be inflected. The judge-advocate will attend to assist in the matter, which he will lay before the board.

*I have the honor to be, gentlemen, your most obedient
and humble servant,*

> *G. Washington*

"Gentlemen, we will now review the evidence put forward, including testimony of soldiers involved in the battle against the *HMS Vulture*, those who captured André, as well as from Mr. Smith, an alleged accomplice and known Loyalist in our custody." stated John Laurance, the chief prosecutor. As every new piece of evidence was introduced, André and his lawyer replied in his defense,

"I had business with Arnold and permissions to pass behind lines in civilian dress."

Next into evidence, was the actual pass confiscated from André at the time of his capture. André jumped to his feet in protest,

"I was under orders from General Clinton at the time of writing this letter." André hoped that Clinton would come to an agreement of exchange with Washington. *If Clinton turns Arnold over to the rebels, then other defectors would turn tail, and we would no longer have their support. It is a no-win situation.*

Next, one of the three men who arrested André came to the stand,

"Now, Mr. Wart, what did you and your company do after you took André into custody?" the prosecution asked.

"We didn't know he was a Major, he gave us his name as John Anderson. He did give us an order, seeing we were dressed like Red Coats. Once we had him in custody, we met the rest of our company at Davis Hill and proceeded to North Castle and surrendered him to Colonel John James."

"Thank you, Mr. Wart, no more questions." The defense attorney declined to ask questions, so the next witness was called. "Please state your name for the board."

"Colonel John James," replied the witness.

"In the previous testimony, it was established that a man under the alias John Anderson was brought to your custody. Can you tell the court what happened next?"

"Well, upon examining his papers I discovered his true identity, Major John André. Then I was faced with a dilemma. In the end I told General Washington who was in the area, and I also informed Arnold in case that it was just a misunderstanding."

THE VERDICT

AS THE BOARD WAS considering their options, Hundley began to fidget, "These people moved almost as fast as me with this trial–"

"Shhh…pipe down," said George, "Greene is about to speak."

"He is either a spy or an innocent man." Greene stood to address the board. "If the latter, to execute him in any way will be murder. If the former, the mode of his death is prescribed by law."

George and Hundley were both struck silent by the heaviness of those words.

André hung his head. He had one more hope and that was that they would oblige his request, and have him shot like an officer and not be further disgraced by hanging.

***

2 OCTOBER, 1780

André, waiting with his servants and the guards, sat listening to the clock slowly ticking. One of his servants began to sob. André quickly corrected him, "come back when you are more put together. Gentlemen, I'm ready when the time comes."

With that a knock came on the door. Maj. Tallmadge was there to escort him.

"The time has come, André" Tallmadge announced with a note of solemnity in his voice.

André put down his teacup and stood up from the table. Tallmadge escorted André down the street towards the execution site. A large crowd was gathered, some familiar faces and others who had decided his fate. As André walked and looked into their faces he thought *at least some have empathy for me and care to let me have my dignity.*

At the gallows, Colonel Scammel turned to André, "Any last words."

André thought for a moment, *"I pray you to bear me witness that I meet my fate like a brave man."*

George and Hundley, who were hiding in Greene's saddlebags. watch on in horror. *This poor young man fought valiantly for his home-land and now is paying the price of betrayal* George thought as he had Hundley turn around, "You don't want to see what happens next

Hundley," George said.

And with that the wagon began to move, and the end came.

ABOUT

JOHN ANDRÉ

John André was born into a wealthy family in London and would come over to the colonies at the start of the Revolution. In Philadelphia, Peggy Shippen (a wealthy loyalist) took notice of him. In 1779, André was promoted to Major and named the Adjutant General of the North American British Army. By April he was the head of the British Secret Service. By 1780, through Shippen, André began to secretly correspond with Arnold. Their failed plot would lead to André being found guilty and sent to the gallows as a spy. He requested that he be shot by a firing squad as a courtesy of war, but George Washington denied his request and he was hanged on 2 October, 1780, in Tappan, New York.

JOHN ANDRÉ

NOTES FROM THE AUTHOR

Historical accuracy is my main focus—quotes, actual letters and actual correspondence are included—although I have taken the liberty to sometimes divide them up in ways to better fit my scenes.

Hundley (the high-spirited squirrel) and George (turtle) are fictional characters that carry throughout my part of this trilogy. Their role is to assist Greene and ensure the victory of the Patriots. Hundley began in the trilogy with a strong desire to be a spy and intercept messages, so their involvement in this installment was better suited for John André. Greene was actively involved in the trial so it felt feasible that Hundley and George could still be there fulfilling their destiny.

In André, the coded letter is in page, line, and word code (i.e. 125.21.6; page 125, line 21, word 6). You will need a copy of *The Epic Story of America Book 2 Trials, Turning Points, and Triumphs* by the Epic Patriot Campers.

GENERAL NATHANAEL GREENE

FIGHTING QUAKER'S LEGACY

by Cameron Graham

A MAN'S MOTIVATION

MORRISTOWN, NEW JERSEY
SEPTEMBER 1780

S IR," THE AIDE APPROACHED the statuesque General Greene and his staff. "News has just arrived, Wilhelm von Knyphausen is moving out of New York. "

Greene began to pace, his limp more pronounced under the stress. He gazed out over the sea of white tents that made up camp and sighed, taking the welfare of his men to heart. The responsibility of overseeing the camp in Washington's absence fully weighed on his shoulders. This news came on the tail of Colonel Alexander Hamilton's letter revealing Benedict Arnold's betrayal to their cause. This betrayal had consumed his thoughts as he remembered all the times he had confided in Arnold personally. Thus far, the army had acted honorably with the unsettling news. Greene, prior to meeting with the staff, had just penned his thoughts to his beloved wife Catharine Littlefield Greene, whom he affectionately called Caty:

The discovery of Arnold's treason before it could be brought to fruition appears to have been providential and convinces me that the liberties of America are the object of divine protection.

With West Point now vulnerable, Greene gave orders for the Pennsylvania regiments to make ready for a countermarch to block the Hessian general's path. The regiment moved into action quickly under Greene's command and made their way up the Hudson Valley, facing Knyphausen in a scrimmage. This short struggle ended in Greene's favor, with Hessians returning to New York, abandoning their plans to capture West Point. A short time after arriving back at camp, Washington rode in, returning from his meeting with French General Rochambeau. Greene went out to meet him.

"Your Excellency, Sir, it is a pleasure to see you again after this long month that you have been away," Greene said, giving a respectful bow. "How were the roads on your journey?"

"They were average for this time of the year and the hosts were very obliging to our every need," Washington replied.

"That is good to hear, General. It is good to have an ally in the fight we can rely on." Greene took a deep breath and turned to a more serious note, "Especially now with Arnold's betrayal of our trust. Any more developments on the situation, sir?"

"I have sent correspondence to the British requesting the exchange of Arnold for their Major John André. He was Arnold's contact, and it seems to me that André planned it from the start. It is almost certain that he did not work alone, but we may never know who else was involved. I do not anticipate a favorable reception to our idea for an exchange, as the British would be forfeiting any future participants in such a scheme once word got around." The weight of these words showed on Washington's face as he spoke.

"Yes, that is true." Greene replied, "It is fortunate that this is the first such betrayal of our cause; it speaks to the integrity of both our men and officers."

"Yes, however, it has caused a gap in our defenses. Washington continued, "and so I have decided to send you, my trusted friend, to oversee André's trial and get the fortifications at West Point back in order. Upon your return, I shall have found another post for you to fill."

"Sir, I will set out at once." Greene headed into his tent and began packing his belongings, careful not to leave behind his pet turtle, George, that Caty had returned to his camp not long ago. George was no ordinary turtle, but became a friend, listening to his troubles and the advancements of the war. *I am grateful to Caty for returning you to me George, I am going to need a confidant I can trust. And with winter coming, I am guessing you need someone you can trust as well.*

* * *

WEST POINT
DECEMBER 1780

Over the following weeks Greene excelled at his new position, drawing on his prior experience. Greene reflected, *Was it only four years ago that I was commander at Fort Washington? Thank Providence this is less disastrous, but the tasks are as exhausting as my quartermaster's post.* One thing was for certain: he had never before had the responsibility of overseeing the trial of a British spy. *The best laid plans sometimes go awry*, Greene thought to himself as he contemplated all that he had heard at the proceedings.

John André had sailed up the river to meet Benedict Arnold. Their meeting continued into the night, longer than they had expected, and André decided to stay at the home of a trusted Loyalist. During the night, Patriots attacked the ship that was to sail him to New York. The ship left André behind, forcing him to utilize the pass given to him by Benedict Arnold for land passage. He began to make his way to Tappan, New York.

Greene brought his mind back to the testimony of events that took place on 21 September, 1780. Three militiamen, looking for added profit, stopped André. Planning only to take his boots, they discovered papers hidden inside one of them and they immediately took him to their superior officer. Uncertain about the authenticity of the pass and unwilling to provoke hostility or question Arnold's authority, he decided to report the situation to both Arnold and

Washington. Arnold fled when he received the news, and Washington was not informed until he arrived at West Point. *We applaud the action of these militia men as if they are not as corruptible or self-serving as the one on trial,* Greene thought as he adjourned court and met for dinner with his close friend, Lafayette.

"A man's motivation is a serious matter of the heart. We place our lives, our families, our futures, and our honor on the line to fight this war. We face Loyalists who fight to stop our efforts at all costs, risking the same. Others are willing to turn a blind eye to their countrymen, but I have greater tolerance for these, rather than those who fight neither in a way to serve our cause or that of our enemy, but instead for pure monetary gains. Those men are nothing more than smugglers and thieves holding themselves to a nonexistent standard of honor."

"*Oui,* my friend. It is a good reminder, and such a pity that it shall fade from history for only the victors and their actions are honored and memorialized by their descendants. As for the occupations that the society deems unfit for gentlemen or ladies to partake of—no matter what their effect on the courses of history—are quite promptly forgotten!" Both men finished their meal in silent contemplation before heading back to the courtroom proceedings.

* * *

The jury, overseen by Greene, had no question about André being a spy and he was to face death. The remaining deliberation was to address the prisoner's request to be shot as a soldier instead of hanging as a spy. Greene addressed the jury,

"André was either a spy, or an innocent man. If the latter, to execute him in any way will be murder. If the former, the mode of his death is prescribed by law." John André hung as a lowly spy, forever remembered as such in the story of history.

After the trial, Greene returned to West Point and continued with everyday operations, no longer allowing the events to occupy his thoughts until news of Gates' disaster in the Southern Department reached him. Greene read the report, summarizing the details out loud to his trusted companion and pet, George.

"In less than a month, Gates decided to attack the British in a direct assault on one of their major supply depots at Camden, South Carolina. After marching in the open countryside, Gates and the army set up camp to eat a hasty meal of half-baked bread, uncooked beef, and molasses—a substitute for rum." Looking up from the report, Greene shook his head, "With those conditions, lack of food or any rest, it was no wonder that the soldiers were breaking ranks all night long as the army made its way to meet with the North Carolina militia. On the morning of the battle, Gates, disciplined in the British way of fighting, lined up his army with his strongest men on the right. He inadvertently lost the battle and half his men, despite outnumbering his enemy." Greene set down the report and paced the tent.

This report portrays Gates in an unfavorable light, casting doubt on his previous campaigns. Greene thought to himself, I *can almost un-*

derstand why Benedict Arnold felt cheated when Gates received full credit for victory at Saratoga when reality told a different story…no matter. I may be able to empathize, but I will not sympathize with him. It is no excuse. These matters were but one thing on his mind.

* * *

Congress was asking for a new commander to be appointed for the Southern Department and had relinquished its power to choose after their previous two choices failed, leaving the choice up to Washington. Greene immediately approached Washington, recommending his long-time personal friend, Henry Knox,

"Your Excellency, all obstacles vanish before him."

"That is exactly why I cannot spare him." Washington responded, The southern campaign is in disarray and needs a skilled, strategic leader I can trust; a gentleman in whom I place the most entire confidence. So, I have chosen *you* to take command."

Overjoyed to be once again in command, Greene ran to share the news with Caty, say his farewells, and travel south. His traveling companion, Baron de Steuben, was appointed second in command. Their first stop was the capital of the young rebellion, Philadelphia. Once there, they set to work, raising support for the southern army, meeting with congressmen and merchants. Greene did not care much about politicians and was greatly annoyed by their slow decision-making process and reluctance to set aside personal views and work together to raise money for the cause, or anything else for that matter. Upon returning after a long day of meetings to their apartment in the city, Greene found de Steuben reading a book.

"It had been happy for me if I could have lived a private life in peace and plenty, enjoying all the happiness that results from a well-tempered society founded on mutual esteem." Greene vented, "But the injury done my country, and the chains of slavery forging for all posterity, calls me forth to defend our common rights, and repel the bold invaders of the sons of freedom. And it is for this reason and that only that I stay on." At which de Steuben nodded his head and returned to his book.

Leaving behind the frustrations of Philadelphia, they continued south to meet Thomas Jefferson at Monticello. However, when they arrived, Jefferson was leaving his plantation as the British were moving into the region, and he was unable to provide support other than his sympathies. With no hope left for political support, Greene traveled on to meet the southern army while de Steuben stayed in Virginia with the local militia to protect the state and raise more troops there.

TAKING COMMAND

O N ARRIVAL, GREENE SOUGHT out Gates. *I wonder if there will be hostility between us in the transfer of command,* Greene thought. *I do hope for a smooth, peaceful transition for the sake of the men.* Greene made his way to the marquee in the center of camp and saw Gates.

"General Gates, His Excellency has sent me with orders to relieve you of your command." Before Greene could finish, Gates extended his hand.

"General Greene, I wish you luck on your endeavor. My aides shall inform you of the situation as I tend to the business of packing." Gates turned and walked away.

Greene immediately met with the aides and became acquainted with his new and very capable subordinates. Greene's next decision went against traditional military thinking as he split his forces in two, a "flying army" composed of dragoons that were led by Daniel Morgan, one of the fine line officers. Greene was well aware a line officer's actions often dictate the outcome of a battle. Greene, anxious to outline his plan to Morgan, sat down in his tent to write him:

It is my order to split into three lines. The first, inexperienced militia, will advance and fire twice and fall back. The second line is to have the same orders and the third line should consist of our most battle-hardened Continental Regulars. With our long rifles, we should be an advantage, not seen before. It is my hope that the enemy will follow us, thus splitting their focus. For it will prove advantageous to us in the end, for we know this country and can maneuver through it with more speed than them.

After he sealed the letter and set it aside, he next wrote Washington, assuring him of his plan:

Don't be surprised if my movements don't correspond with your ideas of military propriety. War is an intricate business, and people are often saved by ways and means they least look for or expect.

Now to see how this plan turns out! Greene thought to himself as he walked out of his tent.

INDEPENDENCE

***

CAMP NEAR CAIN CREEK
17 JANUARY, 1781

Greene had been pacing the camp, awaiting news from Morgan about the situation at Cowpens. His aide-de-camp handed him a message and he immediately began to read.

> *Dear Sir,*
>
> *The Troops I had the Honor to command have been so fortunate as to obtain a compleat Victory over a Detachment from the British Army commanded by Lt Colonel Tarlton. The Action happened on the 17th Instant about Sunrise at the Cowpens. It perhaps would be well to remark, for the Honour of the American Arms, that Altho the Progress of this Corps was marked with Burnings and Devastations & altho' they have waged the most cruel Warfare, not a man was killed, wounded, or even insulted after he surrendered. Had not Britons during this Contest received so many Lessons of Humanity, I should flatter myself that this might teach them a little, but I fear they are incorrigible.*

As he continued reading the letter, he learned that Morgan inflicted heavy casualties against the British forces led by Lt. Col. Banastre Tarleton utilizing the strategy outlined by Greene. Tarleton was taken by surprise when the militia returned as ordered and encircled the British. As he was finishing the letter, a scout arrived.

"General our adversaries, Lt. General Earl Cornwallis and General James Webster have now set out in pursuit of Morgan, and are coming up in number from Charlotte!"

Greene wasted no time, he needed to get his army on the move and get word to Morgan. It was a flurry of activity as men prepared to march, Greene handed his orders to his most trusted messenger. As he watched the rider depart, he wondered if Morgan would get the message in time.

After giving his men some rest, Morgan began his retreat north, knowing they would have to keep a feverish pace if there was any hope. As he was moving his men out, Greene's messenger arrived with his orders: *Meet at Guilford Courthouse.* Morgan immediately crossed the Yadkin River and marched 60 miles into town.

MAKE READY, RACE TO THE DAN

GUILFORD COURTHOUSE
MARCH 1781

THERE TO MEET MORGAN on his arrival was a detachment of Continental Regulars under General Huger along with Lt Colonel "Light Horse Harry" Lee's regiment of dragoons. Greene was strategizing alone inside his tent. *I often wonder if the formalities of the council of wars, which allow for strategic planning, only delay progress and shield us from honest opinions of officers afraid to speak contrary to the discussions.* His thoughts were interrupted by the sound of officers approaching his tent. As they approached, he could hear their conversation.

"Cornwallis is still in pursuit despite our combined force that now awaits him." Lee said to the small group of officers outside the tent.

"Cornwallis may still be advancing, but his horses are going slower than donkeys!" laughed another in a raspy voice, "Besides, the troops are tired. Some of the men do not have tents to sleep in. We have the high ground, I say stay here and fight."

"But as you said, the men are tired and they are not in fighting condition." John Laurens interrupted, "We have boats on the Dan River, I say we cross, then we can rest."

"Gentlemen," Greene stepped out of his tent, clearing his throat. Their conversation stopped short. "Shall we get down to business?" as he invited them inside his tent. "Our men are tired, some have been lacking in supplies, and Cornwallis is still advancing. We will advance to the fords on the Dan River, where we have boats waiting. It is my hope that we will have sufficient boats to get our men across to Virginia before the British arrive to give us time to get our men ready for battle." The men offered no objections and nodded in agreement as Greene, drawing from his personal study in military science, continued. "Have the rear guard split off in a fainting action towards Dixie's Ferry, and then they are to await the orders to rejoin us in our flight northward once we are certain our actions are successful. Do we agree?" With no objections, the meeting dispersed and the troops made ready.

* * *

The tired men began to move out, forced to face constant scrimmages along the march with British dragoons, at some points only a hundred yards away from Greene's men. Despite the fighting along the way, the Patriots were able to cross the Dan River just hours before Cornwallis reached the river. Despite Cornwallis's attempts to speed up his men by burning supplies and baggage, he was left with no boats and no choice but to turn back after an exhausting march.

Six days later, after having his men rest up and get more supplies, Greene was on the move again, and this time, he was the hunter luring his prey into a trap. And with him loose in the Carolinas, the Redcoats were forced to protect both Loyalists and their supply depots across the two states to maintain control and march to meet Greene at Guilford Courthouse.

* * *

BATTLE OF GUILFORD COURTHOUSE
15 MARCH, 1781

Greene intended to engage the 23rd and 33rd regiments earlier that morning at Deep River, close to their current position. However, his scouts reported that the British were making their way towards the courthouse. Greene decided to hold their position and make his stand at Guilford Courthouse. He was joined by the local North Carolina Militia and the Virginia Militia bringing his force to 4,400 men ready to face the 2,385 British force.

Around 10 AM, a battle was taking place at New Garden between Colonel "Light Horse Harry" Lee, father of Robert E Lee, and Lt Colonel Banastre Tarleton. Colonel Lee had the upper hand inflicting many injuries to the British prior to having to retreat and join the Patriot lines. At 12:30 the British began their battle against the Patriot line. Nathanael Greene formed three lines of attack, the North Carolinians in the first line, Virginians in the second line and Greene remained with the battle-hardened Continental Regulars three-quarters of a mile back from the front lines. Before the battle, Lee rallied the North Carolina militia saying, "*My brave boys, your land, your lives, and your country depend on your conduct this day.*"

With the British advance, the militia was ordered to only fire three times before falling back. The militia were faithful to their orders, inflicting heavy casualties on the British prior to being forced back into the woods.

At 1:15 the King's troops reach the Patriot's second line. The Virginians stood firm as the first line continued their retreat. The British were met with stiff resistance. After an hour of fighting, the British suffered heavy casualties. General Webster orders the British to come around and out flank the Patriots on both the left and right flanks. The militia began to fall back; but officers quickly ordered the men to stand and fight. Their efforts were futile, and the British broke through to face the Continental Regulars.

Greene held the superior position, atop a ridge. The British 33rd was the first regiment to arrive and decided to push forward without waiting for reinforcements. Brigadier General Webster was injured during the battle. As they continued fighting, the remainder of the British line arrived. Reinforcements were met with stiff resistance by the 2nd Maryland Regiment; however, they were forced back, and the British were able to seize some of the artillery, leaving the flank exposed. The 1st Maryland division, along with cavalry units, met serious opposition and were engaged in desperate hand-to-hand combat. The British opened fire with grapeshot into the fray, killing both Patriots and British alike, and the 1st Maryland began their retreat. The British strengthened in numbers when the 23rd and 71st regiments joined together, and the Continental Army retreated. The British claimed victory, but the cost was high. They lost the lives of over one quarter of their men for a field in North Carolina.

Greene rode up and down the ranks, overseeing the retreat of his men, encouraging them where he could. Seeing his men struggling with an artillery piece and unwilling to surrender it to the mud, Greene dismounted and came to aid them in their efforts. As they were working, an aide to Greene approached.

"Sir, a message from Colonel Otho Williams's rear guard. Our wounded, along with the British's most severely wounded, are being collected and brought to the Quaker settlement at New Garden."

Greene, getting back on his horse, thought silently with a heavy heart. *These Quakers are still the same as I encountered in Rhode Island they sit idly by unwilling to fight, unaware that peace and freedom come at a cost, one they are reluctant to pay. But I am grateful they are caring for our wounded.* He dismissed his aide, keeping his thoughts to himself with hopes he could get the chance to share them with Caty soon.

Later that night, an aide-de-camp delivered a letter to his tent. He immediately recognized the handwriting; his heart leapt within his chest. He sat down to read the letter, which was from Caty. She was with Martha Washington at the time she had written, which meant she would be arriving soon. In the harsh reality of things, his heart went to a deep regard for her safety, and he set to work immediately to advise her to slow her progress and stay within the protection he could provide:

> *My dearest Caty,*
>
> *I have sent you a company of troops to meet you as you come from Virginia into this quarter and to guard you safely here. I can say the human misery has become a subject for sport and ridicule. With us the difference between Whig and Tory is little more than a division of sentiment and persecute each other with little less than savage fury, distressing the populace. When I compare your situation with those miserable people in this quarter, disagreeable as it may be from our long and distant separation, I cannot help feeling thankful that your cup has not a mixture of bitterness like theirs. Hundreds of families that formerly lived in great opulence are now reduced to beggary and want. A Captain who is now with me and who has just got his family from near the Lines of the Enemy had his Sister murdered a few days since, and seven of her children wounded, the oldest not twelve years of age. The sufferings and distress of the Inhabitants beggars all description, and requires the liveliest imagination to conceive the cruelties and devastations which prevail. I will not pain your humanity by a further relation of, the distresses which rage in this quarter; nor would I have mentioned them at all, but to convince you that you*

are not the most unhappy of all creation. God grant us a speedy and happy meeting, by giving to the Country peace, liberty and safety. I look forward to us meeting again but the exact time to be governed by Providence.

N. Greene

With the matters of the heart taken care of, he turned back to his military duties. With Cornwallis in Virginia and not going on campaigns any time soon, Greene responded with an assault to start retaking the south, starting with the supply depots. Over the course of April, he sent detachments of soldiers under his experienced officer corps to besiege the forts and town where the British had stored food, ammo, and supplies.

***

TOWN OF NINETY SIX
22 MAY, 1781

Greene's army arrived on the outskirts of the town and found that it was defended by 550 Loyalists under Lt. Col. John H Cruger. After surveying the area, Greene found that the town's strongest defense was the star-shaped fort. Kościuszko, Greene's chief engineer, trained in siegeworks, set the sappers (diggers consisting of patriots and slaves) to work. They dug a total of three parallels along with three zigzag approach trenches, mounding up the earth for protection. The zigzag pattern made it more difficult for Loyalists to fire on men in the trenches. Greene had a tower constructed that looked down into the fort, and placed snipers to add to their protection. The work was exhausting, and the sappers finally finished the Third Parallel on 10 June, 1781. Now they were in musket range of the Loyalists. Lt. Colonel Henry Lee had returned to camp just two days prior, triumphant from his fight for Augusta. He disagreed with the plan and encouraged Greene to abandon it and attack the Stockade Fort.

"A British relief party, numbering nearly 2,000 men under the command of Lord Rawdon, is headed towards the fort!" a messenger riding into camp announced, "We should expect them to arrive in a week's time." Realizing time was against him, Greene prepared for an all-out assault against the British Garrison on 18 June, 1781. The fighting was intense with losses on both sides. *Reinforcements are nearing, their arrival will leave us outnumbered and trapped between British lines.*

"Men, retreat!" Greene ordered. Greene and his army slipped away before dawn on 20th of June, moving north. Greene addressed his men:

"We fight, get beat, rise and fight again. This loss is not the end. Hold your heads high, men. We may have lost this siege, but our offensive has weakened the stronghold in the back country."

* * *

EUTAW SPRINGS, SOUTH CAROLINA
8 SEPTEMBER, 1781

Despite the setback at Ninety Six, Greene was determined to drive the British from the South Carolina backcountry. Just as determined as Cornwallis was to remain in Virginia and target Patriot supplies.

"We're right on top of them," Greene smiled.

They were just outside of Eutaw Springs, and the British had no idea. The army had just left camp at High Hills and was now on the march to trap the 2,000 British troops who were under Lt Col. Alexander Stewart. Stewart had failed to send out any scouts and, in fact, sent out a quarter of his men to find food instead. Greene's men, numbering 2,200, quickly rounded up the foraging parties and moved in to attack the camp. Using the three-line approach, Greene pushed ahead and inflicted heavy casualties on the British. Greene, sensing it was time to leave, fell back. Lieutenant Colonel William Washington, second cousin to George Washington, with his mounted troops, charged the British flank. In the struggle Washington was knocked out of his saddle, captured, and taken to Charles Town. Greene and his men were afforded a reprieve once the battle had passed.

A month later, Greene received news that Cornwallis surrendered at Yorktown. Greene celebrated the victory with his men, knowing that the end of the fighting was near. As he returned to his tent, Greene's concern for his men was at the forefront of his mind. *Here we are at the end of the fight, and the problem is still the same. Congress has never understood the cost of our independence. My men know the cost too well. They need food, basic supplies, and owed back pay.* Greene paused and noticed his turtle, George, and smiled. "Well, George, Congress moves into action slower than, I dare say, you do. There may be surrender, but there is still an army to maintain while we wait for peace to come. I have already placed the order for canteens and now I need to get them food and other supplies. These men have paid a higher price than Congress could ever afford. While we wait on their back pay, I must take action. I am sure Caty will understand I must care for my men."

* * *

SPELL HALL COVENTRY, RHODE ISLAND
DECEMBER 1783

Greene looks out over the family forge, the cold winter air blowing snow on the ground. Greene had built this house in 1770, intending on raising his family here. But the war had other things in mind. Loans he had made to support his troops were now due, and Congress refused his petition for financial aid. In the end, the property would have to be sold to someone. *I am grateful that my brother, Jacob, can buy it and keep it in the family.*

Farewells were never easy. Independence is never free. The war had cost more than money; the sacrifice his sweet Caty and his children were making now was just another one of those debts. As Greene gazed out over the horizon, he had high hopes for the future.

"Jacob, take care," Greene said, "and keep watch over your family. I hope that this house will serve you well."

"It will, my brother," Jacob responded, " be safe on your journey, may the Lord be with you."

"You as well." Greene said as he turned to the rest of his family,

"The carriages are ready, and we must be going." With that, his wife and five children settled in for the long journey. As they were pulling away, Greene held Caty's hand, grateful that the things that matter most still remained.

EPILOGUE

GREENE LEFT HIS HOME of his Quaker history and upbringing, to move to his Georgia plantation, Mulberry Grove. The plantation was a gift from the state in recognition of his service and unwavering actions that had saved it—a legacy of a Fighting Quaker. Just as the plantation started to prosper, Greene died from sunstroke after touring his neighbor's rice field (three years after the war ended, on 19 June, 1786).

Following his death, letters were circulated among his closest friends. George Washington expressed his sorrow and acknowledged the significant loss to the newly formed nation. Washington wrote expressing his expectation that Thomas Jefferson, *in common with your Countrymen, have regretted the loss of so great and so honest a man.*

Knox, in a letter to George Washington, wrote:

The death of our common & invaluable friend Genl Greene, has been too melancholy and affecting a theme to write upon.

Catharine waged a steady campaign to get Nathanael's debts forgiven. She contacted every friend she and her husband had ever made, and slowly worked her way through the U.S. government. Alexander Hamilton personally oversaw her case, and although George Washington felt he couldn't intervene due to his position as president, there is no doubt that he privately supported and counselled her. Her actions drew criticism, but Catharine continued undaunted, and her hard work paid off. In 1792, Congress passed a bill awarding her full compensation for all of her husband's debts. Catharine celebrated by writing a friend:

I can tell you, my dear friend, that I feel as saucy as you please—not only because I am independent, but because I have gained a complete triumph over some of my friends who did not wish me success.

There is no doubt that Greene would have been proud of the fighting spirit inside of his beloved Caty.

ABOUT

NATHANAEL GREENE

Nathanael Greene was born and raised a Quaker in Rhode Island, and ran the family foundry before he became a major supporter for the cause of independence. He was close friends and trusted companion to George Washington and Henry Knox. He became known as the Fighting Quaker. His study of military strategy and his dedication made him an asset. He fought his whole career to make sure to care for his men, and at Valley Forge organized men and supplies as Quartermaster General. Most of his fighting days were in the Southern Campaign. He also served as president of the board at John André's trial. After the war he moved to Georgia to run a plantation. There he died of sun stroke on 19 June, 1786.

ABOUT THE AUTHOR

CAMERON GRAHAM

Young historian and reenactor, Cameron Graham, has immersed himself in the life of Nathanael Greene in hopes to share his story with others and ignite their own love of history. Over the course of the *Epic Story of America* trilogy, he has spent many hours pouring over history books, documentaries, and letters written by Greene. Reenactment allows him the unique opportunity to walk, work, and fight alongside those from that era. Cameron is an active member of his community seeking to make an impact, lover of his dog, and a homeschooler who lives in Arizona.

MAJOR GENERAL HENRY KNOX

by Emmanuel Morisset

TO GOD, who turned my fight for life into a story of grace and purpose. To my parents, Jocelyn and Rose, my siblings Mikha'El and Gabrielle, and my grandmother Yvrose, whose faith and prayers remind me daily that nothing is impossible when God holds the pen.

THE WEIGHT OF IRON AND PROVIDENCE

HUDSON RIVER VALLEY
WINTER: JANUARY 1775

THE ROAD WASN'T THERE anymore. What passed for one was frozen ruts and churned mud that grabbed at wheels and hooves like it had a personal grudge. The cannons groaned behind Knox's column, big iron beasts that the oxen pulled with about as much enthusiasm as a man walking to his hanging.

Henry Knox rode up front, ice crusting his eyebrows. The road ahead curved around a rock face, a nasty climb that made his stomach turn. Behind him, one of the cannon sleds had stopped moving again.

"Rusty! Get moving, you four-legged disaster!" Corporal Merriweather shouted.

The donkey planted his hooves and snorted as if personally offended.

"He doesn't like hills," Knox said, climbing down from his saddle. He walked over to Rusty, who eyed him with donkey skepticism. "Come on, boy. We've got a war to win, and it won't wait for your artistic temperament."

Rusty snorted, then nudged Knox's coat. After a moment's consideration, he started pulling the sled forward, making sure everyone knew he wasn't happy about it.

Elijah padded up from behind the column. The bear had been carrying a broken axle earlier, and now he walked alongside like he was guarding it. The soldiers had stopped questioning his presence weeks ago.

A white dove circled overhead, bright against the gray sky. Knox squinted up. "There's Esther."

The bird dropped down and landed on the cannon's muzzle. Knox offered her seeds from his coat. She ate delicately, then flew off toward camp, always from Lucy's direction.

The men were hunched over like question marks, but they kept moving. Some had rags wrapped around their feet. Others limped from frostbite. A few hummed tunes under their breath.

Knox let out a long breath that turned white in the air. "Lord, give me strength enough for all of them," he whispered.

From the ridge above, a hidden pair of eyes watched Knox's every move.

HENRY KNOX

THE SPY WHO HESITATED

KNOX'S ENCAMPMENT,
NEAR THE HUDSON RIVER, JANUARY 1781

A MESSENGER STUMBLED INTO KNOX'S tent, snow covering his coat. "Sir, movement spotted on the southern ridge. Could be British scouts."

Knox stepped outside. The horizon was empty, but something felt wrong. Rusty woke up and started braying, trouble, he seemed to say. Elijah got to his feet, tension in his shoulders.

"Double the watches," Knox told Colonel Wadsworth. "Tonight, we figure out how to move faster without losing half our guns to the mud."

Upon the ridge, hidden in the trees, a boy watched through a spyglass. His hand shook, but not from the cold. His name was Thomas, and he hadn't decided yet which side of this war he was really on.

Thomas pulled the coded message from his coat. British intelligence had been clear: Knox's artillery train was the key to Patriot hopes. Sabotage the wheels, poison the oxen, anything to stop those cannons from reaching their destination.

Below, he watched Knox help a soldier whose boot had come apart, kneeling in the snow to tie leather strips around the man's foot. The gesture was so ordinary, so human, that Thomas felt something twist in his stomach.

"He's supposed to be a monster," Thomas whispered to himself, remembering his handler's words. But the man below was sharing his own rations with a shivering drummer boy who couldn't be more than fourteen.

A tiny hummingbird hovered near Thomas's ear. She'd been following him for days, as if she could sense his inner turmoil.

Thomas's hand moved to the small vial of poison meant for the water barrels. He'd done this before, always from a distance, always to faceless enemies. However, Knox had a face now. So did the drummer boy, the soldier with the broken boot, even the stubborn donkey.

For weeks, Thomas had memorized Knox's face, his gestures. His British handlers said the general was dangerous. But Thomas had seen Knox help a man fix his boot strap, give his food to a wounded drummer boy, even whisper to that donkey like the animal might understand. Thomas glanced down at the coded message again, sighing.

"I know what I came here to do," Thomas whispered. "But nobody told me he'd be like this."

THE CHOICE BETWEEN SIDES

HUDSON HIGHLANDS
SPRING 1781

GREEN PUSHED THROUGH THE thawed earth. Knox's column moved more easily now, but his mind stayed heavy. The British were getting smarter. That evening, as twilight painted the treetops, Knox heard it, a branch breaking underfoot.

"Circle left. No noise," he commanded a sentry.

They caught the boy trying to run. When they brought Thomas forward, the torchlight showed his face, eyes wide, jaw set, sweat beading on his forehead despite the cool air. His hands trembled as he clutched a red scarf he'd kept hidden, now visible.

"You've been watching us for weeks," Knox said. "But I never expected you to walk right into our camp."

A soldier dumped Thomas's pack. British orders spilled out, sealed, half-burned, but readable. "Sabotage. Coordinates. Movement plans."

Among the documents was a detailed sketch of the camp layout, along with a small glass vial, still unopened.

"Poison," Corporal Merriweather said grimly, holding up the vial.

Thomas straightened his shoulders and lifted his chin, meeting Knox's gaze with fierce determination. For a moment, he looked every inch the defiant spy he'd been trained to be.

"You had your chance to use these orders. You didn't."

The defiance cracked. Thomas's shoulders sagged. "I was supposed to," he finally said, his voice a low rasp. "But I didn't know it would be like this."

"Like what?" Knox asked.

"You. The men. The songs. The way you treated them. Even the bear."

Knox stepped closer. "I judge what people do, not what they think about doing."

"I didn't betray you."

"No. But you came close. The fact that you hesitated, that's what saved you."

Knox gestured to his men. "Take him to the supply tent. Give him something warm to eat and a place to sleep. We'll talk more in the morning."

Thomas looked up, surprised by the kindness. "You're not going to…"

"Execute you? Lock you up? No. But you need to think about what you really want to fight for."

At dawn, Knox found Thomas sitting outside the watch tent, no longer defiant. The hummingbird perched nearby, watching.

"They told me you were a monster," Thomas said quietly, looking down at the ground. "That you'd burn villages, kill prisoners."

"And what did you find?"

"A man who shares his food with donkeys and talks to bears like they're people. A man who gave me supper when he could have put a rope around my neck."

"There's the truth," Knox replied.

Thomas looked up, sighing.

"What will happen to me now?" he asked.

Knox almost smiled. "What happens to you now depends on whether you're ready to choose a side. *Really* choose."

Thomas looked toward the camp, where soldiers shared what little they had, helping each other with torn boots and patched clothes. He thought of the warm meal Knox had given him, the blanket, the simple human decency when he'd expected only punishment. "I think I already have."

VICTORY'S PRICE

YORKTOWN, VIRGINIA
OCTOBER 1781

SMOKE ROSE LIKE GHOSTS above the battered trenches. Knox stood on a makeshift earthwork, watching French batteries tear into British positions. Below, American siege lines crept forward like a slow tide.

"More powder to Battery Two!" he shouted.

Thomas, now his trusted aide, hurried up. "General! They broke through Redoubt Nine. Lafayette's pushing for Ten."

Knox nodded. "Tell Colonel Gimat to get ready for another assault."

Esther fluttered above them, cooing softly. She hadn't left Knox's side in days. But suddenly, a sharp cry cut through the noise, high and desperate. Esther dove down, wings frantic.

A scout came running, carrying something in his handkerchief. "Sir! The little hummingbird that's been with the boy; she got hit by a stray shot. She... she didn't make it."

Thomas went still. Knox knelt, gently placing his hand over the small creature. "She flew into battle for us. Even the smallest lives have courage."

By nightfall, Redoubt Ten fell. On 19 October, 1781, the British surrendered.

As drums beat and flags came down, Knox stood motionless. Elijah lay beside his boots. Esther perched on the cannon barrel, a single green feather from the little hummingbird clinging to her breast.

"Blessed be the LORD my strength which teacheth my hands to war," Knox whispered, quoting Psalms 144:1. He looked east toward home, sighing with satisfaction.

THE CONSPIRACY THAT WASN'T

NEW WINDSOR CANTONMENT
MARCH 1783

VICTORY AT YORKTOWN SHOULD have been the end. Instead, Knox found himself staring at problems cannons couldn't solve. The cantonment stretched along the Hudson like a wooden city, six hundred log huts housing soldiers who'd won a war but couldn't go home. Men promised a pay that never came.

Knox, now the youngest major general in the Continental Army, walked between the huts. Elijah padded beside him, older now, muzzle gray but eyes sharp. Thomas had grown taller, no longer the frightened boy spy, but Knox's personal companion.

The anonymous letter circulated through the officers' quarters like a disease, calling for the army to "suspect the man who would advise to more moderation and longer forbearance."

"They're calling for a meeting," Thomas said quietly. "The officers want to decide what to do about Congress."

Knox held the inflammatory letter. "And what do you think we should do?"

Thomas considered the matter carefully. "I think we should remember why we fought this war in the first place."

Word came that Washington would address the officers personally. In the Temple of Virtue, Washington faced the assembled men, hardened soldiers who'd given everything for their country and received little in return.

He spoke with quiet authority about duty, honor, and their country's need. But when he struggled to read a letter from Congress, putting on his spectacles, the moment turned.

"Gentlemen," Washington said, "you will permit me to put on my spectacles, for I have not only grown gray but almost blind in the service of my country."

The room went silent. Knox felt tears prick his eyes as these hardened soldiers remembered what they were fighting for, not just pay, but the idea that free men could govern themselves with honor.

The conspiracy died in that moment, killed by simple dignity.

HENRY KNOX

THE GENERAL'S FAREWELL

FRAUNCES TAVERN, NEW YORK CITY
4 DECEMBER, 1783

THE SMELL OF OAK and smoke clung to the low rafters. Knox stood near the fireplace, gripping the oak table's edge, trying to control the storm in his chest.

Washington entered slowly. No fanfare. Just the weight of history. Officers stood automatically.

"With a heart full of love and gratitude, I now take leave of you," Washington said, his voice steady and strong, resonating through the wooden beams. "I most devoutly wish that your latter days may be as prosperous and happy as your former ones have been glorious and honorable."

Silence filled the room. Then Knox stood. Like long-lost brothers, they walked toward each other and embraced. Memories crashed over them, frost-bitten marches, impossible terrain, grace under fire. Tears rimmed Knox's eyes.

Washington put his hand on Knox's shoulder. "You've made your country proud, Henry. God knew what He was doing when He gave you to me."

Knox's voice caught. "It was Providence that brought us here."

Glasses clinked. Eyes shone. A nation still finding its feet stood taller in that smoky room.

HENRY KNOX

EPILOGUE:
THE LONG PEACE

BOSTON COMMON
WINTER 1895

SNOW DUSTED THE IRON cannon at Boston Common's edge. Children in thick wool coats ran past, unaware of its storied journey.

A teacher stopped, letting students gather around the old artillery piece. "This cannon once crossed frozen rivers and dangerous mountains. Why?"

A boy shrugged. "To fight the British?"

"To deliver liberty. Because Henry Knox believed that impossible things could be done. He hauled sixty cannons across the Berkshires when everyone said it couldn't be done."

"Was he a general?"

"More than that. He was a man who trusted God, who had backbone, who wouldn't quit. He believed the Almighty had a divine purpose behind liberty."

The children went quiet, thinking.

"Remember that the next time something seems too hard."

***

KNOX'S STUDY
MONTPELIER, MAINE
SUMMER 1798

The fire crackled, throwing shadows across the study walls. Henry Knox sat alone, grayer and heavier, but still carrying that same fire for freedom. His journal lay open, leather-bound and weathered.

Thomas, now a grown man with a family, had visited earlier with his children to hear war stories, to understand what their freedom had cost.

Knox picked up his quill and began to write:

If this union is ever threatened again, may these pages guide those who defend it. Peace isn't kept by the sword, but by men who fear and obey God.

He paused, watching the ink dry, then closed the journal with satisfaction. Outside, his small bell rang from the tower, marking another peaceful day. Children played beyond the porch. A cart rolled past, pulled by an old donkey with that same stubborn walk he remembered.

Knox stepped into the sunlight. The Atlantic wind touched his face gently. He looked out over his land, a quiet smile forming, and whispered the verse that had carried him from Ticonderoga to York-town:

> *"Blessed is the nation whose God is the LORD."*
> *Psalm* 33:12

ABOUT

HENRY KNOX

Henry Knox was an American-born bookseller from Boston who became one of the Continental Army's youngest and most trusted generals during the Revolutionary War. A devoted Patriot, Knox's military brilliance lay in artillery tactics and logistics, most famously demonstrated during the winter of 1775-76 when he transported over 60 tons of captured British cannons from Fort Ticonderoga across treacherous terrain to help lift the Siege of Boston. Throughout the war, he served as General George Washington's Chief of Artillery and close confidant, playing vital roles in key victories from Trenton to Yorktown, where his artillery placements were instrumental in the final siege. While General Benjamin Lincoln formally received the British surrender at Yorktown, Knox's contributions were pivotal. A staunch supporter of republican ideals, Knox stood firmly with Washington during the Newburgh Conspiracy, reinforcing the principle of civilian control over the military.

After the war, Knox became the United States' first Secretary of War under the Constitution, helping lay the foundations of the national military structure. He retired to his estate in Maine, living there until his death in 1806.

EMMANUEL MORISSET

Hello. My name is Emmanuel Zacharie Morisset. I am 14 years old and live in Coral Springs, Florida. I was born prematurely in 2011 after a traumatic event in the womb. Doctors told my parents I would only live for a few months. But God had another plan. My parents stood firm in faith and prayed with all their hearts. Fourteen years later, the result of that prayer is a healthy young man who is now a published author. I have contributed stories to two books of The Epic Story of America trilogy and plan to write many more.

I am homeschooled and currently on the honor roll. My passions include reading the Bible, writing, preaching, drawing, editing videos, and building websites. I also enjoy tennis and playing piano, violin, and drums. I speak English, French, and Haitian Creole fluently, and I'm currently learning Spanish, German, and Hebrew. Above all, I'm grateful to Jesus Christ for saving my life and for protecting me every day. I am growing in my walk with Him and learning what it means to follow Him wholeheartedly.

In the future, I hope to become an engineer, a writer, and a pastor. I want my life to prove to the world that nothing is impossible when God is writing your story.

HENRY KNOX

NOTES FROM THE AUTHOR

Writing this trilogy has been an unforgettable journey. It was filled with laughter, friendship, hard challenges, and moments I will cherish forever. I arrived at camp as an aspiring writer and left as a published author with a dream fulfilled. Editing was a challenge at first, but from those blank pages came the most meaningful work I have ever created.

Thomas, a key figure in the story, is a fictional composite inspired by real young operatives and spies of the Revolutionary War whose contributions were often overlooked. His journey reflects the moral complexity and courage of youth during this era.

Most of all, I thank God for opening this door and giving me the courage to walk through it. It was an honor to serve Him by using the gift of writing, and I give Him all the glory. It was amazing. It was unforgettable. It was EPIC.

ADMIRAL COMTE DE GRASSE

by Hannah Schneider

To Mom and Dad. A thousand dedications wouldn't be enough to express how thankful I am.

BATTLE IN THE CHESAPEAKE

1 SEPTEMBER, 1781

FRANCOIS JOSEPH PAUL, COMTE de Grasse, Admiral of the French fleet, sat in his cabin on his flagship, the *Ville de Paris*. His fleet had just arrived at the Chesapeake Bay in the colony of Virginia from the West Indies. *They are not colonies anymore*, he reminded himself. De Grasse smoothed out the creases in the letters in front of him. The first was a letter from the Comte de Rochambeau, which had reached him in mid-July earlier that year.

> *There are two points at which an offensive can be made against the enemy: Chesapeake and New York. The southwesterly winds and the state of defense in Virginia*

*will probably make you prefer the Chesapeake Bay, and
it will be there where we think you may be able to render
the greatest service.*

Comte de Grasse had indeed preferred the Chesapeake Bay. He had written to Rochambeau and the patriot General Washington immediately, informing them of the decision he had made. His fleet, made up of twenty-eight larger ships-of-the-line, seven frigates, and two cutters, would be sailing directly to the Chesapeake Bay, with soldiers, artillery, money, and other supplies.

His black-throated blue warbler landed on the desk, almost hitting his inkwell. De Grasse carefully moved it out of the way.

"Not now, Souverain," he chided. "I told you not to interrupt me while I am working."

Souverain fluffed his feathers importantly. The Admiral had picked up the bird recently while fighting the British navy in the West Indies. It was unusual because his breed didn't usually live in the Caribbean during the warmer months, but even more unusual was the bond they had developed.

Souverain pecked de Grasse's hand in a playful way.

"I understand." De Grasse smiled despite himself. "I can look at old correspondence later." He rose to his feet and headed to the door. Souverain darted past him as soon as he opened it.

Admiral de Grasse and his pet bird arrived on the top deck. Sailors snapped quick salutes or dipped their hats as he passed.

"What do you think?" de Grasse murmured to Souverain at a

stretch of unoccupied railing. His bird looked at him for a moment.

"It's fine so far," Souverain chirped.

De Grasse smiled at the wonder of his special bird. "Do you know what is going on?"

"Of course I do." Souverain bobbed his head. "The French soldiers you brought will join General Lafayette at Williamsburg to help with the assault on Yorktown. George Washington is coming with the Continental Army. Rochambeau is coming with him."

"*General* Washington and *Comte de* Rochambeau," de Grasse corrected.

"If you say so." Souverain wasn't concerned with the technicalities. He looked off toward the shore. "The British fleet will have to get here eventually, won't it?" He sounded unusually concerned.

"I assume so, if they mean to come to Cornwallis's aid. Why? Are you worried?"

"No-o-o," Souverain chirped. "I just don't like flying around when humans are setting off cannons."

"Ah, *je comprends*." De Grasse stroked Souverain gently. "It might not be too bad this time."

"We'll see." Souverain flapped his wings lightly. "Do you mind if I go meet some of the local birds? I need to stretch my wings."

"I was under the impression that you have been *stretching your wings* for the better part of these last several weeks." De Grasse smiled down at him, amused.

"Well – you see–" Souverain stammered, "it's not like flying over land."

De Grasse laughed. "Go and have fun, Souverain. I have to go back to my work."

"Hey!" Souverain hopped towards him quickly before de Grasse could turn away. "Do the work you have to do right now, not the boring work you already did!"

He smiled. "I will, Souverain."

Satisfied, the little bluebird winged away toward the land.

***

CHESAPEAKE BAY
5 SEPTEMBER, 1781

Admiral de Grasse stood on the deck of his flagship, watching the sky. Souverain had spent much of the last four days ashore, talking with the local avian residents.

When a blur of blue and black feathers darted into de Grasse's face, the admiral jumped back. "Goodness, Souverain!" de Grasse cried, clutching his chest. "You almost gave me a heart attack!"

"Sorry," Souverain said, "but I learned something interesting. A British fleet was here already – only two days before we arrived."

"What? Who was commanding? What did they do?"

"Well, a pigeon I talked to said it was Admiral Hood, but you can never tell with pigeons. They can be smart when they want to be, but their attention spans are horrible, and most of them can't keep their feathers in a row, let alone facts." Souverain treated de Grasse to a tiny bird shrug, mimicking the human motion he had seen in the past. "He had about thirteen or fourteen ships with him, from what it sounds like. Of course, no one bothered to count. They say he didn't stick around long. No one to fight, I guess, so he went straight up north."

"Probably to New York," de Grasse surmised. "When the British learned my fleet had left the West Indies, Admiral Rodney likely sent Admiral Hood to stop me. Except…"

"He got here first and completely missed us on the way," Souverain finished, "and he either assumed we weren't here yet, or were still ahead of him, sailing on to New York."

"Of course, he'd have wanted to go to New York anyway." He was interrupted in his thinking when a call rang out from the top of the rigging. De Grasse looked up sharply.

"Ship sighted! Multiple ships on the horizon!" a sailor shouted.

"Perhaps it's Comte de Barras arriving." De Grasse hurried for a good viewing spot, pulling out a spyglass as he went.

Souverain flapped quickly to catch up and landed on his shoulder. "De Barras… Wasn't he in Rhode Island?"

"*Oui*. If his fleet combines with ours, it would be a great help." De Grasse peered into the distance, trying to identify any of the ships that were still mere dots on the horizon.

"I'll go check." Souverain offered. He winged away toward the arriving fleet. Several long minutes later, Souverain barreled back, chirping like mad.

"It's not de Barras!" he gasped. "It's Admiral Hood – and Admiral Graves! Those ships are British! I saw Graves's flagship!"

De Grasse collapsed his spyglass and turned. He hastily began barking orders to signal the rest of the fleet and begin moving into a favorable position for battle. His face was white.

"They have certainly surprised us. If they attack us now, we will be quite vulnerable. How many ships do they have, Souverain?"

"Nineteen." Souverain panted. "They're already moving into battle positions. They saw us first."

"They have the advantage for now," de Grasse said grimly. "Once we're set to shoot our cannons at them, we'll see if it will last."

"I have an idea, if it might help."

"*Quoi?*"

"Well, what if we shot at their rigging?" Souverain asked timidly. "Sails and stuff. The way ships look to me, that seems easier to break than the hulls. And it's just as important."

"You are exactly right," de Grasse complimented him. "*C'est vrai.*" He shouted to the sailors readying the cannons, "Aim for the British sails and rigging. Prepare some bar shot for them. Make every shot count."

Souverain shivered. Bar shot was made of two cannonballs connected by a metal bar. It was ideal for catching and tearing enemy ropes and sails. All cannonballs made him uneasy, but he didn't mind bar shot as much as he minded the cannonballs designed to take out *people*; grapeshot and canister shot.

De Grasse scooped Souverain into his hands and held him close as he continued to give orders to the fleet. The French ships were almost in position now, and neither the Admiral nor his bird could guess why the British hadn't fired yet.

"We are very fortunate so far," de Grasse said. "We were frighteningly vulnerable, but they let their chance slip away from them."

Souverain stirred. "I can fly over the battle," he offered. "I can see if our plan is working."

"Souverain, I want you to stay safe…" De Grasse protested.

"I want to help you!" he chirped back.

De Grasse sighed. He couldn't watch the fleet and Souverain at the same time. "Be careful, *mon petit ami*." He flung the little bird into the air and watched him dart away. De Grasse checked his watch. It was around 4:15 in the afternoon.

The first cannon shots exploded from the enemy side. The French cannons responded in turn. The battle in the Chesapeake Bay had begun.

Souverain flew over the sea in between the two fleets. The French fleet was larger than the British fleet, and the initial surprise had worn off. Cannons fired incessantly, almost deafening him. Some cannonballs fell harmlessly into the water, throwing up waves. Other shots made contact.

The bluebird was pleased to see the results of the barrage. The bar shot snapped rigging and ripped gashes into the sails of the British ships. Meanwhile on the French side, the British cannonballs impacted their hulls. Souverain flapped closer to check. *Excellent! This damage hardly looks critical. Our ships will be able to keep fighting easily!*

The minutes ticked away. Guns roared, smoke filled the air, and occasionally over the din, the screams of men could be heard. Some of them were shouting orders; commands to send signals, to clean and load cannons, and to repair damage. Some of the screams were the screams of the wounded. Two British ships were so heavily damaged at one point that they drifted out of formation, their sails torn and useless.

Souverain was flying over the British ships when another bird almost flew into him. Souverain recognized it as a red-tailed hawk.

"You there!" The hawk shouted at him. "What do you think you're doing?"

"Flying," Souverain responded, darting around the hawk.

The hawk chased him. "I know who you are. You're the special pet of the French Admiral!" he yelled over the cannon fire.

Souverain pivoted in midair to get a look at the hawk. "Yes, I am. And who are you? Are you a Loyalist?" he asked.

"Proud to serve His Majesty's soldiers - and sailors," the hawk added. "My name is Charles, and I've been watching General Cornwallis ever since he first came to Yorktown."

"Well, it's been nice to meet you, Charles, but I don't have time to chat," Souverain apologized. "I should get back to my fleet." He flinched as another cannonball smashed into a British ship.

"Yes, you should!" Charles snapped. "And don't bother sticking around. The Rebels don't need France. They need *England!*" he screeched after the little bluebird.

Souverain darted back towards the French fleet, the hawk ascending higher into the sky to watch him. *He's mad that his side is losing,* Souverain thought with satisfaction. *Any bird could see that.*

Souverain was taking a quick rest up on the top of *Ville de Par-*

is's sails when he saw a new group of ships coming into the battle. The French flag waved from their masts. "Comte de Barras's fleet!" he chirped jubilantly. "It has to be!" He dive-bombed Admiral de Grasse again. "There are French ships coming," he informed him. "About eight or so ships-of-the-line. It looks like de Barras's fleet."

"Excellent." De Grasse looked through his spyglass toward the new ships. "You'll be glad to hear that the battle should slow soon, regardless."

"*Pourquoi?*" Souverain cocked his head. De Grasse smiled at the bird's attempt at French.

"The sun will set soon. We can't fire at the British if we can't see to aim."

De Grasse's prediction turned out to be correct, much to Souverain's relief. At 6:30, as the sun dipped toward the horizon, the bombardment ceased.

"What now?" Souverain asked, watching the British fleet float across from them, stark and silent.

"We will find out how much damage and how many casualties we have sustained. The British will certainly be doing the same." De Grasse turned toward his sailors and called for a damage report.

"Sir, damage appears minor. Two of our ships got it worse than the others, however it seems the British were dealt a more severe blow," a sailor responded in French.

"They sure did," Souverain tittered in de Grasse's ear. "The British ships looked bad. I'd be surprised if they were in a hurry to return for another beating. That hawk must be mad."

De Grasse's brow furrowed. "*Pardonnez-moi? Un faucon?*"

Souverain nodded. "There was a red-tailed hawk out there watching the battle like me. He was a Loyalist."

"Ah." De Grasse looked towards the enemy fleet. "Their fleet is outnumbered, outgunned, and severely damaged," he murmured. "Souverain, I believe you are correct. Admiral Graves cannot possibly want to risk another defeat so soon."

COMTE DE GRASSE

AND I'LL BE WITH YOU

CHESAPEAKE BAY
20 OCTOBER, 1781

SOUVERAIN FLEW AROUND *VILLE de Paris*'s sails, enjoying flashing his feathers in the sunlight. He landed on top of the mast, looking toward the mainland. *I wonder if any of the local birds know how the siege at Yorktown is going.* He was about to take off to investigate when he saw a shape coming toward him.

Souverain quickly discerned it to be the form of a large bird. As it glided closer, he realized it was a hawk. A red-tailed hawk. *Not this Loyalist feather head again.*

Charles swooped in and landed on a different mast, glowering over at Souverain. "I nearly got killed out there!" he snapped. "All of your lot firing off cannons like it's the King's birthday."

"We wouldn't be celebrating the King's birthday," Souverain pointed out.

"You know what I mean," he ruffled his feathers. "All that gunpowder going off, and they're not nearly as good as His Majesty's navy."

"The French are excellent, actually," Souverain said mildly. "And the Patriots *are* beating you, aren't they? You can't have come here to gloat. There's nothing to gloat about."

He had clearly gotten under Charles's feathers. If looks could kill, the hawk would have the entire ship dead from the force of his glare. "I don't usually go after such *small* birds, but I'd be willing to make an exception for you, Frenchie."

Souverain swallowed. "As fun as that sounds, I think I have somewhere I need to be." He dove off the mast and flapped toward the deck as fast as he could. Charles screeched angrily and dove after him.

Feathers! What was I thinking? Hawks can dive faster than songbirds! Souverain pulled level and darted around a sail. Charles's claws ripped a small gash near the edge as he tried to follow. The hawk quickly righted himself. Souverain darted downward again, then ducked under the bottom of the sail and shot upward. Charles lost precious seconds trying to spot him again.

"French pet!" Charles screeched as he caught sight of the warbler again.

"It's not really so bad," Souverain chirped back. "You should try it sometime." He dropped into a dive, shooting past Charles's head.

The hawk twisted around and dove after him.

"Hey, a hawk is chasing the Admiral's bird!" A sailor yelled. Souverain levelled out quickly before Charles could catch him and scanned the deck for the man who had spoken.

There. The humans. Perfect. Souverain flew straight for the sailors as fast as he could. He could feel Charles's breath on his tail. He beat his little wings, closer... *closer...* A sailor stepped in behind him and blocked Charles's path. Souverain flew into another man's hands, which cupped around him protectively. Charles righted himself and flew up to the rigging once more.

"*Fine*, you French pet!" Charles screeched. "You hear me? FINE. I'm not risking my feathers in this battle anymore! If the colonies want to be free so badly – treating His Majesty's soldiers like this – maybe I'll just move to England!"

Souverain poked his head out. "You do that," he said. "Find yourself a lady hawk."

Charles's face was a storm cloud. "You'll see. This little independence experiment will *fail*. The colonies *cannot* survive without Great Britain. They're not ready for it. They'll *never* be ready. Independence is a dream. A happy, unrealistic fantasy."

"They'll show you!" Souverain snapped. "Come back in a couple of years. If they're not ready for independence, then why are they winning?"

Charles snapped his beak shut and flew off toward the mainland. Souverain preened himself.

"Looks like that hawk is gone," the sailor observed. "How about you head back to the admiral, little friend?" He released Souverain into the air, and the little bird flapped straight to de Grasse's cabin.

He squeezed in the door and hopped up onto de Grasse's desk. De Grasse smoothly moved the inkwell out of his flapping range. Souverain was about to tell him what had happened when a sailor knocked on de Grasse's door.

"*Monsieur, une lettre est arrivée.*"

"Enter." De Grasse looked up from his desk. The sailor slipped in and handed him the letter. "*Merci.*" De Grasse nodded; Souverain pecked the man's hand lightly in thanks. The sailor smiled and gave Souverain a quick stroke before taking his leave.

"Let's see what this is," de Grasse murmured, breaking the wax seal on the letter and smoothing the creases. His lips moved slightly as he read, then he exclaimed, "*Le général Cornwallis s'est rendu!*"

"What? What happened?" Souverain leaned over to peek at the letter. "Has Cornwallis surrendered? When?" He smiled, thinking of Charles. *Who needs England, now, feather head?* he thought triumphantly.

"Yesterday," de Grasse said in excitement. "Given that the British fleet hasn't returned and his escape attempts have failed, he cannot hold his position any longer. Yorktown now belongs to the Continental Army!"

"That means they've captured Cornwallis too, haven't they? Thanks to us." Souverain preened his feathers. "If the British navy had been able to help Cornwallis, our armies wouldn't have been able to do a thing. But because of us, Graves had to leave for repairs, and now he's too late! Washington was right. It was smart of us to stay here." He looked at an open letter on the desk that had arrived shortly after the battle in the Chesapeake, from General Washington.

> *I most earnestly entreat Your Excellency farther to consider ... that if you should withdraw your maritime force from the position agreed upon, that no future day can restore us a similar occasion ... Let me add Sir that even a momentary absence of the French fleet may expose us to the loss of the British garrison at York...*

De Grasse stroked Souverain's head. "This is a great victory for the new states," he mused. "They grow closer to *indépendance* with every battle. But soon *we* will have to sail back to the West Indies. France has commanded me to protect her interests there and so I will."

"And I'll be with you!" Souverain chirped.

De Grasse smiled. "*C'est ça, mon petit ami,*" he said. "*C'est exactement ça.*"

ABOUT

ADMIRAL COMTE DE GRASSE

Francois-Joseph-Paul, Comte de Grasse, was born on September 13, 1722, in Le Bar, France, entered French service in 1740, and was given a commission as an admiral in 1781. He sailed to the Chesapeake Bay from the West Indies and engaged in the Battle of the Chesapeake against British Admiral Graves's fleet, emerging victorious and helping to secure Cornwallis's surrender at Yorktown. On April 12, 1782, back in the West Indies, he was defeated by the British in the Battle of the Saintes and taken as a prisoner of war. De Grasse returned to France after the conclusion of the war and his actions were investigated by court martial. Nothing came of the court martial, and de Grasse passed away in Paris in January of 1788, age 65.

ABOUT THE AUTHOR

HANNAH SCHNEIDER

Hannah is an avid writer and ambivert bookworm who enjoys spreading random knowledge and a little bit of chaos. When she is not writing or reading, you can find her gaming, doodling, looking for writing advice, or hanging out with friends. She lives in Virginia with her parents, brothers, dog, and two fat and happy guinea pigs.

COMTE DE GRASSE

NOTES FROM THE AUTHOR

The number of ships in de Grasse's fleet varies depending on the source. The number I have given in the chapter might not be the actual amount, but I have selected the most reasonable number estimate I could find.

Souverain and Charles are fictional. De Grasse did not really own a pet bird, and birds cannot actually talk to humans, unfortunately.

MARQUIS DE LAFAYETTE

CHASING THE SUN

by Mikayla Baderhorst

My chapters are dedicated to Jesus who equips me to do everything I do, my mom who brainstormed my "getting into character" to break my writer's block and listened to the unfolding sagas of my characters, and my friends, Teagan, Haylee, and Makenna who were my real-life inspirations for Marcel–Louis (Lafayette's fictional eccentric sidekick in my story). You guys have been extremely encouraging to me, and I am so thankful to all of you (especially Jesus)!

PROLOGUE

EN ROUTE TO AMERICA ON BOARD LA VICTOIRE
MARCH 1777

MY DEAR ADRIENNE,

I cannot believe I made it out of France without being captured by the king. The ship I am on is called La' Victoire. Fitting, isn't it? I can only hope and pray that it is some kind of sign from God above that this cause for American liberty is just. I opened my Bible this morning to Ecclesiastes 3:1–8. You know it well.

To everything there is a season, and a time to every purpose under the heaven:

A time to be born, and a time to die; a time to plant, and a time to pluck up that which is planted;

A time to kill, and a time to heal; a time to break down, and a time to build up;

INDEPENDENCE

A time to weep, and a time to laugh; a time to mourn, and a time to dance;

A time to cast away stones, and a time to gather stones together; a time to embrace, and a time to refrain from embracing;

A time to get, and a time to lose; a time to keep, and a time to cast away;

A time to rend, and a time to sew; a time to keep silence, and a time to speak;

A time to love, and a time to hate; a time of war, and a time of peace.

That last phrase, my love, spoke to me. I felt God telling me to fight. I suppose what I am trying to say is that I am sorry for leaving you behind, my dear wife. I do not know what's in store for me, but I am willing to learn.

Adieu, my dear Adrienne.
Yours truly,

Gilbert Lafayette

"LAND!" The cry came from the crow's nest above my head. A small speck in the distance slowly grew more visible as I breathed in the briny smell of the glistening sea. I would be glad to be rid of my ship. It was fun at first, but I quickly got tired of it.

"*Belle Amériqueue, je suis arrivé (Beautiful America, we have arrived)!*" I said while my friend, Marcel-Louis Fontaine and I disembarked in busy South Carolina. The city was teeming with life, people chattering and going everywhere at once.

"*Mon bonte (My goodness)*! How can they survive in this *cacopho-nie* of noise? I can barely stand it." I sighed as my friend complained about the noise.

"Oh, come on Marcel. I find this busyness like fresh air after being confined to the ship for so long! *Ici, la vie, c'est aussi frais que l'air, n'est-ce pas (Here, life is as fresh as the air, isn't it)?*" Through the teeming crowds, I spotted our luggage and maneuvered over to collect it, leaving a very unsatisfied Marcel trailing me, grumbling about my comparison of life here to fresh air.

"Perhaps, but even air can smell foul once in a while, *Monsieur.*" Marcel mumbled in protest.

Just as he said that his shoe caught an uneven ledge in the cobblestone wharf, causing him to tip over into a muddy puddle. I rolled my eyes and dragged our baggage to the waiting carriage. Having pulled himself out of the puddle with disgust, poor Marcel drooped after me, sopping and avoiding eye contact with the guffawing sailors nearby.

"Mr. Benjamin Huger's residence, please." I said to the driver as I scooted far away from Marcel in the carriage, trying to avoid getting soiled by his now filthy attire. The carriage driver looked at me with a friendly smile and I immediately felt welcomed. A few minutes into our trip, however, I was willing to revise my original assessment of our driver. He seemed to take us over every bump on the roads at a speed that could have killed us, as well as taking a few turns that had me praying to my Dieu Tous-Puissant (my God) for our safety. Predictably, poor Marcel had the worst time, getting sick as his visage took on a few strange shades of green.

***

CONTINENTAL ARMY CAMP, GERMANTOWN, PENNSYLVANIA, 1 AUGUST, 1777

Ma trés Chére Adrienne,

How I miss you! Our host, Monsieur Benjamin Huger, was kind to me and helped me obtain an audience in front of Congress. I was nervous, no doubt, but I was given the rank of major general without pay. The camp for the army was in desperate condition, if you could even call it an army. Or even a camp. The men were barely clothed and clearly needed food. I could practically count their ribs through their skin. You would have cried if you had been here. They are so young, mostly teenagers, younger than even you. I met a young soldier, Joseph Plumb Martin. He was perhaps sixteen years old, but you would never be able to tell as he spoke far beyond his years. I am on my way to meet General Washington but find that my heart is longing for you. Continue to pray for me, that I grow in wisdom as God takes me on this journey.

Adieu,

Gilbert

***

THE NEXT DAY

"Greetings, *Monsieur* Lafayette and *Monsieur* Fontaine. I am

General Washington, this is General Nathaneal Greene, and our translator, Mr. Hamilton. It is a pleasure to have you here with us." A tall figure in a blue-and-buff uniform and a somewhat smaller man greeted Marcel and me as the translator relayed the greeting to us.

"It is a pleasure and privilege to be here. I can only hope that we can both be of some service." I responded in French as young Hamilton translated everything perfectly, unaware that I understood every word he shared with General Washington and General Greene. I liked the grandiose Generals and their young translator immediately, and elbowed Marcel to get him to smile.

"Ah, perhaps you will be able to teach us something, Lafayette." Washington smiled.

Oh dear. I should not be the teacher here, I thought to myself, my heart pounding.

Perceiving that English was *necessaire* to define my role in America, I sheepishly shrugged my shoulder, saying in English, "Sir, I am here to learn, not to teach."

The General's eyebrows shot up as he silently observed and measured me. I smiled awkwardly, Marcel shifting from one foot to the other next to me. My English was not *parfait,* and I could only hope that it would not hinder me in my quest for glory.

"Ah, well, Mr. Hamilton, please escort our young friends back to their quarters. Make sure they have everything they need." I bowed and said *au plaisir de vous revoir (hope to see you again soon)* to the silent general and his companion, General Greene, before turning to follow Mr. Hamilton. We walked together quietly until I broke the silence.

"You translate beautifully, yet I detect another accent."

"You have a good ear. I am not originally from the colonies, having come over from the Caribbean," our interpreter shared in French.

"Really? How interesting. Our ship was supposed to dock in the West Indies. Well, your French is impeccable." He smiled and thanked me. Our conversation continued on as we shared our similarities, helping me to feel a little less alone and more like I had a friend in this land.

***

CONTINENTAL ARMY HEADQUARTERS, MIDDLEBROOK, NEW JERSEY, 25 DECEMBER, 1778

Chére Adrienne,

Joyeux Noël! The war is going well enough for us. We have had some victories and some defeats, as one would expect in war. The good General Washington brought in a supposed baron from Prussia named de Steuben. He is quite a colorful character and often peppers his sentences and commands with très dégoûtant words and commands. I do, however, admire the way he has whipped our fledgling army into shape. We went from being an undisciplined and scraggly band of ruffians to a truly deadly fighting machine, all in the span of a few months.

Hope has found a new meaning after the battle of Monmouth, where the American army rallied to fight our dreaded foe, the foul Redcoats. The heat was dread-

ful, and soldiers were dropping left and right. General Lee ridiculously called for an early retreat before we had a chance to showcase our newfound fighting abilities. I was shocked when I realized he had called the soldiers to pull back. An angry General Washington showed up just in time to prevent the retreat as I was riding up to encourage a few soldiers to remain and fight. I almost felt bad for the misguided General Lee as I would not like to be on Washington's bad side either. General Washington rode up on his horse, eyes blazing, and proceeded to berate Lee for his choice. I never thought that I would hear my beloved General curse, but curse he did. Rallying the troops to fight, we won the battle, much to the astonishment of the British.

I am to return to France soon and cannot wait to see you and our dear daughter, Anastasie. Marcel sends his greetings and wants me to report that neither of us are hurt, even though a bullet pierced through his coat. He wants you to know that he bravely kept on fighting for liberty and America despite the damage to his uniform. Just between us, he actually fainted after the bullet incident. Give Anastasie a kiss for me and buy her something pretty in my stead.

Je t'aime ma chérie (I love you, my darling),

Gilbert

***

PORT OF BOSTON, MASSACHUSETTS
11 JANUARY, 1779

"General Lafayette!" I paused as I was about to board the *Al-*

liance for France. The young soldier I had met previously, Joseph Plumb Martin, rushed over and handed me a small parcel. "You almost forgot your bag, sir. I wasn't sure if you wanted it, but I brought it in any case." I smiled in gratitude at the diminutive Martin and thanked him.

"Thank you, *Monsieur*. Please keep your eye on *Monsieur* Marcel-Louis Fontaine. He is rather prone to getting into trouble and his family would not be happy with me if something happened to him."

He nodded solemnly and saluted. "Yes, sir! Goodbye, Major General. I hope that your trip goes well and that you return safely, God willing."

"*Adieu*, soldier. Fight on." I saluted this fine young man, appreciating the brave soldier he had become under the tutelage of the somewhat pompous Baron de Steuben.

DON'T DO WHAT I DID

MY SHIP HAD SET sail for America nearly a week ago, allowing me time to desperately miss my wife and children, Anastasie and Georges. This past year in France had been interesting. It started with an eight-day house imprisonment when I arrived home from America. The King had not released me at that time to travel to the Americas, yet I had felt such a compulsion for the revolutionary cause that I left anyway. He eventually forgave me, giving me court time with him as I worked to secure money and troops for the still ongoing Patriot war in America against our common enemy, Britain. Thankfully, my year at home in France brought not only financial and political success, but also time with my lovely wife and daughter as we experienced the joy of welcoming Georges, my son, into the world.

Obtaining more support for the Americans was not easy. The King was reluctant as our own beloved country, France, was in turmoil. Unfortunately, the American situation was time-sensitive as their revolutionary war raged on. King Louis finally relented just two weeks ago, calling me into his study at midnight to discuss France sending more aid to the Americans.

"Ah, Captain Lafayette. Merci for meeting me at this strange hour." I nodded and bowed, afraid to speak. "I have a question for you."

"What is your question, your Majesty? I will do my best to answer it." He gazed off absentmindedly and seemed to forget I was there for a while.

"Is this worth it?" the King asked me.

"Sir?" I said, wrinkling my brow in confusion as I considered his question.

"Is draining your country of its resources, and leaving your wife and children behind for years, to go fight a war in a country you barely know, worth it? How much are you willing to sacrifice for America?"

I was taken aback by the questions, not quite knowing how to answer them. We were silent for a while as I contemplated my response. Finally, he rescued me from having to answer his soul-searching inquiries.

"Ah, no matter. I will send more troops and ammunition to General Washington and his Congress. You are to return to the colonies with this letter giving my promise of further assistance," he said as he waved an envelope in my direction.

"Your Majesty, I will do as you ask." I bowed and took the envelope,

backing out of the room slowly.

"And Lafayette?"

"Yes?"

"Do not make me regret this. You may very well sink both France and America with this venture of yours."

His last words to me resonating in my mind, I gazed at the beautiful waters while the ship sailed further away from my beloved country. Could France and America go down with this endeavor? I certainly hoped not.

"God, give me strength and wisdom. Allow me to be sufficient for this task you've set before me." I muttered under my breath. "And, Father God, protect my wife and children."

***

PORT OF BOSTON, MASSACHUSETTS
28 APRIL, 1780

I once again docked in America on a busy waterfront, the Port of Boston, home of the infamous Boston Tea Party. I heard all sorts of noises and smiled as I recalled the first time I set foot on American soil. Marcel had been so unhappy! Now, I couldn't wait to return to the camps and share my news. General Washington and I exchanged letters during the year I was gone, and my other friends wrote as well. According to Marcel, Alexander, and General Greene, the American Revolution was as unpredictable as the weather. I could not help but wonder how everyone would react to the news of France's continued assistance. They were sure to be ecstatic, I hoped. Not everyone was open to French aid.

I needed to make my way to the army headquarters in New Jersey quickly. Luckily, a carriage was available. I made my way over to the driver and tapped him on the shoulder, asking him to take me to the army camp where General Washington was currently stationed. The gentleman turned around, and my jaw dropped. It was the same driver that had terrorized Marcel-Louis and I on our way to the camp when we first arrived in America.

"Ah, *bonjour, Monsieur*. Would you be available to take me to New Jersey? I must meet up with a few friends there." He smiled a broad smile and clapped me on the back.

"Hey, you are the Frenchie from a few years ago! How are you?" he said excitedly. His smile dropped quickly. "All the way to New Jersey? I don't know. That's far."

"For the right price, perhaps?" I asked, shaking a small bag of coins. His eyes widened, and for the first time, I noticed his clothing looked rough and worn. "What's your name, *Monsieur?*"

"Scott MacLeod, but you can call me Duff. I'd be happy to take you to New Jersey." Duff reminded me of an overeager puppy, much like the men and women at court in France. However, he did not have the same conniving look in his eyes.

"Let's be off, *Monsieur* Duff! My name is Gilbert du Motier, the Marquis de Lafayette, but you may call me Lafayette," I said, introducing myself formally.

***

EN ROUTE TO THE CONTINENTAL ARMY CAMP, NEW JERSEY, 1 MAY, 1780

The carriage rocked back and forth. I attempted to secure my bags on the bench across from me. Adrienne would kill me if she could see how unkempt I looked. Duff had not improved his driving skills much since the last time I was in his carriage. We stopped for the night at a dusty old inn and were nearly finished with dinner when he asked me a question.

"Lad, how old are you?" Duff asked curiously as I sat across from him.

"Twenty-three," I responded, placing my spoon back in the rough bowl. "Why?"

"Just curious. When I was your age, both of my parents had died, and I was married."

"*Oui*. I am. We have two children, a boy and a girl."

"Two children? Sounds wonderful!" Duff exclaimed, causing me to smile.

"Yes. Unfortunately, my wife has been alone for a while because I was called to fight in America." Loneliness and guilt took me by surprise, piercing my heart at this admission to Duff.

"Called? Or chose?" He asked.

Trying to push back my feelings of remorse, I once again stopped my spoon halfway to my mouth and placed it back in the bowl. This gentleman was wise, it seemed.

"Lad, let me tell you something. My wife and I were married for a good 25 years, and I have one regret. I left to go to work in South Carolina because I thought we were short on money. She told me when I left that she would always love me, but she didn't care about the money. My Lily, she just wanted me. I was in South Carolina for five years. During those five years, I would constantly write to her, telling her how much I missed her. Do you know how many times I went home to see her?"

"No, sir." I asked, "How many?" wondering if he knew what Adrienne and I had been through.

"Once. She was trying to convince me to stay and not go back. I didn't listen. She died a year later." His eyes misted and he turned away to regain his composure. "Boy, don't do what I did. I missed what really mattered because I was chasing something I thought was important. All the while, the most important thing in my life was waiting for me at home."

Duff's words stayed with me through the night, as well as through the remainder of our journey to New Jersey, as I wrestled with the personal cost of aligning myself with this noble pursuit of freedom.

* * *

CONTINENTAL ARMY CAMP, NEW JERSEY
MAY 1780

I walked into the army camp, my musings interrupted by a coarse yell coming from the direction of the training grounds. Major General Baron de Steuben was training a new group of soldiers with the help of his large dog, Azor, and Marcel-Louis. Azor darted around, yipping at the soldiers and generally wreaking havoc as Marcel-Louis followed the Baron around the grounds, attempting to assist de Steuben where needed. Azor, the silly dog, in his frivolity, got entwined in poor Marcel's legs and tripped him. The Baron, not seeing what had happened, spun around to witness the unfortunate Marcel sitting in a pile of mud.

"Ach, so you wish to be one with the mud then, Fontaine?" He asked. Roars of laughter erupted from the training soldiers. "Go clean up and then report back here as quickly as you can."

Azor whined and slunk over to me as I chuckled in the shadows.

"Hello, old boy." I ruffled his ears as Marcel passed by me, grumbling about the unfairness of being tripped by a dog and the world in general. "Now, Marcel-Louis, that is no way to treat a dog." Marcel stopped in surprise, gazing into the shadows and breaking out in a muddy grin when he realized it was me.

"*Monsieur* Lafayette? My goodness, I did not realize you were back already!" I turned to walk with him, threw my bag more comfortably around my shoulders, and motioned towards the camp.

"Tell me everything whilst we make our way back to your quarters."

* * *

FORD MANSION, MORRISTOWN, NEW JERSEY
THE NEXT DAY

Eager to share news of my success in France, I ascended the

plain stairs, excitement dancing in my heart. I waited for someone to answer my knock, shifting from side to side. The door swung open, and I was given entry into the mansion that housed General Washington, his wife, and his aides.

"Ah, Major General Lafayette! It is a pleasure to see you again. How did you fare on your journey?" Mrs. Washington asked, smiling. I could not help but smile at the good General's wife. She reminded me of my own mother, who passed away when I was young.

"My travels were *très bien, merci.*" I answered, bowing deeply as I explained it had been a good trip. She graciously nodded her head, gliding away unobtrusively, as Mr. Hamilton stepped forward.

"LAFAYETTE! You have returned to America at long last, my friend!" Hamilton exclaimed in French, grabbing my hand enthusiastically. "Finally! Someone that I can speak to in French who's not annoying!"

"Dear friend," I laughed, continuing the conversation in French, "you have not changed a bit. I hope that all has been well with you. I got your letter in February, but I did not bother to respond as I thought I would be back sooner than this. Down to 8,000 troops? From 12,000? How terrible! How and where is the General?"

"Right behind you." Washington entered the room behind me. I turned and gave him a bear hug, much to his embarrassment. He cleared his throat and stiffly smiled at me.

"Ah, Lafayette. It is good to have you back safely. Tell me, how are your wife and children?"

"Good!" I chuckled, "Adrienne sends her greetings and asks that you make sure that I do not sustain another injury," I said, referring to the bullet that grazed my leg during the Battle of Brandywine in 1777. Alexander and I chuckled at that, and Washington nodded, a knowing look in his eyes.

"Alexander, I will return our Major General to your clutches soon. For now, he must update me on his missions in France." I shrugged at Alexander as General Washington led me into his main office. Once the door was securely closed, he sat at his desk and gave me his full attention.

"Lafayette, I'm anxious to hear how your meetings went with the King. I feared failure to secure support as you have been gone for a year. I understand that a lot is at stake with the unrest in France and your having to leave your family yet again to assist us."

"Yes, General. It took quite a bit of convincing, but the King finally agreed to send an expeditionary force, led by Comte de Rochambeau, to America. He should arrive in July with five thousand additional troops. Another fleet of ships will also be arriving sometime next year. Comte de Grasse should be commanding that. America will be getting our guns and ships."

He sat back, looking as though a weight had been lifted off his shoulders.

"Fantastic news! Your King is very generous." I decided not to confirm to him that France was on the brink of political and financial collapse.

INDEPENDENCE

***

GREEN SPRINGS, VIRGINIA
9 JULY, 1781

We were still licking our wounds near Green Springs Plantation in Virginia when I conferred with Major General de Steuben and Brigadier General Anthony Wayne, following a skirmish three days earlier. There, we had attacked the back portion of the Redcoat army attached to the new British officer, General Charles Cornwallis. *Monsieur* General Wayne and his men, not knowing that it was attached to a far larger unit of Redcoats, had begun firing on the smaller British contingent. Being significantly outnumbered, we eventually retreated under the cover of darkness. De Steuben was not entirely thrilled with our disorganized retreat, but it worked.

"This devil Cornwallis is much wiser than the other generals with whom I have dealt. He inspires me with sincere fear, and his name has greatly troubled my sleep. This campaign is a good school for me. God grant that the public does not pay for my lessons," I muttered in frustration.

"Spoken like a true French officer, Lafayette. Do not fret. It will all work out in the end, my friend," de Steuben said, patting his ever-present and ever-eating dog, Azor, on the head.

"Easy for you to say, sir. You are not the one with the fate of your home country and King depending on you," I said, somewhat vexed by his calmness.

"I hate to say it, but you do have a point, young Marquis," de

Steuben said as I groaned, letting my head fall into my hands. I hated that title, even though it provided many open doors for me.

"General Wayne? What do you think? Where is our elusive Cornwallis heading?" I asked, pacing around our small tent.

"I would say New York. That is what makes the most sense right now."

"Yes, that would seem to make the most sense. If you would be so kind as to give me a moment to pen a line to General Greene, I would be grateful," I said, needing to update my friend and mentor, Greene, regarding the most recent developments.

***

WILLIAMSBURG, VIRGINIA
19 OCTOBER, 1781

We were wrong. Cornwallis went to Yorktown instead. Striving to course correct, I quickly dashed off letters to Washington and the French representative here in America, Chevalier de La Luzerne, detailing how we could trap the British in Yorktown if Washington and the French Navy came as backups. They arrived three weeks after those letters were sent, much to our relief.

I had convinced Hamilton to return to the army after he left in a huff over an argument with Washington. Alexander led his men on small-scale attacks at Yorktown, managing to restrain himself from doing anything crazy during those attacks, thus saving me from getting into trouble for recommending his return to the army. Now, Cornwallis was to surrender to us shortly, signaling the beginning of the end.

I wasn't entirely sure how to feel about the war's ending. On one hand, I was grateful the bloodshed was over, and I would get to see my family and France again. On the other hand, I was grieved to leave my friends here in America and return to yet another country on the brink of revolution.

"Lafayette? Are you ready to finish this cursed war?" asked General Washington. He had become like a father to me, and I would be sad to leave him and all of my other friends here.

"Yes. Let's finish this, General," I responded, blinking back unexpected tears. God bless this General. He had led us well.

***

PARIS, FRANCE
31 DECEMBER, 1781

"Gilbert!"

I turned to see my beautiful wife running towards me, dropping my bags to catch her. I swung her around in a circle. *Ma Chérie!* Oh, how I missed you. I am so sorry for leaving you and our family behind for all those years." She smiled through her tears and cupped my face.

"Papa!" Two little voices rang out shyly from behind their mother, excitedly waiting to see their father after a few years of absence. I swept my now bigger children up into hugs, pausing when I saw Marcel-Louis slinking off in the opposite direction.

"Marcel! Come, say hello to my family! They have missed you!"

He joined us timidly. He clearly felt out of place at our little reunion. Anastasie scampered over to him, holding her arms out to be picked up. He did so, a smile lighting up both of their faces. Adrienne turned to me to respond to my apology.

"My love, I forgive you. You have always wanted to chase the sun and loved the idea of *liberté*. How was I to stand in your way?" she laughed. "Just tell me no more revolutionary wars, *mon amour*."

I gazed off at the beautiful sunset, Anastasie in my arms, as Adrienne leaned into me while holding Georges. My mind wandered back to the carriage driver, Scott MacLeod. His words of advice were still with me, making me grateful to be in the presence of my family. However, I feared another quest for *liberté* was about to begin, this one with dire consequences.

"I don't know if I can promise that. One war for independence may have ended, but I have a feeling another is just beginning," I said as Ecclesiastes 3:8 ran through my mind, "*A time to love and a time to hate; a time of war and a time of peace.*"

ABOUT

MARQUIS DE LAFAYETTE

Marie-Joseph Paul Yves Roch Gilbert du Motier de la Fayette, better known as the Marquis de Lafayette, was born on September 6, 1757, in France, to the elder Marquis de Lafayette and Marie Louise. Tragically, the young Marquis lost his father when he was two and his mother when he was twelve, leaving him a very wealthy orphan. Lafayette met his wife, Marie Adrienne Francois, when he was fourteen, and she was twelve years old, and they married two years later. He came to America at the age of nineteen and fought valiantly for the American cause as a Major General, only returning home once during the war to convince King Louis XVI to send more guns and ships to aid the fledgling American nation in its fight for independence from Great Britain.

When the war ended in 1781, the Marquis returned to a violent France on the brink of revolution and was imprisoned for five years by his fellow countrymen because he tried to defend the queen, Marie Antionette, and denounced the bloody ways in which the French revolutionaries conducted themselves. The Marquis, whose whole life was identified by independence, revolution, and war, passed away on May 20, 1834, at the age of 76 and was deeply mourned in both America and France.

NOTES FROM THE AUTHOR

The letters Lafayette wrote to his wife are fiction, although you can find the actual letters online! They are very interesting to read as they provide a glimpse into his mind! I chose to fictionalize my letters because I wanted to provide a view into Lafayette that didn't include the need to decipher the grammar of the times.

Marcel-Louis Fontaine is unfortunately fictional! He was such a fun character to come up with and write, and I hope you enjoyed him as much as I did.

Benjamin Huger is a real person, and he helped Lafayette get his feet under him when the young Marquis first arrived in America.

History is not clear if Lafayette needed a translator upon arrival, so I chose to use that as an opportunity to introduce one of Lafayette's closest friends, Alexander Hamilton.

The Battle of Monmouth was a truly amazing battle for the Americans, and a shock for the British, who were not expecting such a disciplined force!

Lafayette did indeed sail back to France in 1779 and returned to America in early 1780 as a part of a mission to convince the king to send more guns and ships, leading to a huge shift in the balance that tipped the war more in favor of the Americans. He was also imprisoned for eight days upon his return to France because his first voyage to America was not exactly approved by King Louis XVI.

Scott Macleod is also fictional, but he is based off some of the wisest people (and worst drivers) that I know.

Azor is a real dog that belong to the Baron de Steuben, and he would often eat the poor Baron into debt as he ate enough for a grown man.

The Battle of Green Springs was a real battle and did not go well for Lafayette and Generals Anthony Wayne and the aforementioned Steuben.

Lafayette did originally think that Cornwallis would move his army to New York, but he was wrong, and the British redcoats instead travelled to their doom - Yorktown.

Lafayette was known as Gilbert to his family and friends in France.

As a final note, Lafayette did not believe in slavery and helped free many slaves, and at least one of them chose his last name for themselves. He also said that he would not have assisted the Americans in their fight for independence if he had known that they would not abolish slavery.

ANNA SMITH STRONG

BLINDMAN'S BUFF

by Mikayla Badenhorst

PROLOGUE

SETAUKET, NEW YORK
14 JUNE, 1748

COME ON, ANNA! LET'S play blindman's bluff!" My sister, Rebecca, grabbed my hand and dragged me over to my other siblings. At eight, I was one of the younger ones. Rebecca and Henry were the oldest at thirteen, and my sister Catherine, whom we call Caty, was two. Then there were my half-siblings: brother, Charles, who was a year older than me, and sisters, Elizabeth and Martha, who were four and eleven, respectively. Of all of them, I was closest to Charles and Rebecca.

"Who's it this time?" I said. Rebecca laughed.

"Charles is it!" He groaned but willingly took his place in the middle of the circle. Once the blindfold had been secured, and he had spun around a few times, we began to play. Charles ran around the garden and attempted to chase us.

Finally, he stopped and called out, "Blindman's Bluff!"

We all stopped where we were and called out, "Bluff!"

From there, he began to attempt to catch us. After tagging us all, we made our way back to the parlor to have some lemonade, where we heard voices coming from our parents' bedroom.

"I can promise you right now, the colonies are not going to stay part of Britain," I heard my father say.

"Husband, please. I don't want to talk about this. No one would ever fight with Britain. They are too powerful," my mother said.

"Mark my words. There will be a war before little Anna is 50," he said resolutely.

ANNA SMITH STRONG

MADAM, YOU MISUNDERSTAND ME

SETAUKET, NEW YORK
18 DECEMBER, 1777

MY DAY BEGAN LONG before dawn that morning. Now thirty-seven, I woke up before the birds began their song to get the fire started for breakfast. Then, I made my way out to the coop and garden to collect eggs and pick some vegetables. My house was practically on the water, so I took a second to breathe in the briny sea, grass, and trees that I could not quite see yet. It was my only moment of peace, for my children would soon awaken and wreak havoc in the world. Alright, so that is a little dramatic, albeit true. I do love my children, but with my husband ill, I feel all alone in this world.

"Now, Anna, that is enough! You are to be present for your children and husband. God gave you this life for a reason, and you are to glorify Him in every and any way that you can!" I said, as I gave myself a stern talking to. Sighing, I squared my shoulders and spun on my heels to finish my chores, and tend to my household with my servants, Abigail and Cicero.

The eggs cooked nicely, and I had just finished giving Abigail instructions for cleaning the house when my kids began to file in one by one, starting with my oldest, Keturah, to my youngest, Joseph. Rubbing sleepy eyes, they sat down at our rough-hewn table to eat breakfast.

"Mother, may I go down to the waterside today?" Keturah asked nonchalantly, helping herself to some eggs.

I frowned, unhappy with the request. She knew her father and I were cautious about her spending time with James Woodhull, a man nine years her senior, who was attempting to initiate a courtship. We were also concerned about the presence of soldiers as tensions remained high during this revolutionary period, especially along the water.

"Anne will be there, too, so I won't be alone," she quickly interjected, knowing that her attempt to see James, who was working near the waterside, required a chaperone.

Just then, 15-year-old Thomas chimed into the conversation, trying to help his sister.

"Mama, I can escort Keturah as I'm taking Benjamin and William to school before I head to work." He waited patiently for my reply, knowing that I was wrestling with fear during these turbulent, unstable times.

I looked slowly from Thomas to Keturah, then reluctantly nodded my consent, asking Thomas to also escort Keturah, Benjamin, and William home at the end of the day. The children finished their breakfasts, pecked me on the cheek, and departed. Now, it was just me, my youngest children, my ill and recovering husband, and our two servants. Silently asking God to quiet my fear and anxiety, I quickly signaled Abigail to sweep up the dishes left over from breakfast and clean them.

"Come now my darlings. Go get your slates and schoolbooks and let our lessons begin!" They giggled and scurried up the stairs to get their things. We were about to begin when a knock came to my door, which was odd because we don't usually have visitors.

"Children, go ahead and start while I answer the door."

I opened the door to a very nervous looking Abraham Woodhull, a close friend of my husband's. "Mr. Woodhull! What a surprise! How may we help you?" Now, Abraham was a nervous person as is, but today he looked like he was on the verge of collapsing.

"Anna...I have a favor I need to ask of you." I noticed his eyes, bloodshot and tired, and quickly summoned Cicero, telling him to collect Selah, my husband, and escort him downstairs. My husband and I sat down in our parlor with Mr. Woodhull for coffee a short time later. His hands kept shaking. Finally, he set his cup down and got to business.

Looking around to see if anyone else was in earshot, he leaned forward and quietly said, "General Washington has employed my services to spy for him during this conflict, and I need some help. I have others, but I need one more person."

Trying to quell my fear and maintain my composure, I quietly replied, "Oh, Mr. Woodhull. You should know that my husband is unavailable! Why, it is ridiculous to even suggest that he should help you! He still has not recovered from his imprisonment." He shook his head and held up his hand before I could vent further.

"Madam…you misunderstood me. I am not in need of your husband's services. I need yours." I was speechless. Unfortunately, he took my silence as a signal to keep explaining. Speaking in nearly a whisper, he explained, "I need a messenger to convey information to one Caleb Brewster. You know him."

I heard Selah's sharp intake of breath, and he slowly stood up to his feet and crossed the room to the fireplace.

"Mr. Woodhull," I admonished, "I don't think I can do that. I have my children to think of, not to mention I am trying to nurse my husband back to health."

He sighed as he continued with his plea for help.

"I thought you'd say that. Look, what if I told you I could arrange for your husband and children to stay in a safe place during the war? Please, Mrs. Strong. I wouldn't ask if I did not need your help," he quietly pleaded.

My eyes suddenly filled with tears, and I turned away to regain my composure. I loved my husband and children. Could I really send them away for months or even years? I met my husband's gaze from across the room and felt his approval. Once I had managed to contain myself, I gave him my answer.

"Yes. I will do it."

***

SETAUKET, NEW YORK
17 JULY, 1780

I was starting to regret my recruitment into the Revolutionary War and the Culper spy ring. Every time I went outside to hang up the black or white handkerchief along with my laundry, I would feel a flash of anxiety and debilitating fear. Now I understand how Mr. Woodhull felt. However, I had to keep going for my husband and children, who had recently left for Long Island.

When the pressure of spying got to be too much, I would go and ride my horse, Arabella, for hours on end, always alert to the need to avoid soldiers and unsavory characters. It was a nice way to relax and release all of my problems. Suddenly, Mr. Abraham Woodhull came riding through the woods, pulling up his horse next to me. Out of pure courtesy, I reluctantly slowed to a trot. Here I was, running away from my problems (or rather attempting to), and one just came riding up to me.

"Mr. Woodhull, what do you need now? I have been delivering your messages just like you have asked," I said testily, not appreciating his intrusion into my inner sanctuary of peace.

"Madam, I need to ask a favor." *Oh no. This couldn't possibly be good.* "Would you accompany me to the wonderful city of New York posing as my wife?" Occasionally, I would wish that a woman was allowed to partake in violence to solve problems or answer questions. This was one of those times. I sighed and turned in my saddle to face the problem that was sitting so prim and proper in his saddle.

He sat atop his horse, aware that his request was unconventional and could bring my marriage and reputation into question if anyone became aware of this rendezvous. Yet again, I regretted my involvement in this war, feeling that the sacrifices were becoming too heavy.

"Mr. Woodhull, you're quite aware that you are putting me, my marriage, and my family at great risk with this request, are you not? I was to assist in the exchange of information only," I said as my eyebrow raised, and my voice lowered.

"Mrs. Strong, I am quite aware of the risks. However, for the sake of the Patriot cause, I find it necessary for me to go to New York City and do not believe the British will allow me to pass if they believe me to be single. I simply require your presence as my 'wife' to cross through the check point, nothing more," he earnestly explained. "You have someone to visit with in the city, have you not?"

Contemplating my need to give him an answer, I nodded my head. I did indeed have a close friend whom I could visit and had not seen in ages. Maybe it would do me good to get away from my loneliness and fear and spend some time with my friend.

"Mr. Woodhull, I will accompany you. When do we depart?" I queried.

"Tomorrow. And we will be gone for a week." *A week? Oh, dear Lord, now I was really praying for him to run into a low-hanging branch. But did I have a choice?*

"I will be ready, sir." He nodded and crisply spun his horse, soaring away like he didn't have any care in the world. Or so he thought. He turned around to say something more to me when his head connected with a low-hanging branch. *Huh. Maybe God does have a sense of humor after all. Or just a good sense of justice.*

"Are you alright, Mr. Woodhull?" I asked quite innocently after riding over to check on him.

He waved me off and made another attempt at a graceful exit, succeeding this time. I constrained myself until he was out of ear shot, then succumbed to peals of laughter. Once I stopped laughing, I headed home to pack and place my servant, Abigail, in charge of the household for a week, ducking below the branch on which a very unfortunate Mr. Woodhull had just gloriously hit his head.

* * *

EN ROUTE TO NEW YORK CITY, NEW YORK
THE NEXT DAY

I left early the next morning to meet Mr. Woodhull, ready for the trip to New York. He looked nervous and exhausted. Hopefully he will be able to comprehend my idea for today.

"Mr. Woodhull! Good morning. I trust you had a restful night? I have an idea for us to discuss on our ride to the glorious city." He looked at me suspiciously before answering.

"Madam, I would be happy to discuss your idea, and I had a *lovely* rest last night," he said, grumpy from too little sleep.

"My idea is simple: my friend in New York who is well-connected in high society and knows many officers in the British Army is a secret supporter of liberty. Would you allow me to press her into our group of friends?" I searched his face, hoping that he would agree. He sighed and rubbed his hand over his face, wincing when his hand brushed over the bruise he had sustained from his visit with the tree branch yesterday.

"I suppose that would be all right," he reluctantly said. "Include her correspondences in the messages you deliver to Caleb Brewster as your own." We rode through the day until we spied a redcoat up ahead.

"Halt! Who are you and why are you entering the city?" the soldier said as we neared the checkpoint. Mr. Woodhull smiled and greeted the officer.

"Hello, sir! My wife and I are simply coming to visit an old friend of ours. May we enter?" There was a tense moment as he looked us up and down.

"You may enter," he said eventually. "Enjoy your visit."

We arrived at our destination and quickly sat down to plan our next day. The rooms that we obtained were plainly furnished, but comfortable, with matching green and gold furnishings in each room. We completed our necessary unpacking, each in separate rooms, so I asked permission to walk along the streets for a while, as well as visit my friend. He begrudgingly nodded, and I snatched up my cloak, disappearing before he could change his mind.

Tears pooled in my eyes and threatened to spill out: I missed my husband and children desperately and wished this could all be over.

I arrived at my friend's house. Reaching up, I grasped the lion's head knocker and rapped twice. It took so long for her servant to answer that I almost turned away.

"Hello. I am here to see the lady of the house. Please tell her that Anna is here."

The servant eyed me suspiciously, which, to be fair, was warranted given there was a war going on.

"I will inform her that you have arrived. Come, take off your cloak and put it on the stand. You may have a seat in the parlor while you wait. She will be down presently."

I was ushered into a gorgeous parlor rich in blues and whites. It looked just like the parlor she used to describe to me when we were younger. I was holding a small bust of the king and wondering why she had it in her house when my closest and oldest friend, Charlotte James, swept into the room, looking like a princess.

"My darling Anna! I cannot believe you have arrived! I do hope my servant Samuel wasn't too much of a bother. He can be positively boorish at times. I do apologize for his not welcoming you warmly.

"Samuel," she said, calling for him, "Dear, would you run to the market for some eggs? Thank you, darling." She hadn't changed a bit. Organized and in control, but in a way that felt like you were the one who volunteered to help. He departed as requested, and she leaned in towards me, smiling.

"Did he grant you permission to press me into service?" Charlotte asked once we were alone as she leaned forward and lowered her voice. She and I shared regular correspondence; hence, I had kept her informed of my recruitment by Mr. Woodhull through a code we had developed when we were young.

"Yes. You are to write your letters to me as usual and include gossip or things you overhear from Loyalists, Patriots, those with no allegiance, basically anyone who speaks. Leave nothing out of your letters. No details are too small. Once I get them, I will send them on so, if intercepted, you should be safe. If you don't want to do this, you don't have to as you could be imprisoned or killed."

"Anna, I forget that we are not little girls anymore. I am so proud of the woman you have become." Her words made me feel important. "But of course I will help. I cannot wait to begin." I was about to say something else when the servant, Samuel, arrived with the eggs requested, holding a piece of paper. He handed it to her, and she read it and smiled.

"Tell them I accept the invitation and will bring an extra guest for the party."

"Who?" Samuel asked. She nodded towards me and Samuel began a protest. Clearly, she was a rather lenient slave owner. "But my lady!"

"She is going with me and that is that. Now, don't you have the afternoon off?" she asked, dismissing him as she turned back to me.

We held back our laughter until a very confused Samuel left the room. Charlotte now looked me up and down as her forehead wrinkled at what she saw.

"Now, about your dress."

Hours later, I found myself in a lovely gold dress with a fan and fancy updo. My friend was dressed just as beautifully in a white dress that I would have stained the second I touched it. She called for a carriage, and we set off. The party was being held at a prominent Tory's house, and she thought I should come.

"I must confess that I am concerned I might drop something or embarrass you somehow," I said uneasily, still trying to get out of this, knowing that Mr. Woodhull would likely not be happy with the high riskiness of this endeavor.

"Oh, don't worry! You will be fine. Just follow me, I will watch out for you."

I felt out of place among the other ladies, who seemed to brim with class and manners. Charlotte subtly jousted and joked while getting information out of these ladies. Something one of the rather tipsy ladies said caused my ears to perk up in alarm.

"A gentleman was telling my husband that there is a spy in the rebel army!" I was quite alarmed but disguised it and maneuvered myself closer to the conversation.

"Madam, do you know his name?" One of the other ladies asked the question before I would need to.

"No. He never told me." *A rebel spy?!* Oh dear. This was terrible news.

Later that night, I made my way back to the inn. Mr. Woodhull was still awake, so I filled him in on my discovery.

"*WHAT?* You have to be kidding me. Are you sure you heard the lady correctly?" Noting the look on my face and the way I had planted my fists on my hips, he backtracked quickly. "Alright. I need to send a missive to Washington immediately and inform him of this grave new finding." He turned away and returned to his desk to commence his missive. "You may go. Good job, Mrs. Strong."

I was hurt by his curt dismissal and made my way back to my room to write a letter to my husband. I had come to New York City hoping to escape my loneliness yet found myself desperately missing my husband and children who were still on Long Island.

***

SETAUKET, NEW YORK
ONE WEEK LATER

I returned home expecting a return to my daily routine after a busy week in New York City with Charlotte and Mr. Woodhull. My jaw dropped open and I dropped my basket of laundry as I stepped outside to hang it. There, right in my backyard, was a redcoat camp!

"Not good, not good at all!" I whispered. Before I could escape back indoors, however, one of the soldiers approached me.

"Are you the lady of this house?" he asked arrogantly.

"Yes. Do you need something?" I said, meaning quite the opposite.

"Yes, actually. By order of His Majesty's Army, you are to provide food for us as we take up residence."

"But of course! May I know your name in case of any issues?"

"Of course. I am Captain James Carleton." I tensely smiled my thanks and turned to escape back into my home. "Please inform us when the rooms are ready," he said, then abruptly turned away, not waiting for my reaction.

I had to blink back tears as I practically ran inside. NO! I was not alright with this. I did not want them in my house. I wanted my husband and children back.

✳ ✳ ✳

LONG ISLAND, NEW YORK
25 OCTOBER, 1780

A note came from Charlotte's husband. She was imprisoned on suspicion of being a spy for the Patriots. I had been visiting my family, so I was able to call Selah. My dear husband came running and I silently handed him the note.

"Oh, my dear Anna. I am so, so sorry. I wish that there was something I could do."

"How could this happen? We were so careful. And to make matters worse, she is pregnant!" I lamented. He grabbed me and held me close as I cried. We sat like that for a while until I managed to pull myself away.

"At least we managed to figure out Benedict Arnold's schemes. I am quite sad that we didn't get the chance to see him brought to justice."

"I know. Mr. André was also killed because of his capture." I was nearly inconsolable with the news of Charlotte's imprisonment as I wished and prayed once again for an end to this deadly war for independence.

ANNA SMITH STRONG

EPILOGUE

OCTOBER 1783

THE WAR HAD FINALLY ended, with the Patriots emerging as the victors. Abraham Woodhull and Benjamin Tallmadge (the creator of the Culper Spy Ring), along with their families, and some of our fellow couriers, Austin Roe and Caleb Brewster, all joined us for a celebratory meal. The other women and I had been prepping since before dawn for this meal, and a time of games, as all our neighbors joined us to rejoice in our hard-fought victory. I was grateful to finally meet some of my fellow conspirators.

"Well now, Mrs. Strong, was it all worth it in the end?" I groaned inwardly at Mr. Woodhull's question. "Independence. What a beautiful sound."

My thoughts went to the beginning of the war. I had just been a simple housewife, tending to my children and running my household. Slowly, however, the comforts I had previously enjoyed were stripped away from me. First, my husband joined the army and was imprisoned. I had to turn to my Loyalist relatives to free him. Then, Mr. Woodhull practically strongarmed me into joining the Culper Ring. My children and husband were relocated out of reach, to Long Island, while I was at home, fretting over them and my new job.

My servants and I had held down the fort, so to speak, while the war raged around us, and I conducted my spy affairs. Then, at Mr. Woodhull's request, I travelled to New York City with him and, at my request, asked my best friend, Charlotte, to join the ring as my contact. After all that, my home was taken over by British soldiers. You would think that all of that was enough, but then Charlotte had been captured by the British and imprisoned on the British ship *HMS Jersey*. No one had heard from her, and she and her newborn son were now presumed dead.

"Mrs. Strong? Are you alright?" Mr. Woodhull asked. I smiled shakily and nodded. Children ran past me chattering, leading me to recall all of the times my siblings and I had played for hours in our young innocence.

Independence was such a difficult thing to achieve, but we had made it. God had been the voice calling bluff for our blind men on the battlefield, and in our homes, so we could emerge the victors. Through blood, sweat, and tears, we forged an army and overcame impossible odds. Now we were one nation under God, destined to great things if we kept our eyes on Him.

"Yes. It was worth it. All of it."

Young Joseph tugged at my skirts. "Mama, come play with us."

I crouched down and picked him up. "Of course I will. What are we playing?"

He smiled a toothy smile, causing my heart to melt. "Blindman's Bluff."

ABOUT

ANNA SMITH STRONG

Anna Smith Strong, affectionately known as Nancy, was born in Setauket, New York, on April 14, 1740, to Colonel William and Mary Lloyd Smith. She married Selah Strong in 1760, most likely on November 3, eventually bearing nine or ten children depending on the source. While historians are not certain, most agree that Anna was Agent 355 of Washington's Culper Spy Ring, a Patriot spy who delivered messages which aided in the eventual capture of Benedict Arnold. Anna Smith Strong died on August 12, 1812, at 72. She was a brave woman who risked everything for independence, helping gain freedom for future generations of Americans.

ABOUT THE AUTHOR

MIKAYLA BADENHORST

My name is Mikayla Badenhorst, and I am fifteen years old. I live in the beautiful city of Sarasota, Florida. I like to play volleyball year-round, hang out at the beach, and read and watch the Lord of the Rings trilogy repeatedly (sorry Mom!). I also love to hang out with my friends at my jazz band and youth group and learn more about Jesus! This is my third year participating in the Epic writing camps and I am grateful to have been given the opportunity to tell part of the story of America's fight for freedom with my fellow campers.

ANNA SMITH STRONG

NOTES FROM THE AUTHOR

The names of Anna's siblings are real, and I had so much fun tracking them down!

Anna' children's names are also real, as are the names of her two servants.

Anna Smith Strong's husband, Selah, served in the Continental Army until he was captured by the British, imprisoned, and then subsequently released, thanks to some of their Loyalist family members.

Mr. Abraham Woodhull is described as a nervous character in most books on the Culper Spy Ring, but he was effective in getting people he trusted to join him in his espionage activities.

We are not completely sure that Anna Smith Strong was Agent 355, the lady spy who assisted Woodhull and his associates, but a lot of evidence points to her, including the fact that she supposedly travelled with him to New York City posing as his wife. She was ten years older than Woodhull.

Charlotte James, Anna's New York City contact, is fictional. One of history's greatest questions is the capture of Agent 355. History tells us that she was pregnant, and either died on the prison ship where she was held with her newborn child or survived and was just simply never mentioned again. I could not find a source that could tell me that Anna was the one who ended up in prison, so I added Charlotte as a secondary agent.

The dinner that Anna attended is obviously fictional, but I wanted to foreshadow one of the worst betrayals that occurred during the war: Benedict Arnold, an American general who defected to the British Army.

The British did indeed take over Anna's backyard and house during the war. She moved into a small cabin and remained there until they departed. All the while, the rest of her family was on Long Island.

At the end of the war, Anna was reunited with her family and got to meet some of her fellow spies: Benjamin Tallmadge, Abraham Woodhull, Caleb Brewster, and Austin Roe.

The Culper Spy Ring never tried to be recognized by anyone, and they preferred to keep their endeavors a secret. They all lived, spied, and died quietly. These unsung heroes are only now getting the recognition they deserve as George Washington's original spy ring.

LIEUTENANT COLONEL
BANASTRE TARLETON

by Roxanne Messier

TARLETON'S MEMOIR

TARLETON SAT DOWN AT his desk and smoothed out a sheet of parchment. It was a paper that he had shoved into the back of his desk for months, too afraid to revisit it. Now, however, he felt brave enough to write. Banastre had never written a book before, much less his own story.

He smiled to himself as he thought of how his account might be received. The king would read it, it would be in every bookshelf in the country, and his legacy would be remembered forever. He shook out of his trance and pulled several pieces of paper towards him. The crumpled-up sheet of parchment that he had been staring at was his outline for his memoir. He scanned the paper to jog his memory. He didn't want to write about his whole life, as that would be too much work, but he wanted to write about the most important moments of his life; the American rebellion from 1780-1781. He put his quill to a fresh piece of paper, and the flashbacks started.

RUGELEY'S MILL
29 MAY, 1780

Banastre sat at a little table in his tent, composing a letter to rebel Colonel Buford. He finished with a flourish and set the quill down to review it. He nodded in approval, folded the letter, and slipped it into an envelope. He gazed towards the entrance to the tent where he heard men walking past, talking and laughing loudly. He stepped out of the tent into the bright morning sun. Banastre glanced around at all the men surrounding him. He stepped over to one soldier who did a double take as he realized Banastre Tarleton was approaching him.

"Hello, soldier." Banastre greeted, "Will you carry this message to the rebel troops?" He handed the soldier the envelope, and the man saluted before running off.

He fiddled with his jacket anxiously as he walked back to his tent, not stopping to join the soldiers in their conversation. He knew that a battle was coming, and soon.

It was afternoon when the soldier burst into Tarleton's tent, holding a letter in his hands.

"Sir, Buford has sent you a reply!" he panted.

"Finally, you're back." Banastre quickly grabbed the message and scanned through it. The messenger tried to explain.

"Sir, they delayed me as much as they could so that they could prepare their troops for battle." Banastre groaned as he realized that the rebels would not surrender.

"Very well, then." He tossed the letter to the ground. "We must get ready for battle."

WAXHAWS DISTRICT
29 MAY, 1780, 3:00 PM

The air was thick with anticipation as Tarleton trotted atop his horse through the throng of soldiers, organizing them into a fighting position. He called for them to charge toward the rebels. When he had galloped so close that he could see each person's face, the gunshots were fired. As soon as he heard the shots, his horse collapsed under him, and he fell to the ground. He sat up, glancing around him, and saw the poor animal lying dead. He staggered to his feet, suddenly feeling several different emotions at once: angry, scared, sad. He wanted to punch someone, anyone, but he channeled his rage into pushing forward. He had to fight. He jumped onto the back of a soldier's horse and raised his sword in the air.

He called out to his troops, "No prisoners taken! Kill them all!" His soldiers roared in agreement and pushed forward.

Though many rebels held their hands up in surrender, Banastre and his troops continued their bloodshed. When Buford held out a white flag of surrender, Tarleton turned his head away. He had already stirred up his troops to the point where they could not be stopped, and he didn't feel like taking prisoners.

The battle was over quickly, but the damage was done. Banastre gazed around at the discord he had created. Many rebels lay on the ground, either dead or seriously injured. As enemy soldiers began to carry away the dead and wounded, many gave Tarleton looks of hatred. Nobody had ever looked at him in that way, not in the way that made him feel like snakes were squirming inside of him. He turned his face away, but he could still feel their glares like daggers sinking into his skin.

LIVERPOOL, ENGLAND
1786

Banastre finished writing and quickly read over it to revise it. He paused when he re-read the part about him encouraging his soldiers to attack the rebels. He crossed it out and laid his pen back down, wondering how to make himself sound kinder to the enemy. If he wrote about what he had done, it would be set in stone. His future reputation would be ruined. He brainstormed ideas for a bit before deciding to pretend his horse had collapsed, trapping him underneath, and he wasn't able to order his troops to stop fighting. *Yes, that was it.* Now his name was cleared.

Over the next few weeks, he began writing much more. The next part was the Battle of Cowpens. He sighed as he remembered the conflict...

COWPENS

17 JANUARY, 1781

It was dawn when they faced the enemy on the other side of the field. Tarleton grinned to himself as he realized that the rebels had placed themselves in a vulnerable position. This was going to be quick. As Tarleton's troops approached, the soldiers in front of the enemy lines fired a few shots and then retreated. A few British soldiers fell dead, but Tarleton urged the soldiers to press on. As they marched onward, shots continued to fire, and more of the soldiers collapsed. Banastre glanced around, shocked. He thought the rebels were beginning to retreat, but they had tricked him.

Tarleton's troops were beaten down and tired with little hope of victory. He heard shouts that made his blood run cold.

"Remember Buford's Massacre!" several rebels shouted while charging straight into the British, firing at any enemy close to them. As Tarleton watched in horror, they fixed bayonets and charged, slaughtering the British, and shouting, "Remember Buford's Massacre! Tarleton's Quarter!"

LIVERPOOL
1786

Tarleton shook himself from his memories. It had been his fault that they lost the battle, at least a little bit, but he hated feeling guilty. He decided to place the blame on the soldiers. *It had partially been their fault, right?* He was near the end. He had to write about Yorktown, the end of the 'American Revolution', as the rebels liked to call it.

MONTICELLO, VIRGINIA
4 JUNE, 1781

Tarleton and several of his men crept up the large pathway toward Thomas Jefferson's mansion. Seeing the impressive building reminded him of England and his comfortable life before the war started. Sometimes he wished that he had never gone into this war. Though winning battles and rising in ranks was very satisfying, sometimes he wished he could go back to being a posh, upper-class gentleman. *You will be if you survive*, he thought to himself.

They approached the doors to Monticello. Tarleton and his men knocking loudly on the doors. After a little while, a timid woman opened the door and said,

"If you are looking for Thomas Jefferson, he isn't here."

Tarleton and his soldiers paid no heed to her. They pushed the woman aside and charged throughout the house, turning over every piece of furniture in rooms, searching for him.

After the soldiers had torn the house to pieces, Tarleton finally believed that Thomas Jefferson was gone. Angrily, he reached for a delicate vase placed on a table near him. He threw it to the ground, startling some of his soldiers. The vase made a loud crash and shards of it flew across the floor. He stormed through the house, gathering all his men together and they left Monticello, enraged that Thomas Jefferson had escaped.

GLOUCESTER POINT
3 OCTOBER, 1781

Banastre and several of his men tramped through the wilderness trying to find some food to eat. They heard a rustle in the distance.

"It might be a rabbit, let's move ahead quietly, men," Banastre whispered. They urged their horses to creep forward, but no rabbit was to be found. Instead, they found footprints. Tarleton frowned. "Hmmm, maybe enough foraging for today, men."

Thankfully, the forest led to a main road. As they galloped, they found a house with a beautiful woman sweeping the porch. Tarleton smiled at the rest of the men and called out to her. "Ma'am, have you seen any soldiers come along this road?"

The woman shook her head. "No, sir, but may I ask why?"

"Oh," laughed Tarleton, "I just wanted to see if I could find the French Duke and shake his hand."

The woman narrowed her eyes in confusion but said nothing as Tarleton and his men mounted their horses and rode off.

Tarleton had been trying to find Duc de Lauzun, a French general, whom he knew was in the area. So far, he had been unsuccessful in finding him. As they kept riding, they heard a shout come from behind them. When they turned around, they saw the rebel troops galloping towards them. They immediately prepared to fight. Shots were fired, and Banastre felt himself being knocked from his horse. He collapsed to the ground, stunned for a few seconds, but some of his dragoons helped him to his feet and back onto his horse.

He grimaced to himself as he remembered the last time he fell, but this was no Battle of Waxhaws. This time, as he viewed the chaos of the battle, he realized the British would lose this fight.

Eventually the rebels won, as Tarleton had predicted, and he and his soldiers retreated to their fort at Gloucester Point. They didn't know how hard the following weeks would be.

* * *

A few days later the news came to them that General Cornwallis had surrendered. Tarleton was shaken. He thought the British army was invincible; 'the greatest army in the world.' But some country hillbillies had defeated an army full of trained men. He remembered when he had just arrived in the colonies, having complete confidence that he would win, but times had changed. History books would remember him being on the losing side. This made him angry. All this work for absolutely nothing. All this death, this pain, for *nothing*. But now, as he thought more about it, he grew fearful. He was not a friend to the rebels. Taking one step outside the fort would ensure his hanging.

He quickly wrote a message to the rebel forces and sent it through a young soldier. Shortly after, the answer came that he could stay in the fort and not face execution. He sighed in relief. He had been pacing around, wondering if they would grant him mercy. He would live, which made defeat less bitter.

19 *OCTOBER, 1781*

Tarleton stormed around his room, fuming. All the British officers had been invited to a dinner, except for him. He guessed the rebels and his fellow countrymen were laughing about him around a large table, clinking drinks and having fun. Deep in his mind he knew it was the complete opposite, that it was probably a very tension-filled dinner, but he wanted to feel self-pity.

As he continued to pace, he wondered what might have been if he hadn't done what he had in the war. If he had been more merciful. But he shook those thoughts away. The war would have ended up just the same, with his country losing.

LIVERPOOL, ENGLAND
1786

Tarleton set his quill down and sighed. His arm was weary from writing for too long, and he was tired of the memories that made him feel guilty. He reviewed all of his writings and nodded in approval. His book was finished. He glanced out the window and realized it was dark. He set down his papers and blew out the light.

ABOUT

BANASTRE TARLETON

In January 1782, Lieutenant Colonel Banastre Tarleton returned to
his home country of Britain to praise from his countrymen for his
bravery in the war. He remained in the army while also running to
be a member of Parliament; failing in 1784 but succeeding in 1790.
While in Parliament he argued to continue the slave trade.
He continued to receive promotions well into his career. He became a full general in 1812. He was rewarded a baronetcy in 1815,
and five years later he was knighted by the king. He passed on
January 15, 1833, leaving not as much of a mark on history as he
hoped.

ABOUT THE AUTHOR

ROXANNE MESSIER

Hi! My name is Roxy Messier. I'm 14 years old and I live in South Carolina. I love to read, hang out with friends, and swim. I've been in Epic Patriot Camp one other time in 2023, so it was fun to come back for the final camp! It was interesting to step out of my comfort zone to write about Banastre Tarleton, because I've never really had to write about a villain or an anti-hero before. This was a fun challenge and I hope you liked reading my story!

BANASTRE TARLETON

NOTES FROM THE AUTHOR

I took some liberties on what I wanted to include in the memoir; parts I believe Tarleton would have wanted. Since most materials about Monticello are written from Thomas Jefferson's point of view, I took liberties in telling the story through the eyes of Tartleton.

Banastre Tarleton did, in fact, write a memoir—called *History of Campaigns of 1780-1781*. I'm confident he wrote about all of the events that I wrote about in this chapter, but definitely in greater detail. I don't know if he was telling the truth when he wrote that his horse collapsed on top of him during the Battle of Waxhaws, but according to the Patriots it was false, so I'll take their word for it.

When I wrote about Tarleton and his men trying to capture Monticello, I only found information written from Thomas Jefferson's point of view so I took the liberty to write it through Tartleton's eyes.

CATHERINE MOORE BARRY

PATRIOT SPY

by Madeleine Rose Wenzel

*For everyone who has listened to me ramble incessantly about the
Revolutionary War for the past decade.*

PROLOGUE

ROCKY SPRING ACADEMY, ROEBUCK, SOUTH CAROLINA, 22 AUGUST, 1780

NOW, CAN EITHER OF you boys name a battle that happened here in South Carolina during this war?" Ambroise paced in the dirt outside the schoolhouse, the mouse's paws clasped tightly behind his back as he awaited a reply.

Victor, Ambroise's nephew, met gazes with Lysander, the big brown puppy, who had carried them to the schoolhouse that morning. Neither had expected a lesson of history, but Ambroise, whose current ambition was to be a teacher, was inexhaustible in his aspirations.

The pair of mice and Lysander had traveled to the schoolhouse every morning for the last two weeks, accompanying the two eldest

Barry children as they joined several other children from the area in learning the four subjects taught at Rocky Spring Academy. After a moment of silence, Ambroise turned, frowning as he looked back at his unwilling pupils.

"I suppose, if neither of you answer, I could tell you of my arrival in these fine colonies."

Victor's eyes widened as he quickly shook his head. Nearly every animal in the area had heard some version of how the older mouse had come to America along with Lafayette, back in 1777, and made his way up to the backcountry. Still, no one was certain how much truth his tales held, as they became more extravagant every time he relayed them.

"General Clinton took Charles Town back in May, Uncle Ambroise."

"And there was the massacre at Waxhaws in May, too," Lysander chimed in, his tail thumping on the ground. "Tarleton's Quarter."

"Very good!" Ambroise clapped his hands together eagerly. Both battles had happened only months earlier, so they were fresh in the boys' minds. After a six week siege on the city of Charles Town, General Benjamin Lincoln had surrendered the city and his entire command to General Henry Clinton on the twelfth of May. Only two and a half weeks later, Banastre Tarleton's dragoons overtook Abraham Buford and his men upstate, reportedly slaughtering them as they attempted to surrender. "The Siege of Charles Town, and the Battle of Waxhaws were fairly recent, but what can you two tell me of the Battle of Sullivan's Island?"

"This wasn't the first time that the British tried to take Charles Town," Victor replied, scrambling up to perch on Lysander's head. "Back in '76 they attacked Fort Moultrie, which stood firm even though it was only half completed."

"Those cannonballs were no match for South Carolina's palmetto wood!" The puppy stood up, shaking himself so vigorously in his excitement that he nearly sent his mouse friend flying.

"There were skirmishes here even back in 1775," Ambroise remarked, using his paw to draw on the ground. "We've been fighting here since the beginning of this war, and we'll fight 'till the very end!"

Lysander nodded eagerly as he settled back down. "And the more recent battles?"

Ambroise frowned a little. Things hadn't been going particularly well over the past month. "After the Battle at Camden, Gates' army is in shambles, and Sumter barely escaped capture at Fishing Creek."

Both battles had taken place within the last week, with Camden taking place on the 16th of August, and Fishing Creek two days later. Victor slipped off of the puppy's head as he added, "But then we had Musgrove Mill as well, and that was a victory for our men."

"True," Ambroise nodded. "If only we could beat Tarleton. That would improve the morale of our troops more than anything."

Just then, the door to the one roomed schoolhouse swung open, and the children dashed out. Ambroise and Victor quickly scrambled onto Lysander's back, knowing it was a much longer way home for the legs of mice, than it was for a puppy.

Lysander rushed to meet John and Polly as they stepped out the door, his tail wagging wildly as he pranced at their feet. John, the elder of the children at nine, squatted down to ruffle his ears. "Are you ready to go home, Lysander? I'd like to check on Papa."

"And Andrew is coming too!" Polly piped in, patting the dog on the head. Neither child noticed the mice, who had dropped to the ground as soon as they realized Lysander was going to greet the children. He wouldn't leave them behind, and it was too much a risk for them to be seen if they remained on his back.

"Oh yes, Grandpa says he can come over for the afternoon," John agreed brightly. "He wishes to see how Papa is faring."

The puppy whined excitedly as the two stood up again, waiting for their uncle to leave the schoolhouse. Though Andrew Moore was their mother's younger brother, he was born only a few weeks before John, and the two were good friends.

Finally, the other boy emerged from the schoolhouse, allowing the little band to make their way to the Barry house. Lysander eagerly taking the lead once he'd picked up the mice once more, sniffing at an interesting plant until they'd settled themselves on his back.

* * *

BARRY HOME, ROEBUCK, SOUTH CAROLINA
22 AUGUST, 1780

Kate Barry wiped her hands on her apron as she exited the room, softly closing the door behind her so her husband, Captain Andrew Barry, could rest. He had been wounded in the recent battle at Musgrove Mill, a few days earlier, and she'd been tending to him.

Just as she was about to peek into the children's room, where she'd put her two youngest children down for a nap, the front door swung open and she turned to see John, Polly, and Andrew tumble inside. Kate quickly pressed her finger to her lips before they could say a word, warning them to keep their voices lowered inside the house.

"Charlie and Katie are napping."

"And Papa?" John questioned, setting his bag on the hook by the door. Lysander padded inside behind him, going to lie beside the fireplace.

"Resting," Kate smiled.

"Will he recover, Kate?" Andrew asked as he walked over to hug his sister.

"The wound is healing well," Kate replied, wrapping her arms around her little brother. "Pray it doesn't get infected."

"I will." Andrew nodded solemnly. "Did the doctor take the ball out already?"

"Yes," Kate nodded, then changed the subject. "Did you all have a good day at school?"

"We did, Mama!" Polly chirped. "Can we see Papa?"

"Papa needs to rest," Kate replied gently, trying to usher the children away from the bedroom door. "Perhaps you may see him after supper."

"You may as well let them in now, Kate," the voice of Captain Barry floated through the door, "I'm not sleeping."

"Very well," she nodded, though her husband couldn't see it, and opened the door. "You must shoo them out whenever you grow too tired. I don't wish for you to exhaust yourself."

"I'm wounded, not ill," Captain Barry laughed, wrapping one arm around his daughter as she flung her arms around his neck. "Good afternoon, Polly."

"Are you hurting, Papa?" the six-year-old asked worriedly, burying her face in his shoulder.

"Not too much," the Captain replied, winking at Kate. "Your mama is taking very good care of me."

Kate smiled as her children chattered about their day with their father, watching them fondly as she stood back a little. Even her brother chimed in here and there, adding in details the other two had forgotten.

Eventually, she could tell that her husband was growing weary. Though he managed to keep it out of his voice, his face was pinched in pain. She softly cleared her throat to get his attention, and he nodded.

"John, Polly, it's time to let Papa rest now."

"Maybe I'll be a doctor when I get older," Andrew spoke softly as stood at the foot of the bed, looking over Captain Barry as the other two children instructed their father to rest well.

"I'm sure you'll make a fine doctor someday," Kate said, smiling and ushering the children towards the door. "Come now, papa needs to rest if he's going to heal properly."

* * *

16 JANUARY, 1781

Kate pressed her lips together as she looked at the note in her hands. It was written in Captain Barry's hand, telling her that General Morgan was gathering the militia, and he wanted her to inform his regiment to meet him at her father's plantation.

She'd been scouting for him for a while now, gathering whatever intelligence she could, keeping her ears open for any news on where the enemy may be headed next. She could gather her husband's men and send them to meet him, but there was just one thing.

Her three oldest children were out visiting her parents, leaving her alone with little Katie. If she went to rally the militia, there would be no one to watch her, and she couldn't just leave a toddler who wasn't even two yet home all alone.

Still, there was no way she could let her country down. It was important that she do her part in the fight for independence. Kate rushed back to the bedroom, where Katie was playing on the floor, stooping down to her level. "Katie, Mama needs to go out for a little while."

"Mama!" Katie looked up at her and grinned, raising her arms to be picked up. Kate smiled and scooped her up, holding her for a moment before setting her down beside the bed.

"I need you to be good while I'm gone, okay?" Kate murmured as she brushed her finger over her daughter's cheek. "I shan't be gone long."

"Look at this," Lysander whispered to the mice hiding in the corner as he nudged the note over to them. Ambroise grabbed it, stroking his whiskers as he read it.

"What is it?" Victor questioned, standing on tiptoe to read over his shoulder. "General Morgan is gathering all the troops? Will there be another battle soon?"

"I'm going with her," Ambroise interrupted, drawing his sword, which was just a pin he'd pilfered from Kate, and thrusting it into the air with a dramatic flair. "You two stay here."

"I don't think this is a wise idea, Uncle-" Victor started, only to be cut off by his uncle pointing his sword at him.

"Nonsense. You, my boy, would be a fool to think that I, Captain Ambroise Augustin de Clavel, would miss out on such a chance as this!"

Victor opened his mouth to respond, but the older mouse was already scurrying towards the door. He looked at Lysander helplessly, but the puppy gave no help.

"I didn't know that your uncle was a captain."

"He's not."

"I love you." Kate kissed Katie's forehead as she made sure the toddler was tied securely to the bedpost, handing her her doll. "I'll be back soon."

She turned, looking for Lysander, giving him a tight smile as he stood, wagging his tail as Victor darted under the bed.

"Lysander, stay here and watch Katie, please."

The puppy barked in response, wagging his tail harder as he sat on the floor, determined to do as she asked of him. Kate sighed softly, giving him a good scratch behind the ears before dashing out the door.

Once she was gone, Victor returned to his place at Lysander's paws, looking up at him worriedly.

"I hope they'll be alright."

"We should probably burn the note," Lysander responded worriedly. "That way no one can find it while they're gone.

"Oh, you're right." Victor carefully rolled up the paper, tucking it under one arm. "I'll do that now."

The young mouse hurried to the fire, climbing up to the mantle so he could drop the note in. He watched as it burned, the flames biting at the paper until it was unreadable. "It's done." Victor was satisfied as he returned to the puppy.

"Good."

Kate sprinted out to the barn, quickly leading her horse out of the stall. "We need to gather the militia. Girl, are you up for it?"

The horse nickered in response as Kate saddled her, standing patiently until Kate mounted. Ambroise scurried up the leg of the horse, settling in just behind the saddle, where he knew Kate wouldn't see him.

The cold wind whipped at Kate's face as she rode through the woods towards John Collins' house. She knew where all the men in her husband's regiment lived and the quickest routes to their homes.

Ambroise shivered as he clung to the edge of the saddle, trying to stay properly seated as the horse galloped. He wasn't used to moving so quickly, and it was exhilarating. His heart pounded as he watched the trees fly past.

"To think that I may be making history as the first mouse to ever ride a horse," he murmured to himself. If he wasn't so occupied in holding fast to the saddle, he would have pompously groomed his whiskers.

As soon as she reached the Collins' house, she jumped off her horse, running to the door and knocking hard. It opened within seconds, and she met Mr. Collins'gaze..

"Kate? What's wrong?"

"You're needed to muster at Charles Moore's Plantation as soon as you can get there." Kate panted, standing as tall as she could. "Captain Barry will meet you there."

"I'll be there." Mr. Collins nodded, grabbing his rifle, which was hanging by the door.

"Thank you!" Kate turned and ran back to her horse. There were many other men she needed to rally before her job was done.

* * *

20 JANUARY, 1781

"We won, Kate!" Captain Barry burst through the door, a wide grin on his face as he excitedly embraced his wife. "We beat Tarleton!"

Ambroise and Victor scurried out from their hole in the wall to listen as Kate laughed, gently pushing her husband away so she could look him in the eye.

"So it went well?"

"Better than well, it was an amazing victory!" Captain Barry explained. "Tarleton got cocky; he thought he had us when the militia retreated, but Morgan is a brilliant commander."

"Did you capture Tarleton?" Kate poked at the fire with a stick, stirring up the coals.

"Unfortunately not. He got away."

"But now we know we can beat him in a fight," Kate smiled, laying the fire stick to the side.

"And he knows it too." he laughed, stepping towards the kitchen door. "Are the children inside?"

"Polly and the little ones are," Kate responded, wiping her hands on her apron. "I just sent her inside to check on them, though they should still be napping. John is out hunting."

"I'll go in and see how they're doing." he turned back, walking over to press a kiss to her cheek. "It's been a while since I've seen any of you."

"Can you stay long?"

"Not long, though I promise I'll be able to stay for supper."

Kate frowned. She couldn't wait for the day when her husband was able to be home again, but that wouldn't happen until the war was over. She knew he would fight until the very end. She was certain that someday they would have their independence.

"Did you hear that?" Ambroise turned to his nephew, pumping a fist in the air as he cheered. "We won!"

"Shh!" Victor quickly clamped a paw over the older mouse's

mouth, worried that Kate would hear them. "Yes, I heard."

"This is magnificent!" Ambroise squeaked, wrestling the paw away from his face. "Magnificent, I tell you!"

"Uncle Ambroise, they're going to hear us!" Victor hissed, tugging on Ambroise's arm until he followed him back into the hole in the wall. "Hurry now and get out of sight."

***

MOORE PLANTATION, ROEBUCK, SOUTH CAROLINA
NOVEMBER 1781

"Don't get too close, Uncle Ambroise!" Victor warned as his uncle poked a thin stick into the mousetrap. He wrung his paws together as the older mouse ignored his fussing and stepped closer.

"Absolutely magnificent…" Ambroise muttered as he attempted to trigger the contraption. "Observe how it swings down to chop the stick in two!"

"Yes, I see," Victor shifted uncomfortably as the trap was sprung, the iron bar falling to ram the stick, snapping it in half. "You do understand that this is meant to kill us, right?"

"Ah, yes," the older mouse nodded cheerily as he dropped the stick, wiping his paws on his stomach. "Fascinating how the humans use such methods against us mice, and yet have nothing of the sort for themselves."

"I certainly hope they never invent something like it," Victor shuddered, turning on his heel to scamper back outside, where Lysander was waiting for them. The dog wasn't allowed in the kitchen and, being so large, was unable to sneak inside like the mice were. "Imagine a mousetrap large enough to take the heads off of a human… how terrible!"

"I think someone is coming," Lysander announced the minute the mice joined him outside. "I hear hoof beats."

"I don't hear anything." Victor cocked his head to the side and listened. All he could hear was the birds chirping in the trees. It was a beautiful day, though a little chilly. "Could it be someone coming to check on Captain Steadman?"

"Maybe." Captain Steadman, who was engaged to one of the Moore daughters, and two of his men were being sheltered at the Moore Plantation while the captain recovered from his illness. He had been down with a fever for several days now. "I don't think it's anyone we know."

"What are you hearing?" Victor frowned.

"There's more than one horse, and they're moving quickly this way." Lysander stood up and shook himself off. "I'm going to meet them."

The dog trotted off down the road, but came running back only a few moments later, barking wildly. "Bloody Bill is coming!"

"Bloody Bill?" Ambroise hopped down from the kitchen door, squinting at Lysander. "Are you certain?"

"Positive."

"Rouse the house then!"

Lysander nodded, dashing to the door as he started barking

again, trying to get the attention of the people inside. Major William "Bloody Bill" Cunningham and his band of loyalists were never a good sign.

"Lysander, what is it?" Mary Moore opened the door and stepped out onto the porch just in time to see the men ride up on the lawn. She gasped and stepped back, turning to yell back inside. "Charles!"

Charles Moore, Sr. ran out to join his wife on the porch, took one look at what was happening, and ran back inside to get his gun. Before he returned, the Loyalists were running up the porch and pushing past Mary, entering the house despite her protests. One of the men held her at gunpoint while two others grabbed her husband.

"Where's Steadman?" Major Cunningham growled, glancing around the front room.

Neither of the Moores answered him. They didn't have to. From further inside the house, one of the loyalists called out. "He's in here!"

"Don't hurt him!" Cunningham shouted back, pulling out his pistol. "I wish to kill him myself!"

Mary gasped sharply, closing her eyes as she pressed her hands to her mouth, murmuring a prayer. A shot rang out, and she let a small cry escape from her lips.

***

BARRY HOUSE, ROEBUCK, SOUTH CAROLINA
NOVEMBER 1781

"Kate! Kate!" Her youngest brother, Charles Moore, Jr., ran up to her as she hung the laundry, Lysander at his heels. "You need to get the militia!"

"What happened?" Kate grabbed him by the arm, holding him steady as he panted, turning to yell into the house. "John, ready my horse!"

John ran out towards the barn as Charles, Jr. tried to explain. "The Tories are raiding our home. I ran as fast as I could, but they may be burning it right now."

"I'll find Captain Barry and send him right over," Kate assured him, pointing to the house. "You stay here."

Charles, Jr. nodded and ran into the house, and Kate ran to the barn. John had saddled her horse for her, and she looked at him thoughtfully.

"John, I want you to go into the house and lock all the doors. Don't answer the door for anyone but your father, your grandparents, or me."

John nodded solemnly. "I will. Mama, be safe."

"If anything happens… take care of your siblings."

"I'll make sure they all stay inside until you come home."

"Thank you. Keep Lysander inside with you." Kate rested her hand on the top of his head for a moment, before quickly mounting the horse. John ran back to the house and shut the door tightly as his mother rode off.

"Where's Mama gone?" Charlie stood up as John came inside, dropping the ball he was playing with. Katie promptly scooped it up as it rolled over to her, dropping her doll in favor of her older brother's toy.

"She's gone to tell Papa that the militia is needed somewhere." John forced a smile as he rechecked the lock, not wanting to worry his younger siblings. "She'll be back soon."

Charles, Jr. sat on the floor, resting his chin in his hands as he watched his nieces and nephews. Lysander walked over to him and lay down, nudging the boy with his nose. He leaned over and buried his face in the dog's fur.

"I'm scared, Lysander." The dog whined softly in response, licking his hand.

"I'll go get my ball and cup, and we can see who can catch the ball more." John glanced at him, then walked over.

Charles, Jr. sat up and nodded in agreement.

***

Kate prayed she would find her husband's regiment quickly, knowing that time was of the essence. Dried leaves crunched under the horse's hooves as they galloped down the trail, the woman occasionally having to duck under a low-hanging branch. Most of the trees were devoid of their leaves at this time of the year, but a few still had a couple particularly stubborn leaves clinging to them.

Her heart pounded in her chest as she rode, and she gripped the reins so tightly her knuckles turned white. This was different from all the other times she'd ridden to gather the militia. This time, it was her parent's house under threat. She hoped that her parents and siblings were alright. Charles, Jr. of course, was at her home, but Andrew and her sisters were likely there, as well as the men her parents were sheltering.

Suddenly, she caught a glimpse of horses through the trees, and pulled her horse to a stop, slipping off the saddle. She wiped her hands on her dress, inhaling deeply before starting forward. Carefully, she walked, making sure her footsteps made as little noise as possible as she approached the camp, unsure if these were allies or not.

Then, she caught sight of a familiar face. John McElwrath, one of the men who served under her husband. She relaxed immediately, sprinting towards the camp. Now that she was certain of who they were, there was no time to waste. "Andrew!" Her husband turned at the sound of her voice.

"What's going on?" he said, catching her in his arms.

"There's a raid at my parent's house, you must go quickly!"

The words spurred all the men that heard into action, and within minutes, they were mounting their horses and preparing to ride to the Moore's plantation. She laid her hand on her husband's arm before he climbed onto his horse.

"I have to return to the children. Tell my father Charles, Jr. is staying with us."

"I'll tell him." He nodded, taking one last glance at his wife before riding to join his men.

* * *

Later that evening, Kate sat in the rocking chair, Katie and Charlie on her lap, and the three older children gathered around her feet as she read to them from the Bible. So far, they'd heard no news of what had happened after the militia arrived at the Moore plantation, and the woman tried to bite down her worry.

The candle was beginning to flicker low, and she was just about to put the two youngest to bed when a knock came at the door.

"Go wait in the bedroom until I know who it is," she whispered as she handed Katie to John.

She waited for them to make their way inside before unlatching the door, opening it just enough that she could see who it was.

"Oh, Papa!"

Her father stood on the porch, hat in his hands as he smiled at her sadly.

"I've come to bring Charles, Jr. home. I knew you wouldn't send him back until you knew it was safe."

"What happened?" Kate questioned, stepping aside so he could enter. "Are Mama and the girls alright? And Andrew?"

"Your Mama and siblings are fine," her father assured her. Then, his face clouded over. "Captain Steadman was killed. Bloody Bill shot him while he was lying defenseless in bed. The two others we had sleeping in the barn were shot too."

Kate gasped, wringing her hands together. The children, hearing the familiar voice of their grandfather, quietly crept out of the bedroom to listen. Charles, Jr. ran forward, tackling his father in a tight embrace.

"Papa!"

"We buried the men this afternoon, started a cemetery in one of the fields." Charles Moore, Sr. placed his hand on the top of his youngest son's head. "Your husband's regiment arrived just as the Tories were about to set fire to the house, and were able to put a stop to it before any damage was done."

"I'm glad, Papa," Kate murmured, wrapping her arm around Polly as the girl came over to cling to her skirt. "If only no one had to die…"

"This is war, Kate," her father responded softly.

"I know, Papa… I know."

EPILOGUE

BARRY HOME, ROEBUCK, SOUTH CAROLINA
3 SEPTEMBER, 1784

A YEAR HAD PASSED SINCE the signing of the Treaty of Paris in France ending the war in the colonies. Victor and Lysander sat in the shade of a large oak tree together as they watched the Barry children—now numbering five with the addition of Peggy, who was almost fifteen months old now—play in the grass. Kate and Andrew sat on the porch, chatting as the shadows deepened with the coming of dusk.

"I miss Uncle Ambroise," Victor murmured, leaning back against the dog's side. Ambroise had set off on some new adventure early that spring and had yet to return. It had been quiet without him and his crazy ideas to keep the pair on their toes.

"It feels weird not to have to talk him out of doing something that could get him killed."

"Agreed," Lysander panted, squinting out at the sun, which was hanging low in the distance, partially obscured by the trees. "It's much too quiet now."

"Ah, were you boys talking about me?" Ambroise himself strutted into view, settling down beside them both. Lysander and Victor gasped, and both immediately began to speak at once.

"Uncle Ambroise, where were you?"

"Are you back for good?"

"Shush now, I'll tell you of my adventures later," Ambroise held up a paw to get them to quiet down. "Charles Town has been renamed Charleston since I've been gone, just over a year ago now. Can you believe that it's been nearly two years since the British evacuated Charleston?"

"Has it truly been that long?" Lysander asked, eyes wide. "It can't be, can it?"

"My boy, 14th December 1782 was almost twenty-one months ago." Ambroise laughed, lying on his back and resting his head on his paws.

"Is Charleston where you went?" Victor asked. "How are things going down there?"

"Moving along," Ambroise shrugged, preening his whiskers. "They're learning where they stand now that the war is over."

"We're independent now, aren't we?" Lysander wagged his tail, grinning widely.

"That we are, my boy, that we are."

ABOUT

CATHERINE MOORE BARRY

Margaret Catherine Moore Barry was a Patriot spy and scout for the South Carolina militia during the Revolutionary War. Born in 1752, she was the eldest of Charles and Mary Moore's ten children, and married Andrew Barry in 1767, at the age of fifteen. Between 1780 and 1783, she gathered the local militia for General Morgan before the Battle of Cowpens, spied and scouted for her husband's regiment, while also caring for her four children. After the war, she and her husband returned to everyday life in the backcountry and went on to have six more children. She died in September of 1823, and is buried in the family cemetery at Walnut Grove Plantation.

CATHERINE MOORE BARRY

NOTES FROM THE AUTHOR

Ambroise, Victor, and Lysander are fictional characters added in for the sake of the story.

I am unsure of when Rocky Spring Academy was named, so I went with the name it has today.

Andrew Barry Moore, Kate's younger brother, would grow up to become the first college-educated doctor in the area.

While legend states that Kate Barry tied her daughter to her bedpost before riding to gather the militia before the Battle of Cowpens, there is no historical evidence that it happened. Still, it makes a fun story, so I decided to include it.

There are three Charles' in Kate's family. Her father, Charles Moore, Sr., her brother, Charles Moore, Jr., and her son, Charles Barry. To try to lessen the confusion caused by three people carrying the same name, I've referred to Charles Barry as Charlie, and the Moore's with their suffixes.

Local legend has it that Captain Steadman, and the two Patriot soldiers killed by Bloody Bill Cunningham during his raid on Walnut Grove Plantation were the first to be buried in what is now the family cemetery.

COMTE DE ROCHAMBEAU

LE EXPÉDITION PARTICULIÈRE

by Madeleine Rose Wenzel

PROLOGUE

NEWPORT, RHODE ISLAND
11 JULY, 1780

SILENT. THE WHOLE TOWN was utterly silent as Rochambeau stepped foot onto its streets, a small grey kitten following close at his heels. There was hardly a soul to be seen anywhere he looked. After two and a half months at sea, he'd expected to be greeted on the shores of America when he arrived, but there was nobody.

Rochambeau turned to his quartermaster general, Jacques de Béville, and asked him, "Where is everyone?"

"I don't know, *monsieur*," de Béville replied, pressing his lips together as he glanced around him. Of the troops who had come over from France to aid the colonists in their war, he and Rochambeau were the only two to disembark from the ship that afternoon.

Only a few people wandering the streets, and all went out of their way to avoid the men as they looked for anyone who might know where they were supposed to go. Rochambeau had been told that he was to cooperate with General Washington, but how could he if he didn't know where to send his troops? Every shop they passed was boarded up, and several buildings were damaged by cannon fire. Finally, Rochambeau stopped walking.

"I don't believe that anyone will come," he remarked, disappointment weighing heavily in his voice as he stooped to pick up the kitten weaving around his feet. "Perhaps we should return to the ship."

"Or an inn," de Béville suggested, gesturing to one just down the road. "If we could find one willing to take us, it would be nice to sleep on a proper bed."

Rochambeau thought for a moment, stroking Rosine's back as she purred. Then, he nodded. "Yes, that sounds like a fine plan."

The army had been onboard a ship for three months now. Initially, they had planned to leave France in April 1780, before they were forced to turn back and return to port the day after departure due to contradictory winds.

Finally, on the second of May, the French fleet set sail for the American Colonies. The terrible conditions on board encouraged disease, and many of the men, who were confined to sleeping two to a hammock, fell ill with dysentery, putrid fever, and scurvy. Some had died, but Rochambeau was confident that the majority would recover in a few months now that they were in America.

"I wish to find a place for the army to camp as well," Rochambeau informed the quartermaster, letting Rosine jump to the ground. "I don't want them on the ships any longer than necessary, they need more space to rest."

"Very well," de Béville nodded, and the two resumed their walk.

***

NEWPORT, RHODE ISLAND
12 JULY, 1780

"So, how was your journey to America?" General Heath asked, stirring his cup of coffee. Rochambeau waited for one of his aides to translate for him, a small smile appearing on his lips as he answered.

"Long."

"I'd imagine so," Heath grinned, then continued. "I apologize for not meeting with you sooner, though I fear we all are a little unsure of what's to come now."

"Why?"

"Well, the last time the French were here, it didn't go so well." Heath shifted in his seat, glancing at the ceiling. "Your country's commanders did not get along well with ours, *monsieur.*

"And besides that," he continued, "the British army was here until October of last year; we barely have enough resources left to support ourselves, much less another army."

"I see." Rochambeau nodded, pressing his lips together. That would explain why everyone in the town was so hesitant to greet them.

At that moment, his kitten decided to jump up on the table, mewing at the two. "Ah! Rosine, *non.*"

"Who is this?" Heath smiled as Rochambeau lifted the feline off the table, and set her on the ground. "Is she yours?"

"Somewhat," Rochambeau responded, sighing as he watched the kitten rub around his legs. "She appeared on the ship two days after we left Brest, and since then has attached herself to me."

"A fine cat she is," the governor nodded, leaning back. "Now, what else were you wanting to discuss?"

"My army needs provisions, as well as doctors, and a place to make camp," Rochambeau replied, folding his hands on the table. "I am able to pay for anything we use. In silver."

Heath's eyes went wide at the offer, and he immediately straightened his posture. It was unusual for any army to pay for anything, and the other man was offering to pay straight out. In silver no less, not the worthless continental money. "I will be sure you get everything you need."

"My officers will pay rent wherever they may stay, and the army will be held to the strictest discipline."

"I am glad to hear it, sir."

* * *

VERNON HOUSE
NEWPORT, RHODE ISLAND
28 MAY, 1781

Monsieur,

The British fleet has left, and our squadron is preparing to take leave at the first fair wind. Once I have the liberty to execute the plans we have agreed upon, I will not delay them long. I am with respect and personal attachment, Sir, Your Excellency's most obedient & most humble servant.

Le cte de Rochambeau.

Rochambeau smiled as he set his quill back on the desk, glancing down at the cat curled up at his feet.

"Well, it appears we will soon be leaving here, if all goes well."

Rosine looked up at him and blinked slowly, stretching out with a yawn as he stood up, before rubbing around his heels. He smiled at her as he exited the house and walked down to the wharf, clasping his hands behind his back as he came to a stop. The convoy he was waiting on hadn't yet arrived, and he was growing impatient.

He had met with Washington back in March, and the two had discussed what their plans were as the campaign season of 1781 drew near. Now, he only waited for this convoy, which was carrying more recruits and money, to arrive in the port. For the past month, he had been gathering wagons, horses, and provisions to prepare for the march they were soon to make.

Rosine sat at his feet, looking up at him with a quiet meow. She was quite the talkative cat, and in the eleven months they'd spent in Newport, he'd grown quite fond of her. Finally he sighed, turning on his heel to walk back to where he was staying. There were better things he could do with his time than stand around waiting for the convoy to arrive. He still had preparations he needed to make.

***

NEWTOWN, CONNECTICUT
29 JUNE, 1781

Rochambeau read over the letter that Washington had sent him, rubbing his chin with one hand. Rosine batted at the corner of the tent with one paw, and he spoke to her as he folded the paper back up. "The General tells me that he would have liked to meet me here, Rosine."

The cat stopped her playing and looked up at him with a meow, walking over to rub at his legs, and the man smiled at her.

"Yes, I agree." He picked up his quill and walked over to the letter he'd started the night before, when he and his troops had arrived in Newtown. "I thought I would stay here three days, but this changes plans."

The French army had started its march out of Newport the 18th of June, with one of the four regiments leaving a day before they were all marching. Rochambeau had gone with the Bourbonnais Regiment on the first day, leaving his siege artillery to be loaded onto ships by the other three regiments, and the four hundred men he'd ordered to stay in Newport under Lieutenant General de Choisy.

Rosine hopped up on the desk he was using, and he frowned, moving the inkwell out of reach of her paws. "*Non*, I know what you wish to do."

He opened up the folded letter and began adding a postscript, his quill scratching quietly on the paper.

> *Monsieur,*
>
> *I arrived here in Newtown today with the first regiment, and intend to remain here three days to mend the wagons, and form brigades. I shall set off again on the second of the next month with both the first and second regiments, and on the third, the last two regiments will follow. I already wrote to you to say that I left my siege artillery at Providence, ready to imbark, and only brought the field pieces with me. It is my hope they will arrive safely. I am with respect and personal attachment, Sir, Your Excellency's most obedient & most humble servant.*
>
> *Le cte de Rochambeau.*
>
> *P.S. Major Cobb has brought me Your Excellency's letter just as I was about to send this one. I will stay here today and tomorrow so I can put everything under the proper orders, then set off the day after tomorrow with a small escort to wait on you and receive your orders.*

Rochambeau set his quill down and sprinkled sand from his blotter onto the page, absentmindedly lifting Rosine to the floor as she attempted to bat his quill off the desk. "I will send this letter to General Washington immediately."

* * *

FRANCO-AMERICAN CAMP, NEW YORK
14 AUGUST, 1781

Rochambeau, Washington, and a few aides huddled over a map spread out on the desk, discussing how best to proceed. They had just received word that Admiral de Grasse was headed for the Chesapeake Bay with the French fleet, so their plans were changing.

"We mustn't let the British figure out what we're planning." Washington rubbed his chin as he thought. "We won't be able to hide our plans forever, but the longer we can keep them guessing, the more chance we have of defeating Cornwallis."

"What do you suggest we do?" Rochambeau asked.

"I propose we send a few faux letters," Washington replied. "We'll send them the most dangerous routes, so they're certain to be captured."

"And to cover our march?"

"Some of the men will stay here and act as though we're planning to attack Clinton, while the rest of the troops march south."

Rochambeau nodded as the aides translated Washington's words, stepping back and clasping his hands behind his back. The two armies had joined together back in July, and since then, he and Washington had been debating where to make their attack. He had been reluctant to attack Clinton in New York, believing that their position wasn't good for a siege. The city was heavily fortified and difficult to effectively put under siege. He much preferred the idea of attacking Yorktown. But, while he could debate with Washington over where to attack, it was ultimately the other's decision.

"We'll leave in a few days' time, the sooner we can meet de Grasse, the better." Washington stood, turning towards the door. "I shall finalize the plans tonight."

THE SWORD OF CORNWALLIS

10 OCTOBER, 1781

THE GROUND SHOOK WITH the impact of the cannon fire. Rochambeau sat with his head in his hands as he rested. The allies had arrived to meet Lafayette in Yorktown on the 22nd of September, and since then, there had been a hustle of preparations for what Rochambeau hoped would be the end of the siege, which had begun on the 28th.

"Surely Cornwallis cannot hold out much longer," he murmured, stroking his cat as she jumped up into his lap, purring softly. "They have no way to bring in more supplies, Rosine."

Rosine mewed, and he smiled at her. "We opened fire on them yesterday, so now they have a bombardment to worry about on top of everything else."

He stood, lifting the cat off his lap, and walked towards the opening of the tent. "I am going to make sure everything is moving according to plan."

"I suppose you are coming with me?" He glanced down at the cat bouncing at his feet before stepping out.

***

YORKTOWN, VIRGINIA
19 OCTOBER, 1781

Rochambeau stood at the head of the line of French troops, directly across from the Americans as the surrender ceremony began. Two days earlier, Cornwallis had sent out an officer bearing a white handkerchief, and negotiations started the next day. The silence had been deafening. One wouldn't expect it to be so, but after a week of constant cannon fire, everyone had grown used to the noise.

The British had asked for the traditional honors of war, but Washington, remembering the surrender at Charles Town only a year and a half earlier, stoutly refused. The British had denied the Americans those honors then, so he would hold them to the same. They would march with flags furled and muskets shouldered, and playing an English or German tune.

Cornwallis himself refused to attend the ceremony, claiming he was ill. As such, his second in command, General Charles O'Hara, would surrender his sword.

General O'Hara walked over to Rochambeau, holding out

Cornwallis's sword to him. Silently, Rochambeau shook his head, gesturing to Washington. Although he ranked higher than Washington, he had grown to respect him greatly in the time they had worked together. Besides, this was his war. Rochambeau and the rest of his army were there to help, and as such, Rochambeau felt that the honor of the surrender should go to Washington.

Benjamin Lincoln, who had surrendered the city of Charles Town to General Clinton. If Cornwallis would not have the decency to show up at the ceremony himself, he would have Lincoln accept the sword.

Humiliated, O'Hara bowed his head as he walked over to Lincoln, offering the sword. Solemnly, Lincoln took it. Then, the British column slowly began marching forward, laying down their weapons as they passed by. The air of the battle-weary soldiers was mournful, as many of the men cast their eyes to the ground, refusing to look their enemy in the eye as they marched along.

The combined American and French army trembled with excitement as they stood, the chilly October breeze nipping at any exposed finger or nose. Rochambeau smiled as he watched the column march past him, clasping his hands behind his back as Rosine settled herself at his feet. He wasn't sure what would happen after this, but he was ready to find out. Perhaps it wouldn't be long before the Americans achieved their independence.

ABOUT

COMTE DE ROCHAMBEAU

Rochambeau was a French officer who aided the Patriots in their fight for liberty. He was born in 1725, and served in the Seven Years War before being given command of the *Expédition Particulière* in 1780. He arrived in Newport, Rhode Island in July 1780, and remained there for a year, earning the trust of the colonists and meeting with George Washington while the British blockaded the French Fleet. In July 1781, he began marching his army to New York to join the Continental Army, where Washington hoped to attack General Henry Clinton. Upon receiving word that Admiral de Grasse was headed to the Chesapeake Bay, the two changed plans and began their march to Yorktown, where in October 1781, Cornwallis surrendered. He returned to France in 1782, and continued serving in the French army until 1792. He was arrested during the Reign of Terror (1793-94), but escaped being executed. He was later awarded a pension and the Légion d'honneur by Napoleon. He lived out the rest of his life in peace and died in 1807.

ABOUT THE AUTHOR

MADELEINE ROSE WENZEL

Born in Norfolk, VA, Madeleine moved to Irmo, SC at 18 months old, where she has lived with her parents, younger sister and brother, and numerous pets for the last 18 years. Madeleine loves animals, reading, and history, especially anything regarding the American Revolution. Currently a tide clock builder, she would love to be a historian in the future, and possibly participate in Revolutionary War re-enactments as a surgeon.

NOTES FROM THE AUTHOR

Rosine is a fictional character. To the best of my knowledge, Rochambeau did not have a pet cat.

Both letters Rochambeau writes in this chapter are referenced from real letters that Rochambeau wrote to Washington. The way he signs off on them are direct quotes from the letters, as translated into English.

The Major Cobb mentioned in Rochambeau's second letter is Lieutenant Colonel David Cobb. Though he was a Colonel, Rochambeau's letter to Washington on June 28-29, 1781 refers to him as a Major, so I retained that detail for his writing.

GENERAL CHARLES CORNWALLIS

THE BRITISH COMMANDER
AMERICAN SYMPATHIZER

by Alexandra Roberson

GENERAL CHARLES CORNWALLIS

THE HOUSE OF LORDS

BRITISH PARLIAMENT, ENGLAND
18 MARCH, 1766

COLD AIR SWEEPS THROUGH England as the debates over the Stamp Act's repeal unfolds in Parliament. Among the debaters, Charles Cornwallis, a member of the House of Lords, takes part in these debates.

Cornwallis, born New Years Eve 1738 into a distinguished military family, began his career in 1757 during the Seven Years' War. Initially serving as an aide-de-camp to the Marquess of Granby in Germany, he became a regimental commander by 1761 and earned recognition for his bravery at the Battle of Vellinghausen. In 1762, he inherited the title "2nd Earl Cornwallis," from his father, and joined the House of Lords.

Charles Cornwallis walks through the halls of the upper house of Parliament where the House of Lords resides. With William Pitt the Elder, the 1st Earl of Chatham, and Lord Paulet, the 3rd Earl Poulett.

Cornwallis rubs his sweaty palms and adjusts his wig in unease. *I sincerely wish other members of the House vote in favor of repealing the Stamp Act.*

This will cause unnecessary trouble and angst between England and its colonies.

Lord Paulet is the first to break the tension. "Well, I certainly hope that others come to their senses and agree on the repeal of the Act. It is redundant and we recognize this now from what we see happening in the colonies."

"Undeniably so," William agrees. "This Act will lead to undesirable distress between us and our colonies." He adjusts his coat and buttons his wrists.

Cornwallis breathes a sigh of relief. "I am grateful I am not alone in opposing the Act."

"Most certainly not," Lord Paulet reassures, "There is no way that this act will not be repealed."

The trio continues into the upper house to take their seats. Cornwallis adjusts his wig nervously. *I pray that this act is repealed. If it isn't, it could lead to a full war between us and the colonists. But what if it is repealed and a war still happens? We all know the colonists are unhappy with us, but we don't understand the full extent of their frustration. No one wants a war but is it even avoidable at this point?*

INDEPENDENCE

Despite the repeal of the Stamp Act, the colonists declared independence and initiated a revolution.

GENERAL CHARLES CORNWALLIS

THE PROMOTION

BRITISH CAMP, SOUTH CAROLINA
JUNE 1780

THE BLAZING SUN BEATS down onto Jack and Emily's faces, the foxhound dogs of Cornwallis. It is mid-June, and the weather proves it. The pair follows Cornwallis through a British camp to meet with General Sir Henry Clinton.

"Jack, I wish to rest. I wish to go home, to go back to England. Oh my, I miss the watered down tea. I miss England!," Emily rants while slowing her pace and closing her eyes each time she takes a step as if she is wincing in pain.

"Emily," Jack begins, "please stop. You are hurting my ears. I understand you want to go home but it's not as if I can do anything about it, so maybe stop complaining. Also, it's not like you're the only one who wants to go home." He stops and puts his paws over his ears to block out Emily's complaints.

"Rude much," Emily retorts, side-eyeing Jack.

"Speak for yourself," Jack rolls his eyes at her.

The pair continue on as they walk toward Clinton's tent beside Cornwallis.

* * *

BRITISH CAMP, SOUTH CAROLINA
JUNE 1780

Why is it so hot? This heat is quite unbearable, Cornwallis thinks. He pulls at his neckerchief to wipe away the sweat accumulating on his brow. He continues to walk through the camp to meet with General Clinton.

I pray that whatever he wishes to tell me gets me out of this heat, Cornwallis ponders, grimacing at the amount of sweat pouring down his spine. The rough material of his uniform adds to his discomfort. Jack and Emily, his dogs, walk closely on each side of him, occasionally barking at wildlife. Suddenly, Emily runs off between two tents as a bird lands nearby.

"EMILY! STOP! COME BACK!" Cornwallis exclaims as he runs off after her with Jack beside him.

Multiple soldiers try to help and grab Emily but she slips through their legs and in between them to continue her chase. As she makes it to the log, the bird flies up into the air to get away from its pursuers. Emily lies down to the side of the log, panting in exhaustion.

As Cornwallis reaches the log, he hunches over in fatigue with Jack standing beside him.

"Y-y-you are v-v-very f-f-fast," Cornwallis tries to speak while sitting down next to Emily, "P-p-please don't do t-t-that again."

As Cornwallis feels steady again, he lifts himself up. Jack gives Cornwallis a lick on the hand to let him know he is still there.

"Let's go Emily, you playful girl," Cornwallis as he pets her head.

The trio head back to the tents and the General's quarters. As Cornwallis walks up to Clinton's tent, he is rushed with nervousness and anxiety. *Did I do something wrong? Am I in trouble? Did he find out that I believe this war is unnecessary? Am I getting punished?*

"Sit here," Cornwallis commands Jack and Emily to stay outside the tent.

As the fabric doors of the tent brush his shoulders, he finds General Clinton sitting at his desk sorting piles of papers.

As Cornwallis approaches the general's desk, Clinton looks up and starts,

"Cornwallis! Welcome! My apologies for not acknowledging you sooner! I loathe doing paperwork and end up procrastinating."

"No issue, sir. What is the reason you have called me?" Cornwallis asks, sweating down his neck.

Clinton gives a long sigh, "As you know, we took over Charles Town earlier this month. You played a vital role in this achievement and I personally thank you. Along with this success, I have found another possible solution to gain more force in these frustrating southern colonies."

Cornwallis shuffles his feet in anticipation of what Clinton has to tell him.

"We require a change in leadership. With you as the commander in the southern colonies, I am confident that we can maintain our momentum and achieve victory in this conflict. Your leadership will be vital in gaining further support from our English Loyalists."

Cornwallis is stunned, "Thank you for this opportunity, sir. It is by uniting and by cherishing the public spirit that we can carry an army through great enterprises and to the wished-for happy conclusion."

The general chuckles, "I am pleased to hear that! Now, if you would excuse me, I must return to my paperwork to avoid any issues."

As Cornwallis exits the tent, he rubs his hands together and claps them in excitement for his new role and how bright the future is.

THE HUNGRY FOXHOUNDS

*TOM POLK'S HOME, WINNSBORO,
SOUTH CAROLINA
21 AUGUST, 1780*

ROSS! ROSS WHERE ARE YOU?" Cornwallis calls for his aid-de-camp, Alexander Ross, wiping the sweat from his forehead. The hot South Carolina day made him long for Great Britain. Sitting in his chair at his headquarters, Cornwallis keeps the blinds drawn to limit the sunlight.

After he called, his aide-de-camp walks through the doors of Cornwallis's office, perspiration seeping through his uniform.

"Ready to make the report from Camden, sir." Ross says, picking up paper and a quill.

"Good," Cornwallis replies, "British forces: 2,230; rebel forces: 3,700. Casualties: British 324; rebel 1,900." Cornwallis pauses as he sees Ross struggling to keep up. He adjusts his uniform due to the heat. He sees Ross look up and continues, "Additionally, 1,000 rebel prisoners were taken along with captured artillery and supplies. The battle included an artillery exchange and a bayonet charge." Cornwallis finishes.

"Anything else, sir?" Ross asks.

Cornwallis sees his dogs come into the room, wagging their tails in joy. They walk up around the desk to Cornwallis and sit at his feet.

"Actually, add some dog bones and treats for Emily and Jack," Cornwallis adds petting his foxhound's head, "That is all."

"Yes, Sir." Ross exits the room with the report in hand.

Cornwallis plays with his foxhound until they leave him to his work.

* * *

21 AUGUST, 1780

"YAY! I LOVE TREATS!" Jack jumps on his sister, crushing her in excitement, his paws stepping all over her.

"Ew, Jack get off!" Emily says, pushing Jack off. She runs to Cornwallis's chair as his aide-de-camp leaves his office. She plays around his feet to get his attention. Cornwallis stands up out of his chair and squats down to rub her.

"Yes, yes, that is the spot," Emily giggles. She squirms out of Cornwallis's grasp as she sees Jack come around the chair. She nips Jack on the ear,

"Now, don't you go doing that again!"

"My apologies Emily," Jack puts his paw over his head, "I do not wish to alarm or upset you. Let us go outside to get some fresh air."

The two foxhounds leave the room and head outside as they leave their master to his work.

FIRING THE GRAPESHOT

BATTLE OF GUILFORD COURTHOUSE
15 MARCH, 1781

SIR, IT'S GETTING MORE difficult to hold the field. We need to do something. Change our tactics."

"What do you suppose then? Give us one of your great ideas?"

"Let's fire grapeshot. It's the time for drastic measures."

"No, we would chance killing our own soldiers."

"Stop arguing, both of you!"

Cornwallis is unable to hear his own thoughts due to the loud conversations of his colleagues and the cries from the battle. Him and his associates, Charles O'Hara, Banastre Tarleton, and James Webster, are in North Carolina, engaging in a battle against Major

General Nathanael Greene and the Continental army. Cornwallis is fighting against a North Carolinian with a fearful look in his eyes.

It was a clear and cold morning before the battle. A light frost had covered the field before fading under the sun. The ground was smooth and moist from the lingering winter snow and rain. Now the field is filled with the boots of soldiers fighting one another. Father against son. Friend against friend.

The fighting is now in a crucial situation with brutal hand-to-hand combat and it is getting worse. The battle is getting out of control and Cornwallis knows it needs to come to an end. He knows that there is enough time, just not enough to spare. He only has one thought in mind.

"Stop it, all of you!" Cornwallis orders, standing straighter and with more confidence. "Tell the troops to fire grapeshot."

Cornwallis understood that his decision could lead to casualties on both sides. However, he recognized the urgency of removing himself and his men from the battle to minimize the risk of fatality.

UNWANTED NEWS

LETTER FROM LIEUTENANT COLONEL FRANCIS RAWDON TO CORNWALLIS, THE BATTLE OF HOBKIRK'S HILL, 26 APRIL, 1781

DEAR COMMANDER CORNWALLIS,

Yesterday morning in South Carolina, we were engaged by Major General Nathanael Greene and his troops on Hobkirk's Hill. They first attacked the garrison on 19 April, but our defenses were too strong for them and they retreated to a position north of the garrison on top of Hobkirk Hill.

Then on 25 April, we launched an attack on their army. Our force consisted of about 900 soldiers including the 63rd Regiment of Foot along with the Volunteers of Ireland, the King's American Regiment, New York Volunteers, and the South Carolina Royalist Regiment. Major Greene's forces were about one thousand five hundred and fifty. We encountered the continental's early in the afternoon. We were successful and drove Major Greene and his army from Hobkirk Hill and managed to secure Camden. Unfortunately, we lost roughly two hundred fifty soldiers. We are running extremely low on supplies and urgently need provisions. Abandoning Camden seems inevitable.

Deepest Regards,

Lieutenant Colonel Rawdon

DARK DAYS FOR THE REDCOATS

SIEGE OF YORKTOWN
16 OCTOBER, 1781

*B*OOM.

A vibration blasted through the whole city.

BOOM.

Another one.

Cornwallis feels the tremors flow through his body. Upon the second impact, his knees begin to give way as he crouches in a fortified underground shelter near the southern shoreline of the York River, shaking and starting to collapse. Both American and French forces alike are actively bombing the British and its positions. Accompanying Cornwallis is Charles O'Hara and Major General Alexander Leslie, their aides-de-camp and clerks. Currently, Cornwallis and O'Hara are discussing ways to devise an escape plan from their situation.

"What are we supposed to do? Starve ourselves down here?" O'Hara asks rhetorically.

"Not necessarily," Cornwallis responds, "we just need to find our opening."

"What opening? We are surrounded from the French naval blockade to the American troops. We have no solution," O'Hara says with fear in his eyes.

Cornwallis knows the desperate situation they are in and is hoping to find a solution. Then, one comes to him.

"We will attempt to cross the York River tonight. Gather some soldiers for the crossing."

His aide-de-camps and clerks scrambled to gather the soldiers for the mission.

Cornwallis paces around the room in panic. *This plan has to work. Otherwise, I have no idea what to do.*

* * *

16 OCTOBER, 1781

"No, Jack. You mustn't go. You can't go," Emily cries to Jack, tears forming in her eyes.

"Emily, you heard Cornwallis. If the troops are going to try and cross the York River, I must go with them. I have to, Emily," Jack responds, pacing the bunker.

After they overheard Cornwallis make his decision, they went right outside the makeshift bunker.

"Fine," she sighed." If you feel the need to go, go. But please, I beg of you, come home. Whatever you do, just come back and find me. We will go home, back to England. I know it. You are my brother, and I love you so. Promise me, promise me you will come back," Emily starts to cry, placing a paw over her face so Jack doesn't see.

"I promise, Emily. I will do whatever I can to come home," Jack goes over to Emily and licks her forehead, "I will see you soon, I know it."

Jack leaves the room to find the troops, while Emily stays and hides under a table, sobbing.

* * *

17 OCTOBER, 1781

Cornwallis paces the tiny underground bunker that serves as their headquarters. No news has come about the York River crossing. It is early in the morning, but the sound of explosions still echoes outside. Sweat trickles down Cornwallis's spine in worry. His defensive measures are failing, and this river crossing is his only hope. About 1,000 troops have left to cross the river. Cornwallis sits at a small table with O'Hara, planning their next move. Only one of his foxhounds, Emily, is with him in the room. *I wonder where Jack is, I hope he is safe,* Cornwallis ponders, petting Emily. Then suddenly, a soldier dashes down the entrance to the bunker,

"SIR! News!" the soldier says.

Cornwallis and O'Hara leap from their chairs to hear the anticipated report.

"Sir, early this morning, a horrendous storm hit the York River. Our boats were scattered and some were even driven down the river. Few boats returned with our men suffering greatly from the loss," the soldier lowers his head, "I am so very sorry, sir," he adds, then turns and leaves the bunker. Emily runs out of the bunker after him, her ears pinned back.

"What are we to do?" O'Hara asks, turning to Cornwallis, fear in his eyes, "Surrender?"

"There is nothing else we can do."

***

17 OCTOBER, 1781

Where is He? Where is my brother? Emily runs along the shore of the York River. She starts panicking and barks at the sky.

"JACK! WHERE ARE YOU?!? YOU PROMISED! YOU *PROMISED!*" she screams, beginning to stumble. Her paws cannot hold the weight of her sadness. She treads back into the bunker, weeping, and hides back under the table, crying herself to sleep.

REUNITED

19 OCTOBER, 1781

EMILY IS JOLTED AWAKE. Cornwallis had moved his base from the bunker to a house in town, and Emily had come along with him. Although it is morning, she sees through the window that it is still dark outside. As Emily stands from her sleeping spot beside Cornwallis's bed, her whiskers twitch with a scent, one with which she is familiar. She walks out to the entrance of the house to see a small figure running towards the house.

"Jack!! It's you!" Emily races out of the house to meet him. "Jack!!" Emily embraces him in a big hug, " I thought you were gone! I thought you forgot your promise!"

"You and promises," Jack laughs. "I was stuck on a boat that drifted from the storm. I sniffed my way to that underground bunker but could not find anyone. Then I sniffed my way back here."

"Well, I am very thankful you are back. Let's go to bed so you can get some rest," Emily says, giving Jack a big lick on the forehead.

The foxhounds slowly make their way to Cornwallis's room. Jack plops on the ground while Emily uses her snout to push the door closed before settling down beside him.

THE SURRENDER

19 OCTOBER, 1781

CORNWALLIS WAKES TO SUNLIGHT on his face. Today is the official and public surrender. Now that the base is in the town, Cornwallis appreciates having a bed. He props himself up with his pillows and sees Jack and Emily sleeping on the floor together. *I really do have the best foxhounds. These dogs have seen it all.* He falls back onto his bed, knowing what the day will bring. Then a loud *CRACK* hits his door. Cornwallis stirs in his bed as O'Hara quietly enters. *I don't want to do this, I never wanted this, I won't do this,* he thinks.

"Sir." Cornwallis recognizes the voice of O'Hara. "Sir you must wake, it is time."

"No," Cornwallis creaks with a fake cough, "I am unwell. You go in my place." Cornwallis turns his head so he doesn't see O'Hara's face.

"But sir–"

"No, I cannot go, so you will," Cornwallis says with another fake cough. "Now, please leave me. You will go and surrender on my behalf,"

"Yes, sir," O'Hara responds, closing the door as he leaves.

Cornwallis turns around so he can see his dogs. *I am so thankful for both of you. I am glad you both have been with me through all this.* He tries to fall back asleep, but his conscience keeps him awake.

BITTERSWEET HOMECOMING

ENGLAND
21 JANUARY, 1782

IT'S A CHILLY MORNING in England. Mist settles over the water, fog filling the streets. Cornwallis is arriving home along with his colleague, Benedict Arnold. The two of them are returning home to England after the war.

Cornwallis rubs his hands together, then looks side to side. His dogs are right by him, Jack swaying, almost like he is seasick. Cornwallis paces the ship before they dock. *What if… what if I am blamed? What if I am thrown into the Tower of London? Am I going to be executed? Put in jail?* Cornwallis feels as if he will throw up until Arnold comes to his side.

"You look awful," he says with a smirk on his face. "Don't worry, everything will go well. We will be welcomed back in open arms. All will be well."

"You are right, no reason to fret," Cornwallis responds, feeling a slight form of relief.

Once the ship docks, Cornwallis and Arnold make their way off the ship, Jack and Emily behind them. As the streets are within sight, Cornwallis doesn't feel completely scared. *All will be well, all will be well, he tells himself.*

The streets are deserted, shrouded in nervous fog—blank, silent, and cold.

Arnold is the first to say something, "Wh-where is everyone? Why aren't they here?"

"I don't know, I-I don't know," Cornwallis says, fear creeping into his body, showing on his face.

EPILOGUE

2 OCTOBER, 1780

AFTER CORNWALLIS'S RETURN TO Great Britain, he had not been punished as he feared, nor was his reputation tarnished. He did, however, receive some criticism about the loss of Yorktown. Overall, he was considered a hero upon his return.

But Cornwallis's story didn't end there. He continued his public service for almost 30 more years. From 1786 to 1793, he was appointed governor of India by the British East India Company with the approval of the British government.

In 1798, Cornwallis was appointed Lord Lieutenant and Commander-in-Chief of Ireland by Prime Minister William Pitt the

Younger. He served in this capacity for three years. He returned to India for another term as governor in 1805. Sadly, he passed away within two months of returning for his second term.

Charles Cornwallis lived a full life, leaving behind a legacy of resilience, dedication to his country, and proud leadership.

ABOUT

CHARLES CORNWALLIS

Charles Cornwallis was an accomplished British commander during the Revolutionary War, leading campaigns against Washington's forces from 1776 to 1781. His military career began in the Seven Years' War, where he served as an aide-de-camp of the Marquess of Granby in Germany before returning to England. Following the British victory at Charles Town, Cornwallis was appointed commander of British forces in the southern colonies under General Henry Clinton. After returning to England, he served as Governor-General of India (1786), later became Lord Lieutenant of Ireland (1798), and briefly returned to India in 1805. He passed away within two months of his return to India due to fever.

ABOUT THE AUTHOR

ALEXANDRA ROBERSON

Alexandra Roberson hails from Central Florida where she lives with her family, rescued Labs, Holland Lop bunnies, and hedgehog. She loves reading and always asks for more books to devour. She is a competitive baton twirler and was a member of Team USA in the 2023 World Baton Championship in England. Alexandra is a junior in high school and an active member of her local Children of the American Revolution society. She is also an Eagle Scout and is recognized as a peer minister at her school.

NOTES FROM THE AUTHOR

Cornwallis served as a member of England's House of Lords during the repeal of the Stamp Act, however he was not part of the assembly when the act was initially approved. While it remains uncertain whether he interacted with notable figures like William Pitt the Elder or Lord Paulet, both individuals, alongside Cornwallis, voted in favor of repealing the act.

King George III gifted Cornwallis with dogs. However, the details such as their number and breed are unknown. The dogs are depicted as foxhounds named Jack and Emily. The exact timing of these gifts remain unclear, but for the purpose of the story, it is illustrated as occurring prior to Cornwallis's appointment as a commander in the colonies.

Cornwallis was promoted to a commander shortly after the British victory at the Battle of Charles Town. General Clinton oversaw the promotion which likely took place at a British camp in South

Carolina, though the specific location is not documented. The portrayal of General Clinton as a procrastinator is purely fictional.

The battle report, written by Alexander Ross and Cornwallis, concerning the Battle of Camden was factual. Following the battle, Cornwallis established his headquarters at Tom Polk's home in Winnsboro, South Carolina. While the report accurately reflects the battle's events, the fiction elements, such as Cornwallis including asking for treats for his dogs in the report, were added for narrative purposes.

At the Battle of Guildford Courthouse, Cornwallis ordered his troops to deploy grapeshot, a cluster-based artillery ammunition effective at short range against infantry. This decision resulted in the deaths of both American and British soldiers, with Cornwallis commanding alongside notable figures such as Charles O'Hara, Banastre Tarleton, and James Webster.

Cornwallis received correspondence from Lieutenant Colonel Rawdon regarding the Battle of Hobkirk's Hill. While the wording was changed for the chapter, the topics accurately reflect the original correspondence.

On October 16, 1781, Cornwallis retreated to an underground bunker along the southern shoreline of the York River to evade bombardment. His attempt to escape by crossing the York River was documented, although fictional elements, such as his dog Jack in the crossing, were incorporated into the story.

Cornwallis and O'Hara remained in the bunker on the morning of October 17th, where they learned of the failed river crossing attempt. Cornwallis made the decision to surrender while still in the bunker.

Between October 17 and 19, Cornwallis moved from the bunker to a house in Yorktown. Claiming illness, he sent O'Hara to represent him at the official surrender ceremony.

Cornwallis returned to England alongside Benedict Arnold. While his fear of being blamed for the war's loss was exaggerated in my depictions, it was noted that Cornwallis was ultimately regarded as a hero rather than being held responsible for the defeat. Narrative liberties were taken, such as portraying empty streets to emphasize Cornwallis's fears. It was unknown if the streets were filled or empty, but in the chapter it was written as if they were empty to go along with Cornwallis's fear.

The epilogue is historically accurate.

ALEXANDER HAMILTON

DESTINY'S DOORSTEP

by Edan MacNaughton

To my Lord and Savior Jesus Christ, through whom all things are possible.

LETTERS AND REFLECTIONS

CAMP BEFORE YORKTOWN, VIRGINIA
12 OCTOBER, 1781

THE CANDLE IN HIS tent was burning low. Here on this chilly October night, twenty-four year-old Alexander Hamilton had one last order of business to attend to. The Continental Army was now over two weeks into its siege of General Cornwallis' British forces and was making progress little by little. Each day that came and went saw the Americans inch closer to Cornwallis' position, but the battle was far from over. Just earlier today, Alexander heard from scouts that Cornwallis was preparing some sort of surprise that he would soon try to unleash. While this report was concerning, Alexander was still confident that the Patriots would eventually prevail.

He reached into his bag to pull out a tinderbox and while digging around for it, he came across a different item. This item was an antique watch, and it was far more special to him than a singular tinderbox. It had belonged to his great grandfather and it was gifted to him by his late mother. It no longer kept time properly, nevertheless it was a sentimental item that Alexander liked to keep close by. On the back of the watch a faded word was written and Hamilton smiled seeing this word.

He carefully placed the old watch back into his bag and pulled out his tinderbox. He still had one last order of business to attend to, and he had better do it quickly, before sleep overtook him for the night. Content with the way he relit the candle, he sat down at his wooden desk and submerged his quill fresh in a splash of ink. He began:

I wrote to you two days since My Dear Betsey...

Writing letters to his wife Eliza, (whom he affectionately called Betsey), was a common pastime for Alexander Hamilton. A gifted writer since boyhood, the power of the pen seemed to come to him remarkably easily, similar to his Patriot colleagues, Thomas Jefferson and Benjamin Franklin. However, any similarities between those two men and him ended with writing. Where Jefferson and Franklin hailed from large families and were born on American soil, Hamilton was constantly haunted by his broken family upbringing and traumatic West Indies childhood. Just thinking back to those days when he lived in poverty and was parentless on the island of St.

Croix made a chill run down his spine. This long war, for so many a thing of horror and disdain, was his ticket to destiny and glory.

Alexander put down his quill for a moment as thoughts from the past few years overtook him. He had already tasted a sprinkling of the glory of battle when his artillery unit helped force the British to surrender at the Battle of Princeton back in 1776. This relatively young man had also caught a fleeting glimpse of destiny in the last several years, serving as General George Washington's aide-de-camp. He was honored to serve the general through thick and thin and handle tasks such as his correspondence, but after a while he began to feel taken for granted.

At the beginning of this year, he had finally put his foot down with Washington. Leaving the general waiting for a handful of minutes wasn't intentional, but it provided the perfect opportunity that he had been looking for to leave Washington's side. After turning in his resignation a few weeks later, he had proceeded to pester his former boss for a field command. There was nothing more that Alexander wanted than a chance to shine in battle, with faithful soldiers under *his* command.

Alexander picked up his quill once more and continued writing a letter to his wife back in New York, who was pregnant. She would give birth in only a few months, and he dearly hoped for the chance to be present for the arrival of their first child. Alexander's own father, James Hamilton, had abandoned him at the age of ten, and the two were never close. Alexander was determined to not only help bring this war to its completion, but to also stay alive so that his child could grow up knowing who his or her father was.

Five days more the enemy must capitulate or abandon their present position; if they do the latter it will detain us ten days longer; and then I fly to you...Adieu, My darling Wife, My beloved Angel, Adieu.

A. Hamilton

A DARING RAID

OUTSIDE THE FIRST ALLIED SIEGE LINE
8:00PM, 14 OCTOBER, 1781

THE PLAN WAS SET. What was seemingly another night of lengthy siege was about to turn into a defining moment…or so Hamilton hoped. His chance to achieve battlefield glory was finally here. He, along with Frenchman Vicomte de Vioménil, had been given command of four hundred troops each. De Vioménil and his four hundred troops would lead a march toward Redoubt Nine, while Hamilton and his four hundred troops would do the same, but with the intention of capturing Redoubt Ten.

Once the agreed signal was given, both forces would silently march towards the redoubts until the enemy spotted them. They had agreed on the signal being the rapid shooting of three artillery shells into the air. Both Hamilton and de Vioménil had warned their troops not proceed prematurely. Their strategy was to assault the British and Hessian forces hiding behind and in the redoubts with bayonets. It was just about time to begin. Any second now de Vioménil would give him the signal and they would be off.

Alexander thought of his wife back home one last time. He also contemplated what could lie ahead of him if this attack was successful. Fame, praise, acclaim, positions of influence and notoriety all awaited him… but only if this attack went according to plan. It was now eight o'clock, time to begin marching towards the enemy's entrenched position.

Three artillery shells were rapidly shot off into the sky, that was the signal from De Vioménil! Seeing this, Lieutenant Colonel John Laurens, one of Alexander's closest friends, took seventy troops with him to start curling around Redoubt Ten. The remaining troops, led by Lieutenant Colonel Jean-Joseph Sourbader de Gimat and Major Nicholas Fish, began creeping toward the front.

Heavy shooting broke out. Bullets unleashed by the mixture of Hessian and British troops whizzed through the air, prompting the Americans to crouch low. Men dropped to the left and right of Alexander, but he kept his composure, and carried on. John Laurens' men peeled off farther to the left side, drawing fire in that direction, lessening the heat directed toward Gimat, Fish, and Hamilton. The password for tonight's assault was "Rochambeau", name of the commander of the French Navy. Someone had remarked earlier in the day that it was perfect, because, when said fast, it sounded like "Rush on, boys!"

Seeing that there was no time to waste, Alexander Hamilton took a deep breath and yelled out, "The fort's our own! Rochambeau!"

This galvanized his men who proceeded to holler and scream in warlike fashion the same words for themselves as they charged. "Men, charge bayonet!" Hamilton commanded.

Fighting continued in and around the redoubt for an hour; the inside of the redoubt was pure chaos. Four separate and distinct nationalities were all thrown together inside a bloody condensed space. Men on each side stabbed, slashed, and sliced their enemy with lethal bayonets.

Great courage was exhibited by the American forces as they continued to strike down their adversaries, even as they themselves lost their own troops. The air smelled of gunpowder, dirt, and blood. However, the longer the fighting continued, the better things looked for the Americans.

The Hessian and British soldiers put up a dogged fight, but their numbers weren't strong enough, and their entrenched position made it hard for them to form any sort of counterattack. Alexander Hamilton had made quite the entrance inside Redoubt Ten as he jumped off the back of a kneeling American soldier in order to leap onto the British parapet. Seeing this daring deed from their commander only further stirred the Patriots to charge hard and charge often with their bayonets as they all entered the redoubt at once.

Suddenly the pandemonium—but certainly not the adrenaline—ceased for a moment. The British and Hessians had surrendered. Over at Redoubt Nine the fighting continued for a little longer, but the verdict would end up being the same. Redoubts Nine and Ten now belonged to the Continental Army. The end of the siege at Yorktown was in sight.

ALEXANDER HAMILTON

JUBILATION

GENERAL GEORGE WASHINGTON'S TENT
YORKTOWN, VIRGINIA, 17 OCTOBER, 1781

MY DEAR MARQUIS, IS it true? Are the British on their way to propose terms of surrender?" George Washington asked.

"*Oui* General! Our men on the frontlines reported that after the British cannons ceased fire earlier this morning, a young drummer boy was seen on the parapet next to an officer urgently waving a white handkerchief. *Nous serons victouriex!*" The twenty-four year-old Frenchman punched his fist into the air with excitement.

"At a moment like this, we mustn't forget the bravery exhibited by General Victome De Vioménil and Lieutenant Colonel Alexander Hamilton." Washington said. "Without their daring assault and capturing of Redoubts Nine and Ten, we would not be in the position that we are today. Speaking of Lieutenant Colonel Hamilton, do you know his current whereabouts?

Before Lafayette could answer this question of Washington's, it was answered for them by none other than Alexander Hamilton himself.

"Your Excellency! Major General Lafayette, come quickly! A British courier has just crossed over to our side and there is not a moment to lose!" the aforementioned Hamilton yelled outside with glee. The generals hurried outside to join Hamilton to see if his report was true, and indeed it was. The courier was holding a white flag in his right hand and a note from General Cornwallis in the other. Hamilton noticed George Washington saying a silent prayer of thanks to Providence as he looked out at the scene in front of him.

"Generals, instruct our troops to stay dignified and to contain their exuberance." Washington said authoritatively. "We shall be victorious, and we shall certainly celebrate this moment, but now is not the proper time. We still have business to attend to, the business of solidifying our independence."

***

TRENCHES BEFORE YORKTOWN, VIRGINIA
19 OCTOBER, 1781, 2:00 PM

Alexander Hamilton was awestruck at what was taking place. The great and powerful British army had finally surrendered. Rumors had it that General Charles Cornwallis was so appalled at the thought of surrender that he feigned illness so as not to have to surrender personally to the Americans. *Dastardly fool, that Cornwallis is!* Hamilton thought. *The fact that his idea of a military surprise was to infect slaves with smallpox and then send them our way both sickens and disgusts me.*

He looked over at his good friend, Lieutenant Colonel John Laurens, who was standing to attention alongside other brave American troops. With an uncanny ability to read each other's minds, the two friends mouthed the word "Rochambeau" at the same time. Laurens smiled over at Hamilton with a look of relief that could only come from someone who has endured a long ordeal.

The next person Hamilton made eye contact with was Lafayette, who was seated high on horseback. He was fairly certain that if he read Lafayette's lips right, the Frenchman had mouthed the French words '*cur non.*'

Hamilton was snapped back to attention as cheers and celebration broke out. He turned to his left to see British Brigadier General Charles O'Hara handing over his sword to the American's second in command, General Benjamin Lincoln. The American patriots all shouted "Huzzah!"

Independence was here at last.

ALEXANDER HAMILTON

EPILOGUE:
A LESSON TO REMEMBER

ISLAND OF SAINT CROIX, WEST INDIES
12 OCTOBER, 1766

ALEXANDER, WE HAVE TO get going!" cried out thirteen year-old James Hamilton, Jr in exasperation.

"Just you wait one more moment, James." replied nine year-old Alexander Hamilton. "I am securing the purse of money."

"Well can you do it any faster? Mother asked us to pick up some sugar for her today at the wharf. If we don't stop by now, Henry the sugar merchant will be closed for the evening." James, Jr. retorted with an antsy tone.

The two brothers walked eagerly down to the wharf of Saint Croix. There weren't many perks that came with living on a tropical island in the middle of nowhere; except for the surplus of sugary delights. Despite the abstract location of their upbringing, the boys found creative ways to have fun, such as today when they had skipped rocks on the water.

"I just hope we can make it in time." Alexander said. "It will be a shame if we come all this way for nothing."

The sugar stand, located on one of the many docks at the wharf, was in sight and the boys were relieved to see that Henry was still selling. However, just as they were going to step onto the dock, they heard a loud noise. *Clank clank clank.* This depressing sound stemmed from a group of chained slaves that were being forced to march.

"Keep it moving! Come on now, the ship is in sight." came the fierce yell of the slave driver leading the march.

Seeing slaves sold at the wharf and board ships was nothing new for James and Alexander, but that didn't make it any easier for their impressionable minds to rationalize. The boys stood back, afraid to draw unwanted attention their way.

Ever since he could remember, Alexander had dreaded the sound of chains. Chains were the opposite of freedom and the enemy of independence. With the slave driver and his slaves now on board the ship, the two boys approached Henry.

"Why, if it isn't James Jr. and Alexander? It must have been a fortnight since I last saw you two." came the voice of Henry the sugar merchant.

"Hello Henry, it's good to see you again." remarked James, Jr.

"We would like to purchase a sugarloaf, sir." said Alexander.

"Well then you have come to the right place, that's all I have!"

Henry said with a smile. "That will be one piece of eight."

Alexander reached into his money purse and pulled out one piece of eight. However instead of handing them over to Henry the merchant, he held onto them and gestured towards the slave ship in the distance.

"Henry, why do some people buy and sell slaves? Are not slaves human beings like we are? It seems to me that money should only be used to buy items like sugar, not another person."

Henry's face turned somber. "I cannot in good faith answer the entirety of your question, Alexander. There are many reasons, all of them being evil, for why certain humans choose to buy and sell other humans. However, I can tell you something that may help partially answer your question. You see, boy, I believe that God almighty created each person in His own image. Because of this belief of mine, I also believe that God gave each and every human the fundamental right to their own freedom. This belief of mine is controversial for many of my friends and neighbors, nevertheless I hold that it is true. Independence is a God-given right, but oftentimes it is sold by man for a price. Does that make sense?"

Alexander nodded. Content with this reply, he handed over the money.

"Thank you for sharing that piece of wisdom, Henry." James, Jr. said.

Alexander added. "I know that my brother and I are still young, but after hearing that explanation, I do not want to own slaves when I am older."

"I am delighted to hear you say that. I must close my stand now for the evening, but please come back any time boys." Henry said with a warm smile.

James and Alexander said farewell to Henry before racing each other back to their house with the sugarloaf in hand. "I win again! Huzzah!" James shouted with glee.

"Alright you win. At least I didn't drop the sugarloaf while running, like somebody I know." Alexander said cheekily.

"Hey, you agreed to not bring that up anymore. I'm telling mom!" James ran inside to tattletale to their mother Rachel.

Alexander sprinted in after his older brother, who had already launched into giving an account of what had occurred. "Alexander, is James, Jr. telling the truth? You did promise not to make him feel bad anymore for the day he dropped the sugarloaf." The boys' mother-Rachel- asked.

"I am sorry to say that it is true." Alexander replied. He turned to face his brother. "James, please forgive me for my trespass, that was wrong of me."

"I forgive you, Alexander, but don't do it again." James said before going outside to collect more rocks for skipping.

"Now that you two are reconciled, I want to hear about the rest of your visit to the wharf. Rachel continued. "Did Henry dispense any of his wisdom?"

"He did. Henry told James and I about how he believes that every person is made in the image of God. He also reminded us that independence is a God-given right that is often sold by man for a price."

"It seems like you have already taken to heart what Henry told you, hmm, Alexander?" Rachel asked.

Alexander nodded confidently.

"Well, it makes me happy to hear you speak those words of truth for yourself. If one day you find yourself with an opportunity to fight for freedom, I encourage you to do so. In fact, to help you always remember this lesson, I would like to give you something." Rachel proceeded to open a drawer in the kitchen and pull out an old watch. "This watch belonged to my grandfather, who is also your great grandfather. It is the only belonging of his that I have, but I would like you to hang onto this from now on."

Alexander thanked his mother for her generous gift and proceeded to examine the watch. On the back of this old silver timepiece was a faded word written in French. He squinted in order to get a better look at this word. "I–N-…uh, I think that's the letter *d*." The nine year-old read each letter he deciphered out loud before combining all of them together. "I figured it out! The word is *indépendance*."

ABOUT

ALEXANDER HAMILTON

When the American Revolution began, Alexander Hamilton was a relatively unknown young man who had barely escaped orphanhood in the West Indies. By the end of the American Revolutionary War, he had gained a reputation as a war hero and as one of George Washington's right-hand men. Hamilton was different from other founding members of America because of his youth, foreign birth, and broken family background. However, this did not stop him from accomplishing several monumental achievements that helped shape America. Hamilton's contributions to America's post-war period include: serving as a delegate to the Constitutional Convention, authoring 51 of the 85 Federalist Papers, serving in President George Washington's cabinet as Secretary of the Treasury, and helping determine the location of our nation's capital in Washington, D.C. He also created the First Bank of the United States, founded the New York Post newspaper, and his face graces the U.S. 10 dollar bill. He-and his wife Eliza-had eight children. You can visit the house that he built, The Grange, in Manhattan, New York. Alexander Hamilton died on July 11, 1804 after being shot in a duel by his political rival Aaron Burr.

ABOUT THE AUTHOR

EDAN MACNAUGHTON

Edan MacNaughton is a 20-year-old college student who is passionate about Jesus, writing, and sports.

NOTES FROM THE AUTHOR

The letter that Alexander writes to Eliza in the beginning of my chapter is real. He wrote to his wife multiple times during the siege of Yorktown. I chose to use the letter from October 12th as I loved how it showed his feelings only two days before he would lead the attack on Redoubt Ten.

The scene inside George Washington's tent where Washington converses with Marquis de Lafayette is entirely fictional. It also was a creative liberty of mine later on in part three when Hamilton, John Laurens, and Lafayette mouth words to each other. My intention in including that brief exchange between the three was to showcase their tight knit friendship for the reader. Given that they were all young men in their 20's, I think it's highly plausible that they shared a few inside jokes.

The epilogue in my chapter is almost entirely fictional. The only true to life elements of my epilogue is the fact that Alexander, along with his brother James, Jr. and mother Rachel did live on the island of St. Croix in 1766. Henry, the sugar merchant, is a fictional character, and you may be disappointed to learn that Hamilton did not have a watch from his great grandfather with the word independence written on the back of it.

One of my biggest battles in writing this chapter was the issue of Alexander Hamilton's true birth year. Historians continue to debate whether or not he was born in 1755-or 1757 (as he personally claimed.) I ultimately decided to use 1757 as his birth year, since a great deal of my chapter is written from Hamilton's perspective. This is why I listed him as 24 years old in 1781, and 9 years old in 1766.

The West Indies in the mid-eighteenth century were a place visited by many different European traders. As a result of this, the local economy was flooded with several types of foreign coinage. My research into this subject found that Spanish currency was the most commonly used during the time period, albeit one of many. This is why Henry the merchant asks Alexander for "one piece of eight" to pay for the sugarloaf. I was unable to find an exact point of reference for how much a single sugarloaf would have cost in 1766 on the island of Saint of Croix, so one piece of eight was my best educated guess.

MAJOR GENERAL BENJAMIN LINCOLN

by Chase Adam

*He withdraweth not his eyes from the righteous: but with kings are they
on the throne; yea, he doth establish them forever, and they are exulted.*
Job 36:7

BENJAMIN LINCOLN

CHARLES TOWN
OCTOBER 1779

MAJOR GENERAL BENJAMIN LINCOLN put his face into his tired, callused hands. It had been a long day, and a longer week. For the first time in this war, he did not know what to do. He *always* knew what to do. Washington relied on him and his exceptional planning and management skills. It was second nature for him to organize and prepare for every situation, which made his recent defeat sting all the more deeply. The burden of failure was crushing him. He sighed. Even now, he tried to recall the details of how he got here - his resources depleting, his troops' morale deflating, and his allies on the run.

"What happened?" He muttered to himself, wrestling with his

frustration. "Despite all the odds, the Southern theater was holding firm! We were victorious over the British siege against Charles Town, morale was good. How then did we lose?" He searched his memories further, trying to pinpoint the moment of failure.

"We began the offensive against Savannah…" He recounted the decision with his officials. "Securing Savannah would have been a decisive victory for our Patriot cause." His thoughts then turned to the height of the siege and his over-ambitious French ally, the Admiral Charles Henri D'Estaing. The bold Frenchman had proposed to lead an attack on a key position guarded by the British. The plan he had outlined was simple enough - capture the Spring Hill redoubts to gain a strategic advantage on the British in Savannah.

"He was so confident of a Patriot victory." Lincoln frowned, remembering the Frenchman's non stop boasting.

"It will be a glorious day - *un jour magnifique!*" Admiral D'Estaing's bold declaration had been persuasive. "We will take Savannah and chase the Redcoats back to their filthy island." It was a convincing plan by an overzealous man.

"*Ils sont faibles* - they are weak." D'Estaing insisted. "Mere militia guard the redoubt."

Lincoln shook his head in frustration "I should have known better!" He slammed his fist down on the desk. He had not been as certain as the brash Frenchman. The British proved to be crafty and strong. Yet D'Estaing had persisted, pointing out the locations and tactics to conquer the redoubt, then the town.

"We will win. *Nous serons victorieux!*" D'Estaing had been relentless. And Lincoln had acquiesced.

Regret seeped into his bones as he sat at the desk, his head once again in his hands. The room suddenly felt chilly. The fallout of that tactical disaster washed over him.

The fateful day had risen thick and grey, the faint hope of victory intertwined with the musky fog swirling around the allied camp. The sounds of battle preparation invaded the blanket of quiet. Tensions were thick, but French pride mixed with American hope had fueled the soldiers forward into the mist.

The survivors reported that the eerie fog had slowed the French towards their target, but battle lines were drawn, ammunition loaded and courage bolstered.

Lincoln sighed, remembering how in an instant the silence had shattered, and was replaced with the raging sounds of cannon fire. The French had pressed on, unaware that D'Estaing had been sorely mistaken about the untrained militia guarding the redoubts. Skilled British Regulars and Scottish marksmen also defended Spring Hill. Confidence shifted to desperation as multiple soldiers fell, littering the battlefield.

Lincoln dropped his hands and closed his eyes. Too late, he had received word of the slaughter. The remaining French soldiers were in full retreat when he had finally mobilized the Patriot reinforcements. D'Estaing was badly wounded and the loss of men and munitions continued. The Americans fought bravely, but hope was dwindling.

"And that was the beginning of the end." He exhaled sharply

and shifted in his chair, uncomfortable at the realization. "And that's how we got here."

Lincoln rubbed his head in frustration, shifting his thoughts from the previous week's nightmare. He frowned, looking out his small office window. The combined losses had been so devastating during the failed operation on Savannah that the Patriots had been forced to retreat all the way back to the safety of Charles Town. He shoved his chair back, and stomped closer to the window, fuming at himself and his humiliating defeat. The busy town was slowing down in the twilight. Candlelight in open windows winked out, and the flurry of the town stilled for the night. The heaviness of defeat hung in the air. Washington had trusted him. He desperately wanted to prove himself worthy of that trust. He turned his gaze heavenward.

Please Heavenly Father, he prayed silently, *Give me wisdom. I know not what to do in this desperate hour. We need supplies. We need men. But most of all, we need You.*

* * *

CHARLES TOWN
APRIL 1780

"General! General Lincoln! News from our scouts near Savannah!" Breathless, the courier burst into Lincoln's office and slammed the note down on his orderly desk. The morning briefing stilled and Lincoln's military leadership paused to hear the word.

"Clinton is on the move, sir! He's becoming more bold every day, and he's heading this way—to Charles Town!" The courier saluted and backed away, trying to regain control of his ragged breathing.

Lincoln eyed the note, then the courier, and sighed. In the wake of the Savannah setback, he had spent the last several months recovering men, supplies and morale in the safety of Charles Town. No news was good news. But this was news. He reached for the crumpled note and opened it gingerly, already aware that his failure in Savannah was coming to haunt him. It was only a matter of time. The momentum the British gained after their victory at Savannah had boosted their confidence. Clinton's prideful reputation preceded the British General, who had now set his daring gaze upon Charles Town. He would fight to claim the Southern Patriot stronghold as his own, no matter the cost.

"Clinton marches to Charles Town…" Lincoln repeated, leaning back in his chair, trying desperately to keep his emotions in check. He continued to read. "Forces numbering as high as 14,000 men!" Lincoln looked up at the room of military leaders. Not one of them moved, waiting.

Please Lord, he prayed, *Please show me what to do! I will not, cannot fail again.*

Lincoln slowly rose to his feet, mustering his waning courage.

"We will meet them with everything we have." He hoped the resolve in his voice would bolster the courage in his men. "Fortify the city, set up redoubts, gather up and take stock of all our supplies, and send word that we need reinforcements. Dismissed!"

The room emptied as the commanding officers headed to their tasks. Lincoln looked out his window, watching the city buzz with activity as soldiers mobilized to complete his orders. Lincoln closed his eyes and prayed again.

Please Lord. I cannot fail. I cannot fail. I. Cannot. Fail.

***

21 APRIL, 1780

"Curse it all!" Lincoln slammed his fist onto the desk, his face hot with anger. "The British have gained ground. Tarleton has cut off supplies and reinforcements. My troops are starving! This is unacceptable!"

The commanding officers quietly glanced at one another. They didn't need Lincoln's depressing battle recap. They were already painfully aware of their dire situation having been mixed in the fray, watching their losses accumulate first hand. Lincoln studied his officers, their stoic expressions masking deeper emotions, wishing for all their sakes a different alternative would present itself. His heart sank. Hope was wearing thin in Charles Town and he was running out of options.

Surrender.

The word crashed his thoughts like a boulder, and the reality of it's meaning burned. But the truth was there before him - surrender or continue this winless battle.

"We will surrender to the British." Lincoln sighed, resigned.

"But, sir…"

"General, wait…"

"No, General…"

The protests became white noise in the small office, each commander arguing their reasons for staying in the battle. He understood their resistance. Surrender was the last resort. But more loss of life was not an option. He was out of options.

Defeated, he summoned the nearest courier, hovering by the door.

"Give this message to General Clinton: I will surrender Charles Town if you let every patriot soldier leave—alive and unharmed." He stared the courier in the eye, looking for a reason to withdraw the deflating notice. He found only weariness in the young man's eyes - and the same longing to leave the battle behind and return to a more peaceful life that had been lost to every young man in these times. The courier saluted and left, shoulders slumped.

Time seemed to stand still since the message had been delivered. Lincoln paced his chambers, as he had for several days, anxiously awaiting Clinton's reply. The likelihood of a positive response from the British General was slim. Hope seemed futile. But the waiting was torture.

He made his way through the battered streets to his office where his commanding officers had gathered for their morning briefing. He glanced around the room at their tired faces. His men were battle weary. Quick and clipped updates began another anxious day. It was too much loss and none of them wanted to dwell on the inevitable.

Pounding on his office door broke the mundane despair of the meeting. A courier burst into the tension filled room.

"A message from General Clinton!" the boy announced, gasping. "He has made his decision." The energy in the room shifted in dreadful anticipation.

Lincoln took the notice from the boy. He prayed as he unfolded the paper, somehow knowing the contents of the notice was not good news. Indeed the arrogant British General declined Lincoln's surrender and terms. An emptiness suffocated Lincoln as he relayed the message to his commanding officers. The room grew desperately quiet.

"Dismissed." He said firmly. "You have your orders. Pray and Godspeed." The officers quietly departed to organize what little they had left to continue their fight.

And the onslaught continued. Weeks later, the British bloodhound Clinton, smelling the despair from the Continental army, sent another message to Lincoln. This one even more devastating than the last.

"Unconditional…surrender?" Lincoln read, shaking his head in disbelief. His face turned white and his heart sank within him. "No! I… I can't do this to them - to these men!"

His mind raced back to a childhood history class, one he recalled where Rome demanded unconditional surrender of Carthage. The heathen monsters burned the city for days with salt, thereby making the whole area unfit for agriculture for generations to come. He clenched his fists in righteous anger.

"No man with a gram of morality in their soul would ever demand this of anyone!" Lincoln threw the note down on the desk.

"This dog, how can he do this?" No one dared to answer him.

"No…I cannot do this." Lincoln seethed, "I decline. Tell General Clinton…. No."

* * *

General Clinton scoffed as he read the response from Lincoln. "Every man in the face of great challenges believes he has a chance. We'll see about that." Clinton crumpled the letter and trampled it into the mucky ground. Turning to the many troops lined up behind him, he shouted "Rain heated shot upon Charles Town!"

* * *

Lincoln gazed on the battlefield the following morning, his horse uneasily shifting beneath him. The buzz of cicadas filled the thick air. Already a bead of sweat lined his brow, the doom of battle before him. Gleaming cannons rolled into place all around Charles Town. A sea of Redcoats swallowed the landscape, like the promise of blood yet unspilled. The clanking sounds of cannon balls and weaponry preparation rang through the air, turning the sweat to a chill that dripped down Lincoln's back. He would fight with all he had. And he would pray.

Lord, we need you now more than ever before. If the worst should happen, please fortify my men, Lord. Give us the courage to stay the course, in spite of defeat. I believe in what we started here – a free America. Bolstered by his prayer, Lincoln organized defensive maneuvers for the enemy's inevitable onslaught.

* * *

General Clinton spared no mercy in his preparations to teach this 'brave man Lincoln' a lesson. He ordered his battery troops to heat up the lead spheres to extreme temperatures. The barrage of searing ammunition was too much for the increasingly vulnerable town of Charles Town. Flames licked the walls of homes and storefronts. Screams and fear flooded the streets, adding to the fiery confusion. Frightened civilians clung to loved ones, giving them a false sliver of security amidst the raging chaos.

With each passing day the city burned, Lincoln's hopes fell. Through the smoke and cacophony of sounds he stumbled to raise the white flag. He couldn't bear another death, another wail, the empty, lifeless eyes of a poor soul he didn't know who had obeyed him without question. He waved the flag slowly back and forth. The thundering silence that followed was like a dream. He barely heard the shouts of the Redcoats storming through the city. The taunting sounds of his enemies jeering, stripping his soldiers of their weapons, now prisoners.

He barely remembered being thrown into a cell, prisoner of the enemy of their righteous cause. He stumbled to the ground, the depressing reality of his situation making him nauseous.

Capture. Defeat. Failure.

Time seemed to escape Lincoln as he sat day and night, a prisoner. Freedom felt out of reach. The ideals he had fought for, gone. What would Washington say? What of his family? What of America?

The loss was too much. Despair tempted his heart. What could he do?

"Pray without ceasing, luv," his sweet wife's voice floated through his mind. "For it is God who fights for us." He turned his face heavenward again, his only option in the darkness around him. The desperate words from Psalm 71 filled his mind and he prayed them now.

O God, be not far from me:
O my God, make haste for my help.
Let them be confounded and consumed that are adversaries to my soul;
Let them be covered with reproach and dishonour that seek my hurt.
But I will hope continually, and will yet praise thee more and more.
My mouth shall shew forth thy righteousness and thy salvation all the day...

Lincoln sat quietly in the cell, and paused for a moment, then prayed again, repeating the words of the godly King Jehoshaphat...

"...neither know we what to do; but our eyes are upon thee."

Lincoln closed his eyes, and slept.

* * *

HINGHAM, MA
SPRING 1781

Lincoln walked towards his home from a good day in the fields, still amazed at the mercy of the Almighty. In his darkest hours of despair, he never imagined that God would still bless him so abundantly.

Parole. Was that even possible for a failure? He sighed gratefully at the memory of his hearing before congress, and their sentencing. He had been ordered to return to his house in Hingham, Massachusetts, to his beautiful wife and quiver-full of children. Home and healing. For the past several months he had prayed without ceasing for his men, otherwise captured and held prisoner, a thousand souls left in the south, ill treated. This weighed heavily on Lincoln's heart. Multiple times he had requested from General Washington a prisoner exchange, but the Commander-in-Chief argued the wisdom of such an endeavor. For the first time in the war the British were spread thin. It would be foolish to hand over reinforcements.

Washington then tasked him with recruitment while on parole, which Lincoln did with diligence. The chatter of patriot wins and losses swirled around the small towns of Massachusetts and he caught himself wishing he was back in the fray. He longed to finish what he started. Multiple nights he lay awake tossing around tactics and strategies, resources and potential allies. But he was home. Why then the growing urge to strap on his uniform and head back into battle?

Lord, let me be content in the here and now. He prayed as he walked. *Thank you for this time of healing and rest. Be with my brothers in arms.*

His thoughts were interrupted by his children greeting him and chattering as they entered the bustling house. The large Lincoln family sat down to dinner and quieted in humble reverence, as Lincoln thanked the Lord again for his many blessings.

Amidst the happy hum around the table, he heard the distinct clopping of a horse's hooves. There was a pause before a loud knock at the door. Lincoln looked at his wife and the surprise, then fear that crossed her pretty face. He opened the door to a Continental soldier who saluted him. He saluted back.

"Major General Benjamin Lincoln," the soldier's staccato tone punctuated the now quiet room behind him, "You are to return to the Patriot camp near New York as soon as possible. You have been exchanged. General Washington requires your immediate assistance."

Lincoln saluted the young man and turned back to the table, his family, his wife. Every reason to fight in the war was before him. He swallowed hard.

"I must go." He said quietly. He saw the pained expression on his wife's face. He knew the hardship this would be. His family had struggled while he was away fighting in the war, his wife managing the farm, his children growing up without him. But the Almighty was giving him a second chance; redemption to see this long, drawn out battle through. He could not fail them. His fight was *for* them, for their freedom.

The trip to New York began early the next day. Lincoln's thoughts swirled around, and his past failures taunted him. The guilt became overwhelming and he second guessed whether his presence could actually help Washington's forces. He was a liability, wasn't he? How could Washington trust him again?

The Patriot camp came into view and he slowed his horse. A million ways to start his first conversation with the Commander-in-Chief danced through his mind, but none of them could portray the remorse he felt. He made his way toward Washington's command center. The tent was a flurry of activity. He walked up to the entrance, and could hear Washington's deep voice commanding attention and obedience. His feet heavy as cannonballs, his heart hammering, Lincoln stepped inside and saluted.

"General Washington, I humbly apologize…"

"Lincoln!" Washington's smile interrupted him and the large man welcomed Lincoln closer. "So good to see you dear friend." Lincoln blinked in surprise at the warm greeting. He started again.

"First, I must apologize sir. I failed in…" But Washington cut him off again.

"Enough of that nonsense Lincoln."

Lincoln stood gaping, not sure what to say next. He tried once more.

"But in Charles Town sir, I…"

"In Charles Town you fought with courage and valor." Washington interjected. "You executed your duties to the best of your abilities. That is all I ever asked of you."

Lincoln, shocked, lifted his eyes to meet Washington's. This mercy did not make sense. His mind was so accustomed to internal accusations, reprimanding himself, trying to prove his worth, he could not imagine a world where he didn't live in shame for the rest of his life.

"I-I-I…" Lincoln stammered. His excuses faded into the humid air. He had nothing left.

"Now on to business." Washington continued, stepping over to his desk, "I have a letter of the utmost importance to write to Major General Anthony Wayne. And you General, need to report as well. Lauzun will fill you in on the details. Rochambeau means to take New York, but we must test the British defenses first. Until then, General." With that, Washington nodded his goodbye and turned to his writing.

"Thank you, sir." Lincoln saluted and found his way out of the meeting tent. Major General Anthony Wayne - a legend, and a fighter - had experienced the blow of defeat. But Wayne had also rallied and recovered territory for the Continentals. Lincoln resolved to do the same.

"I do not deserve this second chance, but I will prove myself." He muttered quietly. "Thank you, God Almighty, for this opportunity. I will not fail you, or America."

Lincoln's step quickened, now a little lighter with his new found resolve. He would find Lauzun and help plan his first mission back on the front lines - the recon of defenses in Manhattan. He would prove he was worthy of his post.

***

EN ROUTE TO THE CHESAPEAKE
SEPTEMBER 1781

Dust swirled like a storm cloud ahead and behind Lincoln. His horse plodded along in a steady gait out of Philadelphia. 2500 Continental soldiers under his care and command, were marching south at breakneck speed. The charge barely seemed real, and the task ahead was near impossible.

"Your mission to Manhattan was a success of sorts," Washington had debriefed with the military leadership upon their return from Manhattan. "Do not fret at the need to retreat." He continued, silencing protests from Lincoln and the French Duc de Lauzun. "Your decoy accomplished what was intended. The Redcoats have too strong a grip on New York." Washington nodded to Rochambeau. "Our plans have changed."

"*Oui*" the Frenchman had agreed. Lincoln spoke next.

"What then, General? What is our next move?"

"Yorktown." Washington declared. "On the wind of speed."

The conversation from a fortnight past, was a blur of planning and action. Speed and secrecy was of the essence, as the Commander in Chief had reiterated multiple times. Lincoln worked tirelessly to fulfill every detail Washington commanded.

Which had brought him to this hot march under the burning sun. Lincoln smiled at the difference between his last assignment - the silent, nighttime assault on Manhattan via the Hudson River versus this loud and dusty procession through Philadelphia to the Chesapeake. The reception of his troops had been warm and welcoming in the City of Brotherly Love; another notable difference and a pleasant surprise for the weary Continentals.

Lincoln thanked the Lord again for the wisdom and blessing in co-ordinating this massive movement of troops. The leadership had worked together to ensure supplies and accommodations were readily available throughout the journey. He surveyed the two mile long column of Patriots with pride. They were on pace to make Head of Elk, the northern most tip of the Chesapeake in just a few short days. He turned his horse and fell into step beside the procession. Two thousand five hundred men on foot, 200 miles, fifteen days if he had estimated correctly. Lincoln shook his head at the enormity of it all. The Lord's hand was on them and he was humbled.

God help us. We will not fail.

***

WILLIAMSBURG, VA
SEPTEMBER 1781

"General Lincoln - sir! General Washington is here - he wishes a briefing post haste!"

The messenger saluted Lincoln, and stepped back at the ready. Lincoln looked up from his preparation plans and sighed, tired and not a little frustrated. He was not ready for a briefing with the Commander-in-Chief. What a nightmare the last few weeks had been. It started with he lack of available transport ships to Yorktown for the troops and supplies. Then the start and stop journey due to bad weather on the Chesapeake. They were still anxiously waiting for news from De Grasse if his French fleet had defeated the British navy effectively halting the enemy's supplies and reinforcements at Yorktown.

Lincoln rose as Washington entered his meeting tent. He was surprised at the pleased look Washington wore on his face.

"Impressive Lincoln, very impressive!" The General reached out and gripped Lincoln's hand in greeting. "You have accomplished the near impossible. The troops and stores are in much better condition and with much less loss than could be expected."

Lincoln nodded at the compliment. "Not without trial, sir, but we are here, and we will be ready at your command."

Washington's command to march on Yorktown came only a few short days later. Lincoln worked seamlessly with the multitude of forces descending on the British post, overseeing logistics and the handling of resources, a talent at which he had proven his worth.

Washington had also tasked him with the prestigious post of honor, and the work of opening the first parallel. Gathering his men and supplies, under the cloak of darkness, Lincoln's regiment dug with great silence and secrecy, securing the first parallel of the siege by morning. From here, the saps - the zigzag pattern of trenches - would allow the Continentals to inch their way closer to the fortified city under cover, enabling artillery and soldiers to rain fire on their enemies and breach the British fortifications around the city.

Washington, pleased with the accomplishments of the first day siege works preparations, ordered the cannons to open fire. American hope was renewed with every bullet and ball that met its mark. Lincoln nodded with appreciation at the ferocity of Henry Knox's artillery. So successful was the first day of the allied assault that Washington ordered the second parallel to be dug. Lincoln dared to predict that the British would not hold out much longer than 12 days.

With the French allies to the left and the Patriot army following Lincoln's lead on the right, the barrage of lead continued to rain down on the despair-ridden British. The combined efforts of Lt. Colonel Alexander Hamilton's and Lt. Colonel John Lauren's successful attack on British Redoubt Ten bolstered the Patriot confidence even more. Lincoln threw up prayers of gratitude. The Allied forces continued to gain ground and confidence day after brutal day.

***

OUTSIDE OF YORKTOWN
17 OCTOBER, 1781

"You were right my friend!" Lt. Colonel Laurens laughed as he shook Lincoln's hand, "The Redcoats cannot handle much more." Lincoln agreed with cautious optimism. The British resistance was waning; they would not last much longer.

"I'm leaving for negotiations shortly," Laurens continued. "Perhaps we insist those dogs surrender under the same terms we did at Charles Town?" Laurens climbed on his horse and flashed another smile as he rode away.

The day had arrived. Lincoln placed his tricorn hat on his head. He mounted his horse, a smile playing on his face. The moment of the Redcoats surrender would forever be seared in his memory. The French army in ranks on one side and the Americans on the other, Lincoln felt a collective breath release as they watched the defeated British army parade out of the city, led by a drummer boy and officer waving the white handkerchief of surrender on the tip of a sword. The entire company silenced as General Charles O'Hara, Cornwallis' second in command stepped forward to deliver the formal surrender message.

"I bring the sword of surrender before General Washington." Lincoln stole a glance at Washington, who rightly, was appalled at the British official's words. O'Hara shuffled nervously awaiting a response from Washington.

"Where is General Cornwallis?" Washington demanded. His low and lethal tone silenced everyone around him.

"He is uh.. indisposed, Sir." General O'Hara stammered, staring at the ground.

"That coward!" roared Washington. "So ashamed of defeat he cannot bring me his own sword!" Washington surveyed the scene, making eye contact with Major General Benjamin Lincoln.

"General O'Hara is Cornwallis' second in command. We shall respond in kind. Lincoln—the honor is yours." Washington nodded, signalling the finality of his decision and rode closer to Lincoln.

Lincoln stared at Washington, not sure he heard His Excellency correctly. Washington maneuvered his horse and leaned in for a private exchange.

"Lincoln—this honor is yours." The Commander-in-Chief smiled at the gaping Lincoln. "You have been a leader and comrade in this war. Your organization skills are second to none, procuring and managing resources. You have believed in and helped us in our cause countless times over. Even in Charles Town, I know you fought with everything you had. You are an honorable man, good sir. The Lord looks upon you with favor today, Major General."

Lincoln nodded in disbelief, and urged his horse forward to accept the sword of surrender from the disgraced British officer. He then directed the British out to the battlefield, for the ceremonial grounding of weapons. The enemy munitions were piled up and battle flags were cased. It was over. He paused for a moment, sun radiating off his face, relieved and humbled at the scene unfolding before him.

Freedom. The word settled on him like a cool breeze. *Thank you Lord.* Lincoln breathed his prayer. *And God, may you direct and bless America in the days to come.*

ABOUT

BENJAMIN LINCOLN

Benjamin Lincoln was a Patriot Major General during the Revolutionary War. He was present during all three major American victories - Saratoga, Trenton and Yorktown. He was a devout Puritan, a family man, and well respected within his community of Hingham, MA. He did everything to the best of his ability. Following the Siege of Yorktown he accepted the sword of surrender from British General O'Hara. After the war, he was appointed the first Secretary of War under the Articles of Confederation.

ABOUT THE AUTHOR

CHASE ADAM

A Midwesterner that loves God and Country, wrestling, history, his mom, and eating (not always in that order), Chase spends his summer days lifeguarding, lifting weights, swimming with friends, and chilling with family. In winter, he can be found training to dominate on the wrestling mat and laughing at Seibel's terrible dance moves. Occasionally he makes time for showering and laundry, as well as other life necessities such as fixing his truck, working with his dad and reading his Bible. He looks forward to his junior year of high school, and the adventure that God has in store.

BENJAMIN LINCOLN

NOTES FROM THE AUTHOR

Major General Benjamin Lincoln is indeed an underrated hero from the Revolutionary War. As the author David B. Mattern detailed in his biography of this historical figure, the records have not been kind in the slightest to Lincoln. Many things written about him perceive the man as a gluttonous, lazy fool, while this is simple incorrect. In fact, he was a hard working, well respected man and extremely intelligent patriot when he joined the continental army.

Although it is perhaps a fictitious element, I wanted to highlight and expand the internal struggle of failure, and how a Revolutionary War Leader may handle such a burden. This was a man who did not succeed all the time, but you can be assured he would try with all his might.

The other thing I wanted to highlight is that he was a devout Puritan, he walked the faith in every facet of his life. This is why I chose the verse I did for my dedication. God really does have his hand on the righteous. It is my hope that after reading this story that you will see that Benjamin Lincoln was a man of faith, a man of intelligence and courage, and a true American hero.

BENJAMIN FRANKLIN
& EDWARD BANCROFT

WE HOLD THESE TRUTHS TO BE SELF-EVIDENT

by Christopher J. Watt

"and ye shall know the TRUTH, and the truth shall make you FREE."
John 8:32

BENJAMIN FRANKLIN

ABUSES AND USURPATIONS

HÔTEL DE VALENTINOIS, PASSY, FRANCE
24 APRIL, 1782

S HADOWS DANCED ALONG THE cold walls. Benjamin Franklin knew that the candle was waning, and would soon need replacing, but his mind was too focussed—and legs too relaxed—to get up and do so. He estimated that there was about half an hour left. Plenty of time. Black ink covered the page on the desk, and more was being added as he wrote.

The Proposal to us of a separate Peace with England, has been rejected in the manner you wish, and I am pretty certain they will now enter into a General Treaty. I wrote you a few Lines by last Post, and on the same Day a few more by the Court Courier. They answered chiefly

He stopped at the end of that paragraph. Lowering the quill, Franklin stretched his hand, wincing as his ageing fingers took strain. They had grown strong from many decades of writing, but those many decades came with a price. Picking up the quill once more, he signed the document, engraving the words *B. Franklin* in solid ink at the base of the letter. Following the eventful surrender at Yorktown the previous year, the British were attempting to make peace with their lost colonies. America, however, formed an alliance with France, meaning that a third wheel was added to the negotiating wagon. There were many people to correspond with, and many people to send word to of even the slightest advancement.

The office door creaked, stirring him from his thoughts. He looked up, peering over the spectacles perched on his nose, as a young lad in his early twenties stepped in.

"Ah, Temple, my boy. Come in." He smiled, setting down the quill and wiping the ink off his hands with a bit of cloth. "I had begun to wonder where you were."

"I was looking for you," Temple replied with a deferential bow of his head, then smiled. "Though I knew you were here. It is getting late, sir. Would it not be good for you to retire for the night?"

"No, no," Franklin waved his hand dismissively. "I cannot interrupt my work with rest. I am writing a letter to Mr John Jay, in Spain. The honourable Prince de Masseran offered to courier it for me tomorrow." He stood up from the desk, stretching as his legs buckled slightly. He had sat for longer than intended. "Come, take a look at this."

He handed Temple the document and he looked at it carefully. "Supplement to the *Boston Independent Chronicle*?" Temple's eyes widened as he scanned the words on the double-sided page. "These are some serious allegations against Great Britain, sir. Where did you get this?"

"From the printer, my boy," Dr Franklin replied with a smile. When Temple frowned, he continued. "I made it all myself. As accurate to the real thing as I could possibly get it."

"But why produce such a thing?"

Franklin spun jovially on his heels, turning to sit at the desk again. "I met with the sensible Mr Oswald last week, and we discussed suitable things. He begged me to trust him with the notes I had prepared for our meeting, so that he could relay them to Lord Shelburne. I eventually agreed, and we parted ways as exceedingly good friends." He patted the armrest lightly. It was still warm.

"So then why create this false paper?" Temple persisted.

"I just recently recalled that, in those notes, I had made mention—subtle, but mention nonetheless—of a sympathy that may be owed to the British Loyalists in America." Franklin sighed, shaking his head. *How could I have been such a fool?* "And so this paper was borne out of necessity, to ensure that no sympathy would be due to the British Loyalists."

Temple studied the faux paper again. "Your deception is clever, but will be discovered, sir. Anyone who sees this will recognise the

French typeface and your hallmark italic lettering."

"Not the common eye," he scoffed. "And even then, were someone to discover this trickery, can the English deny these actions? No, they cannot. This paper is merely…an *enlightenment* of what has truly happened in America."

"I recall you firmly campaigning for virtue in the past, sir," he argued. "Should not a war for moral independence be fought *morally*, with truth?"

"If war is won by truth alone, this world would be free of conflict," Franklin replied. "No—war is won by those who *control* the truth."

"Then, what is truth?" Temple asked. His face was painted with innocence, but behind those eyes revealed a carefully calculated, profound young man.

He let the question dawn on him for a moment. *Always a keen thinker, that boy. I have taught him well.* Franklin looked at the young lad from across the table expectantly. He still held the paper in his hand.

"Truth," he began, carefully forming the words on his lips, "cannot be granted, nor decided. But, it can be *made real.*" He stood up from the chair again. "When we made our declaration in 1776, did the British see it as truth? No. Because it was merely *declared.* Anyone can declare anything," he added, walking over to the window. The curtain had only been drawn halfway; a haphazard act to stop the breeze in the mid-afternoon. It was now well after dark, and only a faint outline of the buildings could be seen outside.

Temple shifted on his feet as he waited for the doctor to continue.

"But now we are making that declaration a *reality*. As of October last year, the British have no choice now but to accept this new truth."

"*New* truth?" he asked.

"Yes, a new truth," Franklin replied, "of independence."

EDWARD BANCROFT

WITH FIRM RELIANCE

TUILERIES GARDENS, FRANCE
14 MAY, 1782

BONES. THAT'S WHAT THE gravel sounded like. Dry bones, crunching underneath me with every step. I stepped through another archway that led deeper into the Parisian gardens. There was a soft, gentle breeze that whispered through the trees; calm, casual, and careless. A hint of nausea swept over me again and I tried to inhale it down, as was the custom each Tuesday morning.

Trying to divert my attention, I glanced down at my companion, Shadow. A fine young water dog with coarse ebony fur, she belonged to William Franklin, although his father Dr Benjamin Franklin took most care of her. Today, as with each Tuesday, she provided me with good walking company. *And support.* Shadow's tail swayed with each clumsy step; her ears twitched with a discomforting alertness.

I inhaled again and glanced away. The well-kept path continued to wind through the elegant gardens. Approaching was an intersection. I eyed the right-hand side, which veered off to another wing of the grounds where trees were clustered. I made my way towards the bend, but stopped dead when a figure stepped out in front of me. My heart pounded in my chest as we made eye contact.

"*Bonjour,*" he greeted politely.

"*Bonjour,*" I returned with a brief nod of my head and continued past. The unexpected worker continued on his way, humming a merry tune. I stopped and spun around to face him again. "Pardon me, *monsieur,*" I called, getting his attention. "I am searching for *pastel des teinturiers.* Woad, as we call it in America." We did get woad in America, though it was not native; it had been imported. "Might it grow nearby?"

"Woad?" he replied with a heavy French accent and a thoughtful frown. "A stubborn, infiltrating plant, *oui.* Not the most welcome in these formal gardens."

I swallowed when I heard him use the term 'infiltrate'. *Does he know something?* I shook it off. *Of course not. It is probably the language barrier.* "Oh, but it reveals a patriotically bright colour in the right conditions," I replied.

"Ah, you speak of dyes. Then you must be a scientist, no?"

"Edward Bancroft, at your service," I bowed with a courteous smile.

The gardener ignored my introduction. "*Pastel des teinturiers* likes to hide its own dark little secret inside its bright yellow outside. There may be some over there, by the chestnut trees." He pointed to a cluster of trees in the near distance. Exactly where the right-hand path led.

I swallowed back another wave of nausea and nodded stiffly. "Thank you very much. *Merci beaucoup.*"

"You are welcome, *monsieur*," the gardener replied. He mumbled something else but Shadow shook her head loudly, masking the man's words.

Noisy dog, I thought with a laugh before making my way to the chestnuts, ignoring the knotting feeling in my stomach. *Dark little secret?* I thought. *Not the most encouraging words to hear.* I glanced over my shoulder, but the gardener was nowhere to be seen. *Odd.* I quickened my pace. Though the morning light shone brightly, the chestnuts were a dark and foreboding sight to my eyes. There was a tall fountain that bubbled loudly nearby. The cascading water provided a much-needed moment of serenity. Another quick glance behind me confirmed that no one was watching.

Shadow sniffed the air, then shook her head. Above me circled a black-billed magpie. *Nimbus.* I smiled as he flew above and made two upward circles. All clear.

I placed my clammy palm on the uneven, knobbly trunk of the nearest chestnut tree, examining it closely. Running my hand down, my fingers fell into the small, familiar little hollow at the base of the roots. I pulled out the little leatherbound pocket book from inside my coat, as well as a small quill. Reaching into a second pocket, I pulled out two little glass bottles. One was dark green, corked shut and with a string tied to it. The other was brown and filled with black ink. I placed the green one deep into the hole in the tree's trunk. I turned casually to face the main path again, scanning the view to see if anyone else was around. I was alone.

Thank goodness. A few old leaves stuffed into the hole made it look natural and undisturbed. Standing up, I opened the book and feigned writing notes about the tree. *If anyone does happen to see, he will hopefully presume that I am on another botanical stroll.*

"I hope Mr Wentworth can appreciate this news," I muttered under my breath. "It did not come easily." *Can I request compensation for stress?* I wondered. *That would be nice.*

Not too far away, as promised, were some small tufts of woad. I grabbed a few stems before returning to the fountain, writing false notes again about the plant. Shadow eagerly followed, sniffing the bright yellow plant in my hand. Nimbus chirped above me in what I can only imagine was a magpie's version of a cheer.

"Another set of intelligence dispatched to the Royal Society," I celebrated with the bird. "The Americans have no clue that the English know *exactly* what is being discussed behind closed doors."

DISSOLVE THE POLITICAL BANDS

HÔTEL DE VALENTINOIS, PASSY, FRANCE
2 JUNE, 1782

A SERENE SILENCE HUNG IN the air as Franklin wrote his next letter. Sunlight streamed in from the tall framed windows bathing the floor and office room with its golden afternoon light.

> *Since mine of May 8th I have not had any thing material to communicate to your Excellency. Mr Grenville indeed arriv'd just after I had dispatch'd that Letter, and I introduc'd him to—*

The large door to his office swung open with a creak. Judging by the sound of their footsteps, two people entered the room. One set was confident and youthful, while the other, slightly more mature, was more cautious. He glanced up as Temple and his other secretary, Mr Edward Bancroft, approached the desk and stood quietly before him.

Franklin flipped the pages of the letter a few times, scanning over the scribbles of ink but not actually reading them. "I heard from young Mr Grenville that he had received the authority to negotiate with France *and its allies*, and that he had left a copy of this commission for me in Versailles," he began. "However, when I reviewed the document myself, I found no mention whatsoever of *France's allies*." He looked up, taking the spectacles off his nose and placing them on the desk. "In a preposterous artifice to waste our time, it seems to me that England intends to delay these deliberations for the time being and continue to wage war, rather than pursue peace."

Temple screwed up his face in a frown that displayed confusion. "Why would they want to do that? America won the war. If Great Britain truly wishes to settle things, the pursuit of peace is her only option."

Franklin shrugged. "Perhaps their late success against Count de Grasse may have given them hopes that these peace negotiations may not be necessary."

A few months ago, the British had managed to capture Admiral Comte de Grasse and other French troops in a naval battle off the coast of the Caribbean. The victory, which came not too long after the British surrender at Yorktown, had bolstered zeal for the Redcoats—and worse, the Loyalists still in America.

Temple nodded in silence, understanding the reasoning in the answer.

Bancroft moved over to where Shadow, Franklin's son's black Newfoundland dog, lay sleeping in the warm sunlight. A precious and overly friendly lass, she and Temple were the only two things of William's that he found himself able to appreciate. *That traitorous boy*, he thought. *An embarrassment to the Franklin name, that is for certain.*

He kneeled to pat Shadow's shiny dark coat, eyebrow raised. "What of Grenville's commission, then?" he asked.

"I had the opportunity to confront Mr Grenville about such things yesterday," Franklin answered, standing up from his chair to stretch his legs. Sharp, yet satisfying pain filling the joints. Once again he had sat for too long a time at this desk. Realising he still had the quill in his hand, he lowered it to lie beside the emptying inkwell. "I asked him why his commission did not explicitly authorise him to deal with the United States. He presented a greatly surprised façade when I pointed this out to him, but could not explain any of it to my satisfaction."

"But surely we know the intention was for him to treat and negotiate with us," argued Bancroft. "Those were his instructions from the British Parliament, were they not?"

Curious. Franklin raised an eyebrow at the secretary, who shrank back a little. "That is *precisely* what Grenville told me. He speculated that the omission of *France's allies*—meaning us—in this so-called 'commission' of his is due to England simply copying their old commission given to Mr Stanley at the last Treaty of Peace after the Seven Years' War in 1761.

"I was not so convinced. I dismissed him and insisted that he go back and get a special commission for this; that we would not deal with him until his commission acknowledges our independence." He straightened his back, walking to the window. The lush gardens of the Hôtel de Valentinois helped to settle his rising temper. *The English are ever eager to deny our truth of independence. One would have thought the surrender at Yorktown was enough—but no, they persist with this vain game.*

"So, what happens now?" asked Temple.

"Mr Grenville has written to his court for further instructions. We shall see what response his request will produce. If full power to converse with each of the French allies does not appear," Franklin shrugged, "I imagine the negotiation will be broken off entirely."

EDWARD BANCROFT

DECLARE THE CAUSES

I LOOKED UP IN SHOCK when Franklin's remark hit my ears. "Breaking off the negotiations!" I gasped, eyes wide. "That could have disastrous results for England. If she cannot negotiate with all those at war with her, she risks prolonging the war and facing even greater losses, especially to her economy." My mind raced. *Surely he does not truly mean that. What would Mr Wentworth say, if my next dispatch to him revealed Dr Franklin's threat to potentially end all negotiations, purely for the sake of one document?* I did not know how I would form such a letter. Shadow, who cared more for belly rubs than economics, nudged my hand with her snout in a gesture for me to continue fussing over her.

"He that lies down with dogs shall rise up with fleas," Franklin responded, eyeing my so-called 'obsession' with the overly enthusiastic canine.

I immediately stood up from the lavish floor and flippantly dusted myself off. Shadow gave a surprised snort of disapproval, but soon settled.

The edge of Franklin's lips curled to reveal a wry smile of amusement.

"So," I continued, "if the English should have known to include the explicit mention of France *and its allies* in Grenville's commission, why did they omit it? It must have been a mistake, for they know our terms, do they not?" I asked. If I could influence my friend to look with more warmth towards England, my task would be far easier.

"I imagine that there is a reluctance in the King of England to take this first step, as giving such a commission would itself be an acknowledgment of our independence, which it is clear that the British fear," Franklin replied.

"Surely we want these peace negotiations to go ahead, though!" I argued with an incredulous chuckle. *Surely he does not mean to actually break off these negotiations.* "Is this delay of Grenville's commission not just a waste of time?"

"Absolutely not!" Franklin cried, spinning from his view at the window. The candlelight illuminated his large, foreboding frame as the rest of the room darkened. His voice boomed with an authority I had never heard before.

I recoiled from the sudden outburst. My heartbeat pounded in my head like the incessant echo of cannons on a battlefield.

Franklin looked me directly in the eye. His firm, steely gaze bore holes straight into my treacherous soul. "The British *must* accept American independence before we can work with them," he answered calmly, relaxing his posture once more. The room spun as it returned to its usual warm ambience. "America is now a free and independent nation, whether England acknowledges it or not. By this failure to openly accept our independence, they are deceiving only themselves."

He made his way back to the large, lacquered desk strewn with papers and old books. He raised the quill with remarkable dexterity. "Temple, my boy," he called. "This quill is getting old and I must continue this letter to Mr Adams. We have discussed much tonight that he ought to know. Do go and see if I left my other one somewhere, would you?"

"Of course," Temple nodded obediently and left the room, closing the door behind him as he embarked on his new quest.

Franklin smiled as his grandson left the room before turning to me again. "Our independence is a curious thing. How can one be sure that it *truly* exists?" When I shrugged, he continued. "We declare this to be *true*, but England determines it to be *false*. They kill our people and plunder our villages purely so that they do not have to accept something that has become *fact*, right before their very eyes."

"The surrender at Yorktown last year should see the end of that,"

I reasoned, trying to keep it lighthearted. "Now we merely have to get their acceptance on paper, correct?"

"That is becoming a whole new war of its own." Franklin shook his head, but smiled. He lifted the inkwell and inspected it carefully. "Curious, how ink reveals the true hearts of men."

"Ah, indeed—yes," I replied, stumbling over my words slightly. The room filled with the sound of a throbbing heartbeat again. I glanced around the room nervously, careful to maintain a confident expression. *Ink. True hearts. Does he know?* Countless thoughts hit me all at once. *Surely not.* But Dr Franklin's mind was as sharp as his gaze. *But if he does know, then why has he not spoken up?* I considered the possibilities, but was pulled away by the creak of the door as Temple entered again, victoriously holding a white goose feather quill.

Franklin turned and beamed at the sight. "Ah, what would I do without my secretaries, hm?" he laughed and cordially slapped me on the shoulder. "I say, were it not for you, these negotiations with England would be far more difficult!"

I smiled nervously, grateful for Temple's interrupting arrival. *Oh, Dr Franklin, you have no idea.*

EDWARD BANCROFT

THE TIES WHICH BIND US

ST. JAMES'S, LONDON
11 AUGUST, 1782

HOME SMELT LIKE LONDON. Or rather, London smelt like home. I breathed in the warm air that carried the scents of coffee, summer, and tobacco. The cloudy sky cast dull shadows over the busy streets of St. James's.

Laughter echoed around me as I pushed open the large door to Rentfor's Coffee-House. Men of all kinds either stood or sat around the room, a sea of wigs and powdered hair. A slightly darkened corner at the back caught my eye through the din. A familiar figure sat at the table, watching me. *Paul Wentworth*. Smiling, I made my way to the corner, looking around as I did so. The coffeehouse was large and spacious, accommodating both communal and private conversations.

Four soldiers were seated at one of the benches, laughing. Their uniforms marked them as guards for St. James's Palace. One of them looked up and caught my eye. I swallowed and quickly spun my head, pretending to study the immaculate wooden flooring instead. Shadow's paws eagerly trotted beside me.

"Mr Wentworth, it is good to see you. I sincerely apologise for my tardiness," I dipped my head as I sat down at the table. "I did not expect the walk to be this long."

Wentworth smiled. "Not to worry, my friend. Time stops for no one, but thankfully, a few extra minutes of waiting is no serious problem for me right now." A tall man, his powdered wig and cravat showed that he was well-kept and reputable, but I knew that behind his piercing eyes and warm smile was a clever and cunning mind. His red coat was a stark contrast to my blue one, a reminder of which sides of the war we were supposed to be on.

"Thank you," I replied with a slight chuckle. "Though I have to say, you are beginning to sound like Dr Franklin with that sort of rhetoric."

"Ah, if only," he laughed in return. "I hear the Doctor's gout has begun to improve. Must be all that the air in Passy."

I wrinkled my nose. "Yes, I hope he will return to his work soon. Jay is more conservative with the information he shares; it is not as easy to work with him." I thought back to my recent times in France before coming to London. Over the past few weeks Benjamin Franklin had been ill with gout and kidney stones, which had rendered him unable to assist in the negotiations with the British and French commissioners. John Jay had replaced him, but was not as agreeable and had conflicting ideas. This had caused friction between the two of them, especially around France's motives. Jay was suspicious of what the French may want in return for their help. Franklin was more relaxed.

"Yes, I hear that Jay has proven himself a bit of a nuisance, playing the same card to Mr Oswald that the Doctor did to Thomas Grenville," Wentworth persisted.

I nodded. "Indeed. He objected to Richard Oswald's commission because it did not recognise America as an independent nation. When he and Franklin approached Vergennes about this, Vergennes saw no problem, as did Franklin, and this led to a rather heated debate between Jay and the Doctor when they returned to Passy in the evening." I shrugged.

"How are things with Franklin's stance on his advisory negotiating points?" asked Wentworth, leaning in closer. "Does he still desire Canadian territory?"

I paused to think carefully. In early July, Dr Franklin had met with the British commissioner, Richarch Oswald, and proposed eight provisions for the negotiating table with America: four necessary ones, and four advisory points. The French did not want America to negotiate without their consent, so this was done with utmost secrecy. With these suspicions in mind, Franklin only made one copy of this proposal and gave it to Oswald.

The Doctor would have never thought that I would find out—espe-

cially not from the British side. I shrugged. "I have no news about the Canadian proposal specifically. But Doctor Franklin is pragmatic, open to negotiating these advisory proposals, so long as America's independence is recognised outright."

Wentworth shook his head and glanced down at Shadow, who wagged her tail enthusiastically in response. Her whole body jiggled. Keeping his eyes fixed on the dog, he sighed. "*Independence…*it is a heavy word, is it not?"

Inhaling a deep breath of coffee-scented air, I nodded slowly. "Indeed. But Franklin knows that peace without independence is merely a truce. It would not be long before something else tipped the scale and war would return to America."

Wentworth gave a curt nod and stood up abruptly, startling Shadow who was lying at his feet. She leapt up, and her excited tail swung across the tabletop and hit Wentworth's mug of coffee. The pewter cup fell to the hardwood floor with a resounding *clank* and nearby customers turned to see what the commotion was about, eyebrows raised.

"Good thing I drank it quickly and my mug was empty," he chuckled, then pointed to Shadow, who was still wagging her tail. "A mischief-filled canine you have here, my friend."

I smiled, rising from the table too. "Indeed. Though she belongs to the Doctor's son, actually. We are taking care of her for now."

"Ah, I see," replied Paul Wentworth with a hint of disinterest. Picking up the mug and returning it to the table, he motioned towards the exit. "You are not just a courier of information, Edward.

You are a witness to *history*." A determined frown was knotted on his brow, but the hint of a scheming smile betrayed his lips. "Better make sure you are on the right side."

My mind raced as I followed the spymaster. A low *thud* pounded from my chest into my ears. *Make sure I am on the right side? What is this, an accusation? A warning? Against what? …Against whom?* The time it took to reach the door allowed me to think. "You ask me for truth, Mr Wentworth," I commented as he ducked out the doorway. "But these days, truth is only a matter of timing."

Wentworth knelt down, stroked Shadow fondly, then stood up and took a few steps down the street before spinning back with a pause.

"Have you forgotten something?" I called.

He held up his hand to quieten me. I clamped my mouth shut, then listened. The bells of Westminster tolled in the distance, loud and clear.

"Truth and illusion, Edward," he called with a smile. "You will find both in Paris."

I waved farewell, but inside my stomach churned. Thankfully, Shadow's loud shaking snapped me out of another daytime nightmare. I turned down the street in the opposite direction. *Dr Franklin relies on me for the birth of a new country; the Royal Society for the survival of an old one. Whom do I serve?* Dark clouds filled the sky as evening settled over London.

Shadow trotted ahead, tail wagging and nose high. *I am glad Dr Franklin allowed me to take her with me,* I thought with a smile.

She makes fine company for a spy. I caught up to the black dog as she stopped by the window of a bookseller. In the window were some of the new literary publications. My heart sank as I read the first title.

REFLECTIONS
upon the
PRESENT STATE OF ENGLAND
and the
INDEPENDENCE of AMERICA.
By Thomas Day, *Esq.*

Independence… such a heavy word. My mind raced to Wentworth's words. *You are a witness to history… Truth and illusion.* My face stared back at me through the reflection in the window. Thunder crashed in my treacherous mind. *These Patriots are the first disciples of America's future,* I realised. *And I am Judas.*

BENJAMIN FRANKLIN

ABSOLVED FROM ALL ALLEGIANCE

JOHN JAY'S RESIDENCE, PARIS
29 NOVEMBER, 1782

ONE MONTH HAD PASSED since the formal peace negotiations had begun with the British delegates at the end of October. The commissioners met regularly, to discuss the next steps in securing peace between America and Great Britain after the war's end. They had come a long way since the beginning of the peace talks, the British now agreeing to all four of Franklin's necessary points of negotiation. The other points were more advisable than necessary, and proved a challenge to fully come to an agreement on.

The office room in Jay's residence was spacious and ornate; adorned with columns, paintings, and golden filigree spread lavishly over the ceiling. A blazing fireplace burned beneath a large mirror that imitated the halls in Versailles. Wide windows with curved frames allowed for the autumn sunlight to stream in over the fine French flooring. At the centre of the room was a large table, with legs curved to resemble those of a lion, and five sturdy yet elegant-looking chairs stood on either side.

On Franklin's side were John Adams, John Jay, Temple Franklin, and Henry Laurens, who had just arrived from London. On the other side sat British negotiators Richard Oswald, Henry Strachey, Foreign Minister Alleyne Fitzherbert, and Secretary Caleb Whitefoord.

The table was layered with a thick red cloth that matched the cushions on the chairs, and on top of the tablecloth was a piece of parchment, decorated with scribblings of ink—a draft for the preliminary peace treaty they were discussing. Franklin eyed it carefully as he leaned back into his chair, placing his hand firmly on the armrest.

"Pre-war debts," Oswald announced, sliding the document across the table towards the American commissioners. "Those that are still owed to English merchants."

Beside him, Franklin heard Adams lean back and sigh.

"There is considerable concern in London," Oswald continued, "regarding these outstanding financial obligations. As you know, many Americans still owe our merchants—debts from *before* the war began. The traders are growing restless from wondering whether or not they will be repaid."

"Mr Oswald, you know our standing on this," Jay answered in disdain.

"I know very well your intentions on the matter, but the problem has not been resolved," he replied. "It is not merely a monetary matter of finances, but rather a commercial matter of *integrity*. If someone owed you, would you not want him to repay you? It is your *right* to demand settlement for the debt he owes you, on the terms which you had both agreed upon." He looked between the commissioners. "You must remember that most of the English merchants have suffered greatly from this war. Surely you do not want to rob them of something that is rightfully theirs."

And yet the Crown robbed us of liberty, which was rightfully ours, thought Franklin. "You remind us of English suffering," he began, "and yet you forget American suffering. The ashes of our towns, the plundered farms and homes, the ruined livelihoods and sacrifices made in pursuit of independence—why must we repay those who took so much from us? Great Britain demands payment of these debts while ignoring the destruction inflicted by its own forces."

Jay nodded in agreement. "Lord Dunmore burned Norfolk at the beginning of the war. Two years ago, General Clinton devastated Charles Town after a prolonged siege. Lord Cornwallis and his forces led multiple further campaigns in the South, wreaking havoc across the Carolinas and Virginia. If there is any debt that still stands, it is that Great Britain owes *us* for these losses."

He leaned back in his chair, staring at the thinking eyes of the British negotiators across the table.

"I disagree," interrupted Adams, breaking the silence.

Franklin sighed quietly. *Of course he does.*

"The British forces in America have done considerable damage to the lives and homes of the people, and that cannot be denied. *However*, a free and independent nation such as the United States of America must conduct itself in a manner worthy of honour," he added, looking directly at Oswald. "Therefore, I agree with Mr Oswald that we honour debts owed before the war. If we wish to be a nation of integrity, we must uphold such virtues. To renounce the debts owed to English merchants simply because we are no longer English ourselves would undermine our moral standing and label us as a nation that does not keep its word. Being portrayed as such would jeopardise any future relations we may seek with other nations." He turned to face the other commissioners. "Mr Jay, Dr Franklin? Is this what you wish for our new nation?"

Jay shrugged. "Of course not."

Adams nodded. "Precisely. We are fighting a moral war, are we not? Thus, we must uphold moral values."

Franklin nodded slowly. *He makes a strong point, unfortunately.*

"Mr Adams's argument is valid; we must ensure America's remains intact," added Jay, quietly.

"So," Oswald called. "Is it settled, then?"

Franklin looked between the commissioners. They looked at him and gave brief nods. "I believe so, yes," he answered, though reluctantly.

Alleyne Fitzherbert's posture relaxed and Oswald smiled.

"Well, that leaves us with one final provision," Henry Strachey announced. He glanced up from the page and looked up at Franklin directly. "Unfortunately, it is the most *sensitive* one."

He sighed, this time loud enough for his colleagues to hear. *Here we go again.* He grew tense as Strachey opened his mouth to utter his next few words.

"Compensation for His Majesty's loyal subjects in America whose estates have been confiscated by the colonists."

The hairs on the back of his neck stood up as Franklin tightened his grip on the armrest, knuckles turning white. *Ridiculous; the negotiating commissions finally recognise American independence, and yet they still call our citizens mere 'colonists'.*

"I am sure *Dr Franklin* would like to begin," Strachey concluded, leaning back in his chair with a sneering smile.

Franklin ignored Strachey's retort and instead made eye contact with Oswald. "You demand that the truth of America's financial integrity be discovered. I ask that the truth of Loyalist actions be recognised." He sat up in my chair and glanced at each of the negotiators. "Compensation is given as a courtesy for something that was lost or damaged following an unanticipated event, *not* as a benefit to those who actively seek to suppress the liberty of a free people."

"His Majesty's people suffered many losses during the war, which to them was an unanticipated event," argued Strachey, a disinterested look crossing his face.

"To them it may have been unanticipated, but to us it was inevitable," shrugged Franklin. "A matter of perspective can do many things, but it *cannot* change the truth—and the truth is, while the Loyalists may have suffered losses, they aided and abetted an even *greater* damage suffered by Patriots throughout this war." His expression darkened and he clenched his jaw in a challenge. "The British Loyalists are enemies of American independence. Compensating them for their so-called 'losses' is an insult to the sacrifices our Patriots made for the sake of independence."

"*However*," Adams spoke up, "while I share the same sentiments as Dr Franklin regarding a general position on compensation for the Loyalists, in specific cases where Loyalists have unfairly lost property, we are willing to consider a compromise—"

"No, we are most certainly not," snapped Franklin. *No more compromises.* He scooted forward to get a better view of his fellow Americans. "In August, I found myself with a horrid case of gout and kidney stones."

"Thank you very much for telling us," replied Henry Laurens.

Ignoring the retort, Franklin continued. "In the time that I was incapacitated, Mr Jay assumed my position as lead negotiator." He turned to face his colleague. "Mr Jay, do you not recall that, while lead negotiator, you challenged the credibility of Mr Oswald's commission to treat with us?"

Jay nodded without hesitation. "Yes, that is correct."

"I can attest to that," Oswald added, earning a slight chuckle from one of the other British negotiators.

"The main point of argument was that Mr Oswald's commission did not explicitly acknowledge America as a free and *independent* nation. Likewise, in June I confronted Thomas Grenville for the very same reason. Throughout these initial discussions about peace, we were focussed on one thing—" he stopped to look around the room again— "*independence*. Independence from the powers of Great Britain, the Crown and the English monarchy. Freedom and liberty to act *independently* as our own nation." He placed his finger on the document that lay on the table and tapped it lightly. "Compensation for the Loyalists is a *betrayal* of that independence."

Adams swallowed, eyes wide, but did not say anything. He knew that openly disagreeing with his colleague now would give the impression of inconsistency and conflict within the American commission.

Betrayal. The stinging word had left a bitter taste on his tongue. He knew all too well what that felt like. Franklin shot a glance at Temple. The young man bore an uncanny likeness to that of his father, too much for him to bear at this moment. He looked back to the table, his mind racing as fast as his heartbeat. A prodigal son who left his father but never returned. *William.* Once a name of pride and honour, now a word of shame and disgrace—treachery, some might even say. *Not anymore. Not now. Because now is when I fight back.*

The interruption came from Richard Oswald.

"Lord Shelburne is eager to demonstrate His Majesty's affection for all who have supported Great Britain and the monarchy," he stated matter-of-factly. "He wants to honour anyone who has supported the Crown."

"Who will pay for this compensation, then?" asked Franklin.

"The Crown?"

Oswald opened his mouth to speak, then hesitated and shut it.

"Precisely," he answered. "Lord *Shelburne* also knows that he might lose his ministry and seat in office if he does not satisfy the claims of all his Loyalist emigrants." he was convinced he could almost hear the negotiators gasp as he made the bold declaration. Before anyone could continue, Franklin stood up from his seat. Shadow followed, sitting up eagerly and watching his every move. He reached into his coat pocket and pulled out a folded piece of paper, dropping it onto the table on top of the preliminary treaty draft.

Henry Strachey scowled at the abrupt movement. "What is this, Dr Franklin?"

"This," Franklin pointed to the page, "is a copy of a letter I sent to Mr Oswald on Tuesday. Inside, you will see that I clearly outline my terms for negotiations. When considering restitution for the lost Loyalist estates, we find that the extensive devastation inflicted by the British forces on our American citizens is a barrier. If the Crown desires any indemnification for its Loyalists, it must also recompense us for all of the American towns destroyed, villages burned, and goods taken by the Redcoats." His mind raced back to the image of his library in Philadelphia being looted. Laughter as books were taken, imaginary flames rising from the rooftop. He winced.

Henry Laurens cleared his throat. All eyes turned to face him. "My home of South Carolina suffers significantly from the cost of this war. The people there have endured the most severe battles and occupations in recent years. Our greatest plantations have fallen and cities have been shattered. Civil war broke out following the Siege of Charles Town as Loyalists rose up against their Patriot neighbours."

The British negotiators remained quiet, but their faces were grim.

Franklin continued, nodding in wholehearted agreement. "Houses have been burnt, lands ravaged, families murdered, lives destroyed—these are the costs of the fight for our independence; the consequences of British military actions—endorsed by Loyalists to oppose our fight!" he cried. "Why should the Patriots, who bled for this freedom, now be forced to pay those who opposed our very existence? No—if you insist on compensation for those who opposed us, then we, in turn, insist on compensation for those who suffered under the hand of your leaders."

Shadow nudged him with her nose, but he ignored her. She moved over to where Temple sat, and plonked herself down next to him.

Benjamin Franklin made eye contact with his colleagues. "Let us be clear, gentlemen: we have come too far to falter now." He stood up straight, now looking directly at the negotiators across the large table. Strachey, Fitzherbert, Oswald, and Whitefoord. "But if an equitable agreement cannot be reached on this matter; if you *insist* on rewarding those who sought our execution and encouraged our suffering, then I assure you that I will make no hesitation to lay an end to these talks and terminate the treaty. Do not take me for a fool, for I will do it. These negotiations will end, and the war will continue, no matter the cost."

Silence filled the room.

Adams, who usually would have objected outright, remained quiet. Jay, who was sharp-witted and quick to respond, kept his mouth shut. Laurens, who had many thoughts around the treaty, stayed in his seat. Temple sat quietly, softly stroking Shadow. They all knew this was no longer their fight.

Finally, Fitzherbert rose from his seat, followed by the other negotiators and Whitefoord. "Please excuse us for a moment." Together, they made their way to the adjacent room. Shadow leapt up and trotted behind them, sliding in through Strachey's legs as the door closed. There soon came a muffled cry of surprise from inside the room, but the door remained shut.

Adams snorted back a chuckle at this.

"Shadow would make a great spy," Temple laughed.

The other commissioners chuckled.

"She would indeed," Franklin replied with a smile.

* * *

Half an hour had passed when the door to the adjacent room finally clicked open and out came Whitefoord, followed by Oswald, Strachey, and Fitzherbert. Shadow walked beside them as they returned to their seats across the table.

"Well," Oswald began, "we have come to a decision." He glanced at Fitzherbert, who nodded to continue. "Rather than a full commitment to compensation, we will accept a promise from you that your

Congress would earnestly recommend to your individual coloni—er, *states*—that they make whatever restitution and indemnification for His Majesty's Loyalists as they see fit."

The other British negotiators nodded in agreement.

Franklin held back a chuckle at this. Henry Laurens was less fortunate and snorted back a laugh, which earned a raised eyebrow from Strachey. *The Congress will not take significant action on this, nor will the states. In fact, I would be surprised if any Loyalist across the nation receives any form of compensation at all.* Knowing this, the American commissioners exchanged glances and nodded.

"Very well," returned Franklin. "We accept and will agree to those terms, ensuring that Congress allows the states to recompense Loyalists as they deem appropriate."

Oswald smiled.

"*On one condition,*" Franklin continued, leaning forward in his chair.

Adams sat up and shot a glare at him.

He ignored him. "We will only agree to this recommendation, so long as it will not apply to Loyalists who bore arms against the United States." Through this caveat, the fate of the prodigal son was sealed. *Some betrayals are too much even for a father's forgiveness to overlook.*

Adams muttered under his breath.

Oswald inhaled deeply, Strachey rolled his eyes, and they looked to Fitzherbert for direction. He shrugged, then nodded, a silent but clear message.

"Very well," Oswald answered with a sigh, tired from the day's back-and-forth arguments. "We accept your terms."

BENJAMIN FRANKLIN

EPILOGUE:
LIFE AND LIBERTY

ON BOARD HMS SIRIUS, DUTCH CAPE COLONY
13 OCTOBER, 1787

OCEAN SPRAY ROARED UP the side of the ship. The incessant rocking, which was once calming, now stirred Shadow awake. She blinked a few times before shaking her head. Standing up from her makeshift bed of rope, she stretched, yawning loudly.

"Took you long enough," cawed a familiar voice. A black-billed magpie fluttered down from the mast. He landed beside her on the quarterdeck. "I was beginning to wonder if we may have lost you to the sea sickness."

"Good to see you too, Nimbus," Shadow murmured. "I was only asleep for a few hours."

Nimbus chuckled. "A few hours can feel like days when you are stuck in the middle of the ocean."

"True," she replied with a canine shrug.

"Ah, I see you are awake," called another voice from behind. Shadow turned and wagged her tail to see a tall man in a shiny blue coat with gold buttons standing beside her. Captain Arthur Philip leaned down to stroke her on the head. "And perfect timing, too. Look, we have just arrived."

She followed his gaze to the front of the ship and caught her breath. There, on the horizon, was something she had not seen for weeks. *Land.* Wide and majestic, a long coastline was faintly tracing itself before them. "Well, you will not have to be stuck on a ship for much longer, Nimbus!" she exclaimed.

"Indeed!" he cheered. Flying up to the main mast, he sat upon the Union Flag that flapped in the sea breeze. "And look!" He cawed, pointing with his wing.

Rising steadily up against the horizon loomed an enormous, grand mountain. Its flat top made it an unforgettable sight, two sharp triangular points guarding it on either side.

"Welcome to Table Bay, my friends," Captain Arthur Philip called, trotting down to the main deck excitedly. "We shall stop here for some time to replenish our supplies before continuing to New Holland."

"Huzzah!" cheered the officers stationed below. Unsurprisingly, they were eager to return to land once more, despite the long journey still ahead.

"New Holland," Nimbus repeated, returning to sit atop the helm next to Shadow on the quarterdeck. "What an adventure."

"Indeed!" Shadow barked in excitement, standing up and wagging her tail again. "Great Britain may have lost America, but in America's place has risen a new opportunity—the *great southern land.*"

"It'd better be worth all the time we have spent at sea," Nimbus muttered.

"I'm sure it will," she replied. "But in the meantime, we can enjoy the delights of the Cape of Good Hope. A wonderful name, is it not?"

"It is," he agreed. "And a wonderful place too, I hear." He hopped around to face the back of the ship, leaning over to glance at the other ten ships behind *HMS Sirius*, the flagship of the fleet. "The convicts on board these ships suffer greatly," he commented sadly. "We must hope, for their sakes, that this new colony will be a fruitful endeavour; a chance for them to start over in a new land."

She nodded. "Indeed. And who knows?" she opened her mouth in a canine smile. "From what we have learnt from our time with the Americans, perhaps we can teach these folk a thing or two about liberty."

"Aye," Nimbus cawed. "And independence."

"Of course!" Shadow barked again excitedly. "HUZZAH!"

ABOUT

BENJAMIN FRANKLIN

Benjamin Franklin was an American-born writer, scientist, inventor, and statesman. He played a crucial role in creating the Declaration of Independence and securing America's alliance with the French forces. Bitter from the betrayal of his son William, Franklin took a vehement stand against the Loyalists in negotiating the Treaty of Paris, which was agreed upon in 1782 and signed in 1783. Franklin eventually returned to America, where he served on the Constitutional Convention and became an advocate against slavery. He died in 1790 at the ripe old age of 84.

ABOUT

EDWARD BANCROFT

Edward Bancroft was an American writer and chemist. A good
friend of Benjamin Franklin in the scientific world, he was made
secretary of the American delegation in France in 1776. But unbe-
knownst to them, Bancroft had been recruited by Paul Wentworth,
a spymaster in the British Secret Service, to gather information
on American activities. He provided this intelligence by making
dead drops in the Tuileries Gardens each Tuesday morning, and
would sometimes travel to London under the guise of helping the
Americans. Franklin, a keen discerner, may have suspected something of Bancroft at times, but Bancroft's identity as a double agent
remained secret until over a century later.

CHRISTOPHER J. WATT

With a passion for historical fiction and fantasy, Christopher J. Watt loves nothing more than a good, well-written book. He is a keen swimmer, devours countless novels, and drinks far too much hot chocolate in one day. South African by birth, Christopher resides with his family and black Labrador retriever, Shadow, in Australia's capital. Learn more about him and his mission to write something worth reading at
www.ChristopherJWattAuthor.com

NOTES FROM THE AUTHOR

Edward Bancroft and Paul Wentworth: This was not a recorded encounter, but we do know that Bancroft often travelled between Paris and London around this time, presumably to share information with the British spymasters. "Rentfor's Coffee-House" is a fictional name, but it's almost certain there would have been a real coffeehouse in St. James's at the time, and noblemen would have frequented it for many reasons.

Peace Negotiations: I decided to write about the commissioners discussing the treaty, rather than signing it, because I believed it was important to convey the intense, back-and-forth negotiations that took place before any documents were signed. These preliminary negotiations took place at John Jay's residence, so I assumed that this significant scene happened here too. The final treaty was signed in September 1783, at the *Hotel d'York*.

Shadow and Nimbus: Shadow and Nimbus are fictional characters who feature as British spies throughout my writing in *The Epic Story of America*. The final idea for this year was to have them turn and become Patriots, but due to space and time limits I didn't get the opportunity to express this, so I left it open for the readers' interpretation.

Benjamin Franklin did have a dog during his time in Paris. It belonged to his son William, who was a backstabbing Loyalist living in London at the time, so it is very probable that "Shadow" was there for some of the negotiations and travel. Historically, she was a Newfoundland.

Spelling: If you notice that some of my words are spelt differently (for example *Dr*, *realised*, *focussed*, *honour*, etc.), it is because I write in British English. Yes, I know I speak the language of the Loyalists, but deep inside I'm a Patriot at heart!

GENERAL GEORGE WASHINGTON

by Payton Grace

I dedicate my chapter to every single one of my family and friends. And yes, I mean everyone. Oh, and all of the people who are kind enough to read my chapter! That means you, even if you've just landed here by accident and are in the process of turning to a more interesting page. In any case, thank you!

CANDLES

NEW YORK CITY
28 AUGUST, 1781

The American columns and 1st. Division of the French Army arrived.

WARM CANDLELIGHT FLICKERED AGAINST the calloused surface of my hand, which led the quill in a gliding dance across the parchment, leaving ribbons of ink in its wake. With each word transcribed from my brain to the paper, I reflected on the events that had been floating within my mind, the events that had led me here, from monitoring activity in British-occupied New York, to steadily heading to Virginia alongside the French army. My diary entry today was shorter than some, but it evoked the sentiments all the same. It was always an odd feeling, those small moments in time when I found myself highly aware of my situation, of who I was, of who I was known to be.

General George Washington.

From a surveyor, to a colonel, to general of the Continental Army, leading my country and its soldiers, those who put their lives on the line for the hopes and dreams of our people, in the physical battle for independence. I'm not sure I ever imagined I would make it this far.

I'm not sure anyone thought *we* would make it this far.

The war, all of this, had caught many of us unaware, forcing a rag-tag bunch of colonists to work together against a world power, a battle that one would naturally assume had an assured outcome. Mankind's predictions and calculations of probability meant nothing against the will of the Lord, however.

Our colonies were divided, in regions and beliefs. As were our colonists themselves- we could hardly discuss most topics without facing a series of disagreements and conflicts.

Somehow still, it all lined up in the end, the path towards independence becoming increasingly vivid, set out for, beckoning us to traverse it. There were just a few more obstacles that we had to clear out first. And not all of them wore red coats and firearms. Most battles were indeed physical, but a large part of them were waged within as well.

The Continental Army had its fair share of division. Our generals did not always see eye to eye, and the aforementioned regional discord was also reflected among the soldiers. Between that and the different ethnic groups that had also joined the battle, from European immigrants to Black men, rallying everyone together hadn't been easy. Especially in the beginning, there had been a lot of infighting and arguments, unsuitable for a respectable army. Which we were anything but.

Even so, we did our best. I, to unify the group of barely trained, un-uniformed men and prepare them for war, and the soldiers, ranging in age, personality, and just about everything else, to become the army that I was so proud of years later. Yes, there had been an unfortunate number of men who'd left right after their terms ended, or whenever they pleased, which did nothing to help the deficiency of manpower we had in comparison to the British, but there were still those who stayed, who stood up and continued to fight.

I, too, had grown along with my men. I learned from past mistakes to make better decisions in the future, developed my understanding of military strategy, and employed new techniques.

I think I would be quite proud of myself, if I could have peeked into the future as a boy. However, as always, there was still a long way to go, so much more improvement and life ahead of me, of all of us. Though I wasn't sure how much longer I would be around, if the next time I entered the battlefield would be the last, one thing was certain.

I would spend every second of my life doing all I could to be worthy of the respect I was given, to fulfill the duties and the place in the world that God had given me, to the very best of my ability.

Stretching, I blew gently on the now stub of a candle, which stood much shorter than its original form. How lucky we human beings weren't like candles, doomed to follow a predetermined path of reduction. Unlike them, we could choose to better ourselves, shining brightly, while standing just as resolutely as before.

GEORGE WASHINGTON

LIGHTS IN THE DARKNESS

YORKTOWN, VIRGINIA
9 OCTOBER, 1781

9th. About 3 o'clock P.M. the French opened a battery on our extreme left, of 4 Sixteen pounders, and Six Morters & Hawitzers and at 5 o'clock an American battery of Six 18s & 24s; four Morters & 2 Hawitzers, began to play from the extremity of our right—both with good effect as they compelled the Enemy to withdraw from their ambrazures the Pieces which had previously kept up a constant firing.

WE HAD TRULY BEEN given a blessing through the French's assistance in our own Revolution.

Twirling my pen between my fingers, I thought back to the past few weeks. Our arrival in Virginia near the end of September had been one of the integral parts of a plan that had long since been set in motion. We could not have done it, surely not as easily, if not for the foreign help we received.

Despite my initial reluctance to go along with Rochambeau's plan of requesting Comte de Grasse's support against the British in Virginia rather than retaking New York, I had to admit that de Grasse's naval forces had been vital in blocking British escape from Yorktown by sea. That, and everything else, from the deception tactics used to trick the British into focusing on New York to the successful French and American surrounding of Yorktown, was going exceptionally well.

Today, I had started off the battle with the *crack* of my musket, setting off a series of explosions and an outburst of action and sound. With the British trapped in Yorktown, we had the advantage, and we would surely continue to make the most of it.

It pleased me to see the French fighting for a liberty that was not even theirs. Whether these foreigners were doing it as a duty, as a kindness, or with some other sort of motive, they fought alongside us as if they themselves were Americans, as if our cause were their own.

Especially Lafayette.

I smiled to myself as I considered the young French marquis, whose conviction and vigor for our fight for liberty surpassed that of which I had seen in most Americans. From the very moment he had set foot on our shores— even before then, or so I had heard, he was eager, so very eager to join our battle, to live and die for, as he said, "liberté." How I hoped that the darkness of war would not consume that brilliant light.

Speaking of lights… my thoughts wandered to my very own light in my life, my beloved Martha. Even just the mere idea of her warmed my heart. As much as I missed her, it comforted me, to know that she was safe at home, away from the bloodshed that I faced almost daily. There was so much that I could not do without her.

Ever since I became general, she had done her part and more, time and time again, to rally support for and lend a hand to my army, procuring greatly needed and appreciated supplies and funding, and encouraging other women to do the same. All the while, she would still spend money on travel, making the time to visit me in camps or wherever else my position took me.

My men gladly welcomed her presence, as she was amicably friendly, which helped me form stronger connections with others, but none so much as I did. Though it was extremely worrying, concerns over her safe journey flooded my brain, she always made it to me. Then, after staying for months at a time, she returned to her family back at Mount Vernon. Of course, she also had an assigned guard to watch over her, and multiple trusted friends often assisted her travel.

I longed for the days when we could sit at home together, no war, no running around the country, just us right where we belonged, in each other's arms. Still, we belonged to our own respective identities as much as we belonged to each other. I as a general leading an army, and she as a leader with her own accomplishments, inspiring others, as good leaders do.

I did not regret who I was, nor did I aspire to forsake my responsibilities and run away. Finished with another diary entry, I carefully closed my copy of the *Virginia Almanac*, storing it and my inkwell safely away once again.

Another day, another British army to defeat in the name of liberty.

BLOOD AND BREATH

YORKTOWN, VIRGINIA
14 OCTOBER, 1781

ONLY WHISPERS IN THE darkness and moving shadows hinted of the hundreds of blue-clad men steadily advancing beneath the cover of night. The sun had dipped below the horizon, leaving behind the perfect shroud for the evening's plans. Our American and the French soldiers were surprising the army of Charles Cornwallis, the British general who was currently occupying Yorktown, with a nice little date- in which sparks would indeed be flying.

The plan would be, if carried out successfully, a vital step towards winning this battle. Cornwallis had been in Virginia for months, preparing and developing Yorktown into a makeshift base for the

British and Hessian soldiers under his command, operating with the confidence that he would emerge victorious in the end. It was that confidence that would seal his fate. Confidence, as a whole, can be an admirable trait, however, a person, especially one with so many lives and factors in their hands, must know when to rein it in. Such arrogance could cloud one's judgement, the almost flawed assurance, wishful assumption that everything would work out the way one hoped it would.

Our troops, however, had greatly prospered from this ill-placed confidence. Since our arrival in September, we had managed to secure multiple British fortifications- most of which they had abandoned for defenses nearest to Yorktown. With Rouchambeau, Lieutenant Colonel Alexander Hamilton, Deux-Ponts (the German regiment under Rochambeau), and the other interchanging officers in command, such as Lafeyette and Lincoln surrounding Yorktown, Cornwallis was, by all definitions, boxed in. Even across York River, another French general, Marquis de Choisy, had confronted and subdued the British in Gloucester, who were under the command of Lt. Col. Banastre Tarleton, effectively cutting off what would have been Cornwallis's means of assistance and escape by water.

Tonight, the goal was to overtake two of the remaining British redoubts, Redoubts Nine and Ten, which would clear the way for us to complete the erection of our second parallel, and further weaken the British. Hamilton would attack Redoubt Ten, and the French, Redoubt Nine. It certainly was not an easy undertaking, and not all would make it out with their lives.

Yet this was the price we paid, exchanging blood and breath for freedom.

GEORGE WASHINGTON

THE SONG OF WAR

YORKTOWN, VIRGINIA
17 OCTOBER, 1781

ARTILLERY FIRED IN A constant stream, creating a cacophonous thundering that shook the very earth. Across the battlefield, dirt flew, and the British lines fell as they struggled to counter our attacks. Cornwallis was surrounded, his men were low on rations, and the endless bombardment from our side was rendering them increasingly helpless. It was a wonder he did not surrender sooner, though his mistakes resulted in what seemed to be becoming an American victory.

The morning sunlight shone down upon us, illuminating an overall bittersweet scene. There was, of course, the overwhelming notion of the enemy's impending defeat, yet there was so much death preceding it. British casualties far surpassed our own, but in the end, we were all human, all had families and people waiting for us to return. I kept my eyes on the task ahead, shouting orders to my men as we advanced on the fortifications. War was such a terrible thing, yet it was a necessary sacrifice that many were willing to make.

It was hard to imagine a world without the sound of cannons and the sight of fallen soldiers. Shouts and explosions were nearly background noise after all these years, constant alertness and motion far more natural than inactivity. It was quite noticeable, when the firing began to cease, revealing another sound that broke through the silence.

A drum.

Upon a parapet, a single, red-coated drummer and an officer holding a sword bearing a white handkerchief appeared; the piece of fabric waving in the wind. The drummer beat steadily, the rhythmic booms the most beautiful sound we had all heard in a while. He was beating a parley.

The British had surrendered.

GEORGE WASHINGTON

NEW BEGINNINGS

PRINCETON, NEW JERSEY
2 NOVEMBER, 1783

WHO HAD KNOWN THAT that victory would be one of our last?

I looked out upon the sea of faces. There stood the Continental Army, the men whom I had led and fought against in a long, brutal war against the Crown. We had fought for liberty, the freedom of our people to claim independence from Great Britain, a country that had tried to continually assert its power over us from across the sea.

At first, it had seemed like a dream that would never reach fruition, a lovely ideal, a skirmish that would end in an instant.

Two months ago, in September, that very same dream had become reality.

The Treaty of Paris. Four wonderful words to describe a remarkable document- if not *the most* critical document in American history. Or it would be, at least, as our country grew and developed, writing its story, *our* stories, stroke by stroke.

Signed, 3rd of September, 1783, the treaty had secured the colonies' independence from the British Crown, officially naming America as its own separate country. All of that rallying, all of the fighting, the bloodshed, the hard nights and days away from the people we loved, everything we'd worked for in the past seven years, had finally gotten us *here*. It was like standing on a mountain after a long and grueling hike, relishing the view that we thought we might never see.

We did it. My heart whispered to me, to the soldiers before me, to my fellow countrymen and women. To everyone who had doubted us, who had feared, thought, for just one moment that we would not make it. To all those who had upturned their lives, fought, bled, and died for us to see this day. To those who were no longer here to take these next few steps forwards into the wondrous unknown, but would not ever, *ever* be forgotten. Even now, they surely smiled down upon us, cheering for the birth of America.

Yet this was not the end.

Countless challenges awaited us on the road ahead, ones that would test every single aspect of our young country. So much growth, so many things to develop, and improvements to make. So many problems, discord, and missing pieces. If we had proven anything in the past few years, though, it was that we had spirit. Perseverance, determination. The will to hold strong to our beliefs, and fight for them with all our strength, all we had.

It definitely wouldn't be easy; we wouldn't get through whatever the future had in store for us without a fair share of mistakes. But I had faith in the Lord, and in the hearts and souls of Americans.

I turned my attention back down to my current task; giving these brave men the farewell they deserved. These troops, this patriotic band of brothers, whom I was so, *so* proud of. All we could do was take things day by day. Today was a day of bittersweet goodbyes and heartfelt congratulations.

The journey here had been a long one. However, this was not the end of anything. Rather, it was the start of a nation. A nation that would be shaped, and had been shaped, by countless, countless hands.

To new beginnings. Wind brushed past my cheek, and with it, I sent my prayers up to the sky. Wherever we went from here, it was up to us all.

ABOUT

GEORGE WASHINGTON

George Washington was born on February 22nd, 1732, as the eldest of six children, with four older half-siblings. Despite not receiving the formal education of his half-siblings, he studied hard, and became quite accomplished in land surveying and mathematics, becoming a surveyor before following in his half-brother's footsteps to seek a militial position. From there, he rose from second-in-command of the Virginia regiment during the French and Indian War, to Commander-in-Chief of the Continental Army, leading America's troops in the fight for liberty. After that, the rest of his story is pretty well known. From General George Washington to the first president of the United States. A prominent figure in America's history, he helped to shape the nation and build the foundation that we stand on today, a nation that, though it has its problems, remains a land of hope and freedom for many, a place we can call home thanks to the efforts of those who came before us.

ABOUT THE AUTHOR

PAYTON GRACE

As always, I had no idea how to even begin writing my author biography. No matter how much I grew and changed over the years, that was one of the constants in my life, it seemed. When I thought about it, I realized—there were really no constraints or requirements specifically outlined in one of those either. Usually, I'd welcome the lack of guidelines and word limits in my writing, but in that case…I wasn't sure whether to count it as a blessing or a curse. I supposed I'd just do what I always did; ramble on for a bit about how much I didn't know what I was doing, then list information like a resume. 16 years old, now…odd to think about, yet a fact no matter how it made me feel. Still lived in Oahu, Hawaii, which was another invariable throughout my existence. …There was a lot less information than I thought there would be. I still loved reading and writing? But why would anyone need to know that?? Perhaps, if they'd perused the earlier books, they would, for some reason, be interested in reading author bios and seeing what may have changed. Which was, come to think of it, an interesting concept. Maybe I should do that sometime. One thing I could say, however, was that Epic Patriot Camp, no matter how many times I did it, was always a wonderful and valuable experience as an aspiring author. The next time I wrote one of these, I hoped, sincerely and strongly, that it would be in a novel of my own. After all, that would mean that I'd accomplished one of my life's biggest and most dearest dreams.

VOICES FROM THE PAST

THE UNTOLD STORIES

IF WE FEATURED EVERY name and historical figure who impacted the American Revolution in 1780–1783, this book would never end. It was a tough choice having to cut certain characters who'd played such significant roles in previous years, but "killing your darlings" is one of the most important things to learn as a writer. However, there were some cases where names and people kept returning to our minds, and it became self-evident that we needed to include their stories somehow.

GOVERNOR PATRICK HENRY

I spent the latter stages of the war advising Thomas Jefferson in his new post as Virginia's governor. I was offered a position at the Constitutional Convention, but had to decline due to health reasons. However, when Washington sent me the finished document asking for my support I replied, "I have to lament that I cannot bring my mind to accord with the proposed constitution." This led to scrutiny by my peers as to why I had not attended to present my ideas. Frankly, despite my health challenges, I had to tell people one reason was, "I smelt a rat." Later I would write the Anti-Federalist papers alongside George Mason and Samuel Adams. These papers resulted in the addition of the Bill of Rights and the first ten amendments to the constitution. With these additions, I was much more obliged to support it. Later I made amends with Washington on our political differences. Washington desired for me to join his administration, but I refused to take any post. I wished instead to return to my plow and plantation where I would die on 6 June, 1799.

MAJOR BENJAMIN TALLMADGE

A major in the 2nd Light Dragoons and the spymaster for General Washington. His activity in the Culper Spy Ring, whether sending messages from British held New York or supplying invisible ink, was critical. Tallmadge was suspicious of John André and suggested to his commander to detain him rather than send him on to Benedict Arnold at Westpoint. Thus he prevented André from having the opportunity to escape like his accomplice. Word would soon come of Arnold's betrayal, along with orders from Washington for Tallmadge to escort André to Tappan, New York for his trial. During the journey, Tallmadge and André grew in respect for one another as they observed each other's conduct. Tallmadge would remain as guard to André until the conclusion of the trial and André's subsequent hanging. Tallmadge continued fighting for independence. Once the war ended, he returned to his home in Connecticut. His post-war professions included banker, postmaster, landowner, and congressman (*1800-1817*). He died at his home on 7 March, 1835 at the age of 81.

SIR HENRY CLINTON

12 May 1780–I led 8,700 men into battle and took Charles Town, capturing seven rebel generals. My orders were then to travel to New York as French forces were expected there in the coming months. I began to improve fortifications in preparation for their arrival.

During the stalemate in the northern theater, I was approached by Benedict Arnold regarding his desire to be of service to the crown. I immediately assigned André to serve as a liaison between us. In September 1780, I offered Arnold £20,000 and a command of his army in exchange for control of West Point. This was critical to the British victory as I would be able to control the river and cut off supplies between Albany and New York. Unfortunately for me I would be betrayed. André was caught and left me without the glory or honor of such a fine success. In New York, I waited and watched as the combined Patriots and French forces made their way to Yorktown and surrounded Cornwallis. I regret my decision to not stay engaged, but I am going back to my homeland and hope they won't blame me.

In 1795, I received the governorship of Gibraltar. It was a new beginning for me. No longer was I surrounded by people who say I lost the war. I could put it behind me and move on. (*Before Clinton could assume his new post he died 23 December 1795*).

COMTE DE VERGENNES

The Foreign Minister of France, had the foresight in 1774 to see that if the colonies gained independence from England they would be reliant on foreign interest to support their economy. He worked with Lafayette to send 15,000 muskets and an army of 7,500 soldiers to the colonies to support their efforts. He also convinced King Louis XVI to send six million livres to Congress and dispatch a squadron of twenty ships, accompanied by 3,000 marines, across the Atlantic. As the war continued through, he began to worry. The Russians and Austrians were ready for the war to end, and they were planning to meet to discuss a treaty that would establish the current line of battle as the new border for each of the countries involved. This would devastate the colony's economy. News of Yorktown's victory ended the talks of premature peace and Vergennes would help negotiate the Treaty of Paris. However, the results were not as profitable as he had hoped due to more shrewd negotiations from the colonies than was expected. (*Died 13 February 1787, just two years before his nation would have its own revolution*).

JOHN ADAMS

I, John Adams, have been in almost constant correspondence with my wife, Abigail, since my arrival to France in 1778. She has been doing well managing our estate, the children are well and she has expressed her interest in my current position. Franklin and de Vergennes have been dismissive of me and now Vergennes has informed me that France does not approve of Congress's plan to address inflation by devaluing the dollar. Both have requested that I return at once to express their concerns. I opt to send the necessary written correspondence to inform Congress and find myself no longer welcome in the court of King Louis XVI. I traveled on to the Netherlands in 1781 to seek a loan. With the news from Yorktown, they are much more receptive than when I first started my negotiations.

In 1783, I was with Benjamin Franklin and John Jay in Paris at the meeting with the British emissary, Richard Oswald. We have successfully negotiated the terms for the Treaty of Paris. I have yet to inform de Vergennes about this agreement but I shall leave that to Franklin seeing that they are such good friends. In 1785, I was appointed as the first United States Minister to Great Britain in charge of establishing diplomatic post-war ties. I will later go on to become the 2nd US President of our new nation. Abigail focused on family but became a strong activist for women's rights. (*Abigail died 28 October 1818; John died 4 July 1826. Both died at their home in Quincy, Massachusetts*).

THOMAS JEFFERSON

Jefferson began in 1780 writing what would be his one and only book, *Notes on the State of Virginia*. It was his response to French diplomat, François Barbé-Marbois, and his personal thoughts on the future of the state. It took him five years to complete it.

On 3 June 1781, as the British were closing in on his Monticello home,, a local militia man, Jack Jouett, alerted Jefferson after he spotted a company of dragoons coming to capture Jefferson. At this alert, Jefferson sent his family off to a farm to hide. He was able to escape, thanks to a neighbor's second warning, just as the British were coming up the hill. Jefferson presumed with the British taking over his home, that he was no longer governor and remained with his family. Sadly, the family home was not the only loss for the family. His daughter Lucy Elizabeth, died at the age of one. While the State Assembly would later investigate his actions and find him innocent of any wrongdoing, the stain on his reputation was permanent and his political opponents continued to question him and use it against him.

The next year was also filled with moments of joy and grief. Jefferson was able to return to his Monticello home, but shortly after they returned, his wife of ten years, died giving birth to a second Lucy Elizabeth.

Before the war ended he would be elected to Congress. This was just the beginning. In 1801, he was elected President, orchestrated the Louisiana Purchase, and approved the Lewis and Clark Expedition. These were just a few of his accomplishments while he served until 1809. (*Jefferson died 4 July 1826, 50 years after the birth of the country*).

KING GEORGE III

In 1780, I received the most troubling news from New York. My intelligence officers there have informed me of a rebel plot to kidnap my son. My son serves in my royal navy and is currently holding court in New York. I am most distressed as his safety is at the forefront of my mind.

In 1781, I take heart knowing that my son's guard has been doubled and is on high alert. I have personally been tracking the movements of the French fleet and artillery. I fear Yorktown will become a great loss for us in our efforts to retake control of the colonies. My only hope is that the idea of this rebellious colony does not spread.

In 1782, my heart grieves with all of England at the death of my son Prince Alfred, only one year and ten months.

In 1785, I express my desire to enter into a trade partnership with John Adams. My hope is that we might profit far more by trading with them freely than we did through taxation. I have just lost my daughter Amelia to tuberculosis and I grieve for her greatly. (*King George III's health will continue to decline from his grief and he dies at the age of 81 on January 29th of 1820.*)

You can read about more characters, plus find bonus content, by scanning the above QR code or visiting the official *1780–1783* book page at
www.ChristopherJWattAuthor.com

GLOSSARY OF WORDS AND PHRASES

Colonial Terms

Sugarloaf	Blocks of sugar
Pieces of Eight	Another way of saying "Spanish Dollar", which was the predominant currency used in the West Indies in the 1700's

French Terms

Adieu	Farewell; goodbye
Au plaisir de vous revoir	Hope to see you again soon.
Belle Amérique, je suis arrivé!	Beautiful America, I have arrived!
Bonjour	Hello
Cacophonie	Cacophony
C'est ça	That's right
C'est exactement ça	That's exactly right
C'est vrai	That's true / It's true
Cher	Dear (masculine)

Ici, la vie, c'est aussi frais que l'air, n'est-ce pas?	Here, life is as fresh as the air, isn't it?
Je comprends	I understand.
Je t'aime ma chérie	I love you, my darling.
Joyeux Noël	Merry Christmas
Le général Cornwallis s'est rendu	General Cornwallis surrendered.
Liberté	Liberty
Ma chérie	My darling (feminine)
Merci	Thank you.
Merci beaucoup.	Thank you very much.
Mon bonté!	My goodness!
Mon petit ami	My little friend
Monsieur	Sir
Nécessaire	Necessary
Nous serons victorieux!	We will be victorious!
Oui	Yes
Pardonnez-moi	Pardon me
Parfait	Perfect
Pastel des teinturiers	Dyer's woad (plant used for dyes)
Pourquoi	Why
Quoi	What
Souverain	Sovereign
Très bien	Very good
Très dégoûtant	Very disgusting
Une lettre est arrivée.	A letter has arrived.
Un faucon	A hawk

BIBLIOGRAPHIES

To ensure historical and scholarly credibility, all authors were asked to provide a bibliography of their top sources. We hope this may assist in further research you may do!

ALEXANDRA ROBERSON

American Battlefield Trust. 2017. "Battle of Camden Facts & Summary." American Battlefield Trust. January 27, 2017. https://www.battlefields.org/learn/revolutionary-war/battles/camden.

History Central. https://www.americanhistorycentral.com/entries/

charles-cornwallis/.

"Copies of Letters from Lord Rawdon to Lord Cornwallis
Referring to an Attack Made upon Captain Greene on
Hobkirk's Hill - Colonial America - Adam Matthew
Digital." 2025. Amdigital.co.uk. 2025. https://www.
colonialamerica.amdigital.co.uk/Documents/Details/CO_5_8_
Part_1_038?utm_source=chatgpt.com.

"No Way Out: Lord Cornwallis, the Siege of Yorktown, and
America's Victory in the War for Independence | Gilder
Lehrman Institute of American History." 2025. Gilderlehrman.
org. 2025. https://www.gilderlehrman.org/history-resources/
essays/no-way-out-lord-cornwallis-siege-yorktown-and-
americas-victory-war.

"Surrender of the British General Cornwallis to the Americans,
October 19, 1781 | Gilder Lehrman Institute of American
History." n.d. Www.gilderlehrman.org. https://www.
gilderlehrman.org/history-resources/spotlight-primary-source/
surrender-british-general-cornwallis-americans-october.

Team, Quotesanity. 2025. "Best Charles Cornwallis Quotes:
Inspiring Words from a British General." Quotesanity. March
12, 2025. https://quotesanity.com/charles-cornwallis-quotes/.

CAMERON GRAHAM

American Battlefield Trust. 2000. "Home." American Battlefield
Trust. 2000.

https://www.battlefields.org/.

General, Nathanael,. 2025. "Proceedings of the Board of General Officers Respecting Major

André, September 29, 1780." Digital Long Island. New London, CT: T. Green. 2025. https://www.digitallongisland.org/record/4499?ln=en&v=uv#?xywh=-1606%2C0%2C6403%2C4631&cv=.

"Founders Online: Home." 2019. Archives.gov. 2019. https://founders.archives.gov.

Golway, Terry. 2007. *Washington's General.* Henry Holt and Company.

CHASE ADAM

"Benjamin Lincoln's Fireside", American Revolution Institute 11, Oct 2020. https://www.americanrevolutioninstitute.org/benjamin-lincoln/

"Yorktown, Siege of Yorktown" American Battle Field Trust https://www.battlefields.org/learn/revolutionary-war/battles/yorktown

Mattern, David B. "Benjamin Lincoln and the American Revolution" First Edition. University of South Carolina Press, 1995.

BIBLIOGRAPHIES

CHRISTOPHER J. WATT

Isaacson, Walter. 2003. *Benjamin Franklin: An American Life*. New York: Simon & Schuster Paperbacks.

Vaillancourt, John P. 2007. Review of Edward Bancroft (@ Edwd. Edwards), Estimable Spy. Center for the Study of Intelligence 5 (1). https://www.cia.gov/resources/csi/static/Edward-Bancroft-Estimable-Spy.pdf.

The majority of my research was taken from summaries, context, and quotes from official letter transcripts, all found at Founders Online (founders.archives.gov).

EDAN MACNAUGHTON

Burdick, K. (2020, April 7). *What they saw and did at Yorktown's redoubts 9 and 10*. Journal of the American Revolution. https://allthingsliberty.com/2020/04/what-they-saw-and-did-at-yorktowns-redoubts-9-and-10/

Chernow, R. (2005). *Alexander Hamilton*. Penguin Group.

Kennedy, L. (2025, June 30). *How Alexander Hamilton's men surprised the enemy at the Battle of Yorktown*. History.com. https://www.history.com/articles/alexander-hamilton-battle-yorktown-revolutionary-war

National Archives and Records Administration. (2025). *Founders online: From Alexander Hamilton to Elizabeth Hamilton, [12 October 1781]*. National Archives and Records

Administration. https://founders.archives.gov/documents/
Hamilton/01-02-02-1199

Ronemus, A. (1995, July 4). *Alexander Hamilton*. ushistory.org.
https://www.ushistory.org/brandywine/special/art08.htm

ELLA QUILL

Sheinkin, Steve. *The Notorious Benedict Arnold; A True Story of Adventure, Heroism, and Treachery*. Flash Point, imprint of Roaring Book Press, 2010, Harrisonburg, Virginia.

Philbrick, Nathaniel. *Valiant Ambition; George Washington, Benedict Arnold, and the Fate of the American Revolution*. Penguin Random House, 2019, New York, New York.

Malcolm, Joyce Lee. *The Tragedy of Benedict Arnold; An American Life*. Pegasus Books, Ltd., 2018, New York, New York.

Flexner, James Thomas. *The Traitor and the Spy*. Harcourt, Brace and Company, 1953, United States of America.

"Peggy Shippen." *Wikipedia*, https://en.wikipedia.org/wiki/Peggy_Shippen

"Benedict Arnold" *History.com* https://www.history.com/articles/benedict-arnold#Benedict-Arnold's-Wife

EMMANUEL MORISSET

American Battlefield Trust. "Fix Bayonets! The Revolution's Climactic Assault at Yorktown." Battlefields.org. Accessed June 28, 2025. https://www.battlefields.org/learn/articles/fix-bayonets-revolutions-climactic-assault-yorktown.

American Battlefield Trust. "Henry Knox." Battlefields.org.
Accessed June 28, 2025. https://www.battlefields.org/learn/
biographies/henry-knox.

Mount Vernon Ladies' Association. "Henry Knox." George
Washington's Mount Vernon, Digital Encyclopedia. Accessed
June 28, 2025. https://www.mountvernon.org/library/
digitalhistory/digital-encyclopedia/article/henry-knox.

Mount Vernon Ladies' Association. "New Windsor Cantonment."
George Washington's Mount Vernon, Digital Encyclopedia.
Accessed June 28, 2025. https://www.mountvernon.org/library/
digitalhistory/digital-encyclopedia/article/new-windsor-
cantonment.

U.S. History.org. "Henry Knox." Valley Forge: Who Served Here?
Accessed July 1, 2025. https://www.ushistory.org/valleyforge/
served/knox2.html.

Biblical References Cited

The Holy Bible, King James Version. Psalm 33:12.
The Holy Bible, King James Version. Psalm 144:1.

HANNAH SCHNEIDER

"Comte de Grasse." n.d. American Battlefield Trust. https://www.
battlefields.org/learn/biographies/comte-de-grasse.

"Founders Online: From George Washington to François-
Joseph-Paul, Comte de Grass …." n.d. Founders.

archives.gov. https://founders.archives.gov/documents/
Washington/99-01-02-07017.

Yorktown, Mailing Address: Colonial National Historical Park-
Yorktown Battlefield P. O. Box 210, and VA 23690 Phone:898-
2410 Contact Us. 2021. "Battle of the Capes - Yorktown
Battlefield Part of Colonial National Historical Park (U.S.
National Park Service)." Www.nps.gov. January 25, 2021.
https://www.nps.gov/york/learn/historyculture/battle-of-the-
capes.htm.

Ruppert, Bob. 2016. "The Three Letters That Determined the
Campaign to Yorktown." Journal of the American Revolution.
November 9, 2016. https://allthingsliberty.com/2016/11/three-
letters-determined-campaign-yorktown/.

"George Washington's Mount Vernon." 2018. George Washington's
Mount Vernon. Mount Vernon. 2018. https://www.
mountvernon.org/library/digitalhistory/digital-encyclopedia/
article/battle-of-the-chesapeake.

MADELEINE ROSE WENZEL

Catherine Moore Barry

Hilborn, Nat, and Sam Hilborn. 1970. *Battleground of Freedom*.

"Margaret Catherine Moore Barry." 2024. American Battlefield
Trust. 2024. https://www.battlefields.org/learn/biographies/
margaret-catherine-moore-barry.

"Margaret Catherine Moore Barry." 2025. The Liberty Trail.
2025. https://thelibertytrail.org/history/biographies/margaret-

catherine-moore-barry.

"The American Revolution in South Carolina - Captain Andrew Barry." 2024. Carolana.com. 2024. https://www.carolana.com/SC/Revolution/patriots_sc_capt_andrew_barry.html.

"The American Revolution in South Carolina - Moore's Plantation." 2025. Carolana.com. 2025. https://www.carolana.com/SC/Revolution/revolution_moores_plantation.html. Comte de Rochambeau

"Founders Online: To George Washington from Jean-Baptiste Donatien de Vimeur, Co ...." 2025. Archives.gov. 2025. https://founders.archives.gov/documents/Washington/99-01-02-05886.

"Founders Online: To George Washington from Jean-Baptiste Donatien de Vimeur, Co ...." 2025. Archives.gov. 2025. https://founders.archives.gov/documents/Washington/99-01-02-06208.

Perkins, James Breck. 2023. "Chapter 16 - the Arrival of Rochambeau | France in the Revolution - AmericanRevolution.org." AmericanRevolution.org. 2023. https://www.americanrevolution.org/france-in-the-revolution-chapter-16/.

Stearns, Jim. 2023. "Why Newport Scorned the French 1780." The Battle of Rhode Island Association. February 2023. https://battleofrhodeisland.org/why-newport-scorned-the-french-1780/.

"The French Arrive: 1780." 2022. Portsmouthhistorynotes. July 22,

2022. https://portsmouthhistorynotes.com/2022/07/22/the-french-arrive-1780/.

MIKAYLA BADENHORST

Anna Smith Strong

Kilmeade, Brian, and Don Yaeger. *George Washington's Secret Six: The Spy Ring That Saved the American Revolution*. New York, NY: Sentinel, 2013.

Medved, Michael. *The American Miracle: Divine Providence in the Rise of the Republic*. New York: Crown Forum, 2016.

Nagy, John A. *George Washington's Secret Spy War: The Making of America's First Spymaster*. New York, N.Y, NY: St. Martin's Press, 2016.

Rose, Alexander. *Washington's Spies: The Story of America's First Spy Ring*. New York: Bantam Books Trade Paperbacks, 2014.

Shorto, Russell. *Revolution Song: The Story of America's Founding in Six Remarkable Lives*. New York, NY: W.W. Norton & Company, 2018.

Marquis de Lafayette

"La Fayette." Palace of Versailles, April 9, 2021. Accessed May 28, 2025. https://en.chateauversailles.fr/discover/history/great-characters/fayette.

"Lafayette and the Virginia Campaign 1781." National Parks

Service. Accessed July 8, 2025. https://www.nps.gov/york/learn/historyculture/lafayette-and-the-virginia-campaign-1781.htm.

"Lafayette Recommends Hamilton for Advancement, 1780." Hamilton Education Program. Accessed July 8, 2025. https://hamilton.gilderlehrman.org/supporting-document/lafayette-recommends-hamilton-advancement-1780.

"Marquis de Lafayette." American Battlefield Trust. Accessed July 8, 2025. https://www.battlefields.org/learn/biographies/marquis-de-lafayette.

"Marquis de Lafayette." George Washington's Mount Vernon. Accessed July 8, 2025. https://www.mountvernon.org/library/digitalhistory/digital-encyclopedia/article/marquis-de-lafayette.

ROXY MESSIER

"Banastre Tarleton." 2017. American Battlefield Trust. January 23, 2017.https://www.battlefields.org/learn/biographies/banastre-tarleton.

"Banastre Tarleton (U.S. National Park Service)." n.d. Www.nps.gov.

https://www.nps.gov/people/banastre-tarleton.htm.

American BattleField Trust. 2017. "Battle of Guilford Court House Facts & Summary."

American Battlefield Trust. January 27, 2017. https://www.battlefields.org/learn/revolutionary-war/battles/guilford-court-house.

"Waxhaws." n.d. American Battlefield Trust. https://www.battlefields.org/learn/revolutionary-war/battles/waxhaws.

American Battlefield Trust. 2017. "Battle of Cowpens Facts & Summary." American Battlefield Trust. January 27, 2017. https://www.battlefields.org/learn/revolutionary-war/battles/cowpens.

PAYTON GRACE

American Battlefield Trust. 2018. "Battle of Yorktown Facts & Summary." American Battlefield Trust. December 5, 2018. https://www.battlefields.org/learn/revolutionary-war/battles/yorktown.

Graff, Henry, and Allan Nevins. 2018. "George Washington | Life, Presidency, & Accomplishments." In *Encyclopedia Britannica*. https://www.britannica.com/biography/George-Washington.

Library of Congress. 2015. "The American Revolution | Timeline | Articles and Essays | George Washington Papers | Digital Collections | Library of Congress." The Library of Congress. 2015. https://www.loc.gov/collections/george-washington-papers/articles-and-essays/timeline/the-american-revolution/.

"Founders Online: The Papers of George Washington." 2012. Archives.gov. 2012. https://founders.archives.gov/about/Washington.

"The Redoubts at Yorktown." n.d. Warfare History Network. https://warfarehistorynetwork.com/article/the-redoubts-at-yorktown/.

ACKNOWLEDGEMENTS

They say it takes a village to raise a child, and the same goes for putting together a book. Thank you to *everyone* who encouraged, supported, and inspired every one of the campers throughout this whole journey.

CAMERON GRAHAM

First and foremost, I would like to thank my parents and especially my mom for helping with not only my chapters of John André and Nathanael Greene but also for providing support for the 2025 Patriot Writing Camp.

Second, to Jenny L. Cote and Libby McNamee for believing in us as writers with stories to tell. Your support over the last three years has been amazing and life-changing. Because of you I took a chance to write and through your mentorship became a better writer. Thank you for the privilege and honor of selecting me for the leadership team for this third installment.

And finally, thanks to Christopher J. Watt and Ella Quill, two amazing authors in their own right, who were brave enough to take on leadership in a big way and have championed us all to the finish line.

CHASE ADAM

God has blessed me with many people that have invested in my life.

Braden Sehr has been a great friend and role model for the past year. His influence in my life has made me stronger both physically and spiritually. Thank you - I'm never here "just for the perogies."

My friends, Wyatt for the laughs, Jace for the lore, Slayton for excessive zoology facts, and Rylan for nerding out with me. You guys are the best.

I have the most amazing wrestling coaches - Silverback Swen, Swanson, Mikey, Seibs and Braden. Thank you for everything. Your presence in my life has shaped me forever.

My mom because she's awesome.

I'm grateful for the opportunity to be part of this incredible project of researching amazing heroes from our country's past, and gaining a deeper appreciation for the historical value of their contributions to the freedom we now enjoy.

ACKNOWLEDGEMENTS

CHRISTOPHER J. WATT

I would like to thank my parents, John and Christl, for supporting me through this entire experience. Words are not enough to express my gratitude for being with me every step of the way; through times of joy and moments of frustration. Much love to both of you, as always.

I thank Jenny L. Cote and Libby McNamee for the gift it has been to not only do this again, but to get to lead this venture too. Thank you for the words of wisdom and encouraging me to take the Next Step. Jenny, thank you for believing in me and always pointing me to the Author of it all. Libby, thank you for you kindness, generosity, and for supporting this fellow English nerd to keep writing, no matter what. Love you both.

A special mention to Aunty Heidi, for showing so much support during the final stages of running EPC, and for reminding me to take breaks when I (really) needed them!

And finally, to my colleagues Ella, Edan, and Cameron—all of you have been such a tremendous help in this entire project and I don't know where I'd be without your enthusiasm and ideas!

EDAN MACNAUGHTON

To my family, thank you for your love, support, prayers, and generosity. Without you, I wouldn't have been able to write this.

To my EPC friends, thank you for all the endless laughs, helping me develop further as a writer, and for all of the amazing memories we made together.

To the EPC25 leaders, thank you for everything that you did to make this book a reality. I am honored to serve alongside you all.

To Christopher J Watt, thank you for tireless devotion, hard work, leadership, and pure genius in directing this camp and book. You have made me a better writer and person. I am so thankful for your friendship.

ELLA QUILL

I would like to thank several amazing people!

THANK YOU to God, the Savior of my life, and my Best Friend. Thank you for hearing all of my endless prayers about this camp.

THANK YOU to Christopher, Edan, and Cameron! You guys are seriously the best team I could ask for! It's been EPIC to work alongside you all!

THANK YOU Jenny and Libby! I sure missed you both, but I thank you for all of your encouragement and support along the way! I hope your eaglets have made you proud.

THANK YOU to all of the awesome Epic Patriot Campers of this year! You all have been the most amazing group of writers and friends and I thank you for the wonderful times we had together!

SO proud of all of you!

EMMANUEL MORISSET

I thank my Lord and Savior Jesus Christ for guiding this journey. To my parents, Jocelyn and Rose, my brother Mikha'El, my sister Gabrielle, and my grandmother Yvrose; your encouragement gave me courage to keep writing. I am grateful to my mentors, the Epic Patriot Camp team, and the historians whose work shaped this story. And to every reader, thank you for joining me on this adventure.

HANNAH SCHNEIDER

Thanks to Christopher, Gemma, and my teammates for checking and editing my work. Thanks to my mom, for supporting me and letting me do this, even though I didn't let you read any of my drafts. And thanks to Dad, for helping me with my French and making sure I don't pronounce my own character's name wrong. Souverain is grateful.

MADELEINE ROSE WENZEL

To my family, who have suffered through numerous history related trips, and hearing me talk non-stop about the Revolutionary war since I first became interested in it.

To the people at Walnut Grove Plantation. Without you I would still be lost trying to find information about Kate Barry!

And to Mr. Joe and Ms. Hilary at the Confederate Relic Room. I look forward to many more lectures and Revolutionary War days in the future!

PAYTON GRACE

Endless oceans and skies, galaxies and universes of love and thanks to my family and friends, those who I have or will come across in the past, present, and future. Every single one of you has had an important, unique part in my life, impacting it, and the person whom I am, and am turning out to be. Which I hope is a good thing. I am truly thankful that I've had the honor to know each and every one of you—as well as just for your overall existence, so, of course, I also have to give thanks to the Lord whom, without, none of us would even be here in the first place. I wouldn't be here being thankful for this wonderful world and the people within it, and neither would anything and everything I know and love. So thank you. Always wishing you all the best in life, through the struggles and the beauty, the smiles and the tears. Never give up, know that you are loved and able, deserve amazing things, and are never, ever alone (*in the least creepy way possible.*) (*I promise it's not in a creepy way*).

On behalf of ALL the Virtual Epic Patriot Campers across 2022, 2023, and 2025, we acknowledge and thank Jenny L. Cote and Libby McNamee for their support, encouragement, and mentorship in a love-filled Declaration of Independence. HUZZAH!!

To learn more about the history of Virtual Epic Patriot Camp, visit www.EpicOrderOfTheSeven.com

Now the Lord is that Spirit:
and where the Spirit of the Lord is, there is LIBERTY.
2 Corinthians 3:17